The Little Door

Stormy Lynn

Copyright © 2021 Stormy Lynn Knaak

All rights reserved

The characters and events portrayed in this book are fictitious. Any similarity to real persons, living or dead, is coincidental and not intended by the author.

No part of this book may be reproduced, or stored in a retrieval system, or transmitted in any form or by any means, electronic, mechanical, photocopying, recording, or otherwise, without express written permission of the publisher.

ISBN-13: 9798520864127
ISBN-10: 1477123456

Cover design by: Art Painter
Library of Congress Control Number: 2018675309
Printed in the United States of America

Dedicated to Caleb Hintz, who supported me every annoying step of the way and refused to let me quit even when I really wanted to. You believed in me far more than I believed in myself, and I love you for that.

Contents

Title Page
Copyright
Dedication
Chapter 1 — 1
Chapter 2 — 15
Chapter 3 — 27
Chapter 4 — 49
Chapter 5 — 81
Chapter 6 — 101
Chapter 7 — 124
Chapter 8 — 146
Chapter 9 — 168
Chapter 10 — 183
Chapter 11 — 205
Chapter 12 — 218
Chapter 13 — 230

Chapter 14	245
Chapter 15	263
Chapter 16	277

Chapter 1

The Dream

    I was drowning.
    I could feel the liquid leaking into my lungs. I blinked into the sunlight reaching toward me through a thick layer of water. The river seemed to be thrashing past me at every angle, yet I wasn't moving. I could hear the distinct sound of the roaring water bellowing overhead, but it seemed to be a hundred miles away.
    My arms lay out at either side of me as my body levitated over the riverbed. I rolled over, feeling a certain calmness that seemed peculiar to me for someone

who was bound to be dead any second now. As I rolled my body sideways, I noticed the riverbed seemed farther away than it should have been. Rivers are only supposed to be a few feet deep, yet this river went on for miles. If I squinted through the water, all I could make out was a vast, never ending blue that darkened the farther it got from me. I dove deeper, wondering how long I might have to swim before I reached the bottom. Then the thought struck me, how do I know I'm going downward? Or is this sideways? I rolled around again to face upward, but perhaps that was the direction to go toward the riverbed. Wait, would I want to go toward the riverbed? No, I certainly should be looking for the direction out of the water, not in deeper. I began thrashing my legs, suddenly filled with a desperation to get out of the cold embrace surrounding me.

That's when I filled with panic. The calmness that caressed me only moments before broke and I realized I was dying. I spun around again, searching through the deep waters for a way out. Something had to be here to help me find my way out. Where had the light gone that had just been reaching for me? I pushed my body forward through the coldness, searching through the vastness of the dark water. I appeared to be in an ocean, but somehow my brain knew this was a river. I pushed forward again just as a strong gush of water hit my shoulder and flung my body around in a new direction.

Then, as though it had been there all along, the riverbed appeared right in front of my face, close enough for me to reach out and sink my hand into the muddy surface below. Through the twigs and rocks, I saw a little door. It was an old door made of a dark brown wood, a small black handle reaching out toward me. For a second, I nearly grabbed it, forgetting I was drowning. I remembered, though, and thrashed backward as though the handle were trying to trick me. I spun around, knowing I had to swim up, up, away from the riverbed and the taunting little door. I peered up and realized the river was no longer vast and never ending. In fact, I could see streams of sunlight and feel the warmth on my face. If I squinted hard enough, I could see a boulder looming over me. And, perched upon the boulder, peering over the edge, and looking through the water straight at me, I could make out the figure of...a boy? Yes, that's what it was, a young boy staring down at me through the water. I kicked forward, rising to the surface of the water, taking a closer look. Distorted through the ripples of the water, I made out wide, shockingly blue eyes watching me from a face that sported sharp, elf-like ears. A hand extended from the elf-boy, reaching toward me, breaking through the surface of the water, making to touch me—

Rose woke with a start, bolting upward in her bed and panting as though she had just run a marathon. In her sleep she had kicked the comforter off her bed, yet she was still coated with a cold sweat that darkened the gray night shirt she wore.

Rose glanced at the alarm clock on the nightstand beside her bed. The numbers glowed red against the darkness of the room, telling Rose that it was 3:24 in the morning. She let out a huff of air and flopped back down onto her pillow. She knew she had dreamt about drowning again, although the details were already slipping away from her memory. She'd been having the same dream for a decade. When she was only four years old, she had almost died by drowning in a river. Her subconscious mind never quite got over the event.

Slowing down her heartbeat was always a challenge after the dream. It required several minutes of taking slow, deliberate breaths and trying to not think of the gushing water surrounding her body. Just as she was starting to regain control of herself, Rose heard a sound. She listened carefully and was able to make out her mother's rising voice.

"—how do you think that makes her feel knowing—" Rose caught, hearing the voice rising from the first floor of the small, suburban house. With a low groan, Rose rolled to her side and pulled the pillow over her head, clutching it to each of her ears. Similar snippets of conversation had woken her up in the past. At first, Rose would always climb out of bed and prop her door open just a crack so she could hear the shrieks of anger coming from her mom and dad. She had spent hours eavesdropping on the arguments. They were always the same, though. Well, always the same three, anyways. The first was always financial. The second always related to the divorce and who would be getting custody of Rose when it all went through. The final was the real kicker, the one that haunted Rose the most and had likely been the reason the dream came back after all those years. How could Rose's dad be so irresponsible, he almost let Rose die as a little girl because he had been so busy watching a football game and hadn't noticed Rose going toward the raging river…

Not that Rose can remember it happening, anyways. Or at least not clearly. She had some vague images of thrashing through water, and the intense feeling of water filling her nose and lungs. Most of her memories, however, came from stories Rose had heard about it. Her dad had taken her to visit Grandma and Grandpa Greenwood, her dad's parents, who lived in a little cabin in a beautiful wood. Dad and Grandpa were watching a football game while Grandma cooked dinner. Mom had been called in for a night shift at the restaurant she bartended, so she had to back out of the trip at the last second, but Dad and Rose had still gone. Rose was bored out of her mind, of course, but she had discovered the river that ran through the woods only about thirty yards from the back of her grandparents' cabin. Rose never even knew it had been such a big deal for her parents until about nine years after, and about one year ago, when Rose first overheard her parent's argument.

When Rose tried to conjure the memory of the day she fell into the water, she came up only with the images from her dreams. Which, clearly, those weren't entirely accurate, seeing as how there had never been a blue-eyed elf-boy the day Rose had fallen in…

At some point in Rose's musings, she must have drifted off into what was, thankfully, a dreamless sleep, because the next thing she knew her mom was shaking her awake and sunlight was filtering in through the blinds that covered her window.

Rose blinked through the sunlight until her eyes adjusted and the hazy figure of her mom leaning over her came into focus. Finally, the blurry outline of her mom sharpened, and Rose could make out her mother's freckled face staring down at her.

"Rose, you need to get up or you're going to sleep through your last day of junior high," Mom said, her voice crisp as though she were well-rested and hadn't at all been awake and arguing with her husband through the night.

Rose rubbed the sleep out of her eyes, letting her mom's words sink in. Then the full realization of it hit her and she bolted upright. Today was her last day of eighth grade! After today, she would have several months of night games and late nights with her best friends from school! She felt like a newborn puppy full of reckless energy as she jumped out of her bed and ran to the full mirror on her dresser.

"Your dad made bacon and eggs," Mom said, giggling a little at Rose as she leaned down to pick up her comforter off the floor. "Is your fan not working? You keep kicking your comforter off your bed at night, you must be getting hot in your sleep."

Rose paused with her hairbrush halfway through her tangled brown hair. She had almost forgotten about the dream. When she was young, she would always tell her mom whenever the dream had returned. But she stopped getting the dream when she was about nine years old, and when it came back a year ago she hadn't told her mom for fear that it would make the fighting even worse.

"It's working," Rose finally replied, continuing to yank the brush through a matted part of her hair and staring distractedly at herself in the mirror. She had the same freckles as her mother sprawled across the entirety of her nose, earning her the nickname of Freckles with most of her friends and family members. "I guess I just kick a lot in my sleep."

Before her mother could reply, Rose ran out of her bedroom and down the stairs toward the smell of bacon and eggs. As she flitted down the stairs, she stole a glance at her dad who was sitting at their round kitchen table, sipping coffee, his eyes glued to the small television set on the kitchen counter. The sound of a football announcer fell from the television set and filled the kitchen. Rose's dad was a handsome man, visibly aging based on the salt and pepper beard and the wrinkled laugh lines surrounding his mouth. From him, Rose had inherited a ski-slope shaped nose that stuck up a little at the end. Unlike Rose and her mother, Dad didn't have a single freckle or face blemish of any sort on his face, and his skin was a far darker complexion than Rose's or her mom's. He also had a carelessness about him that differed from the ladies of the family. He often spent his day laughing or joking around. Rose's mom considered this part of what made him irresponsible. He didn't take much of anything too serious.

"Mornin', Freckles," Dad chirped when Rose joined him at the round table, looking up from the TV and giving Rose a wide grin. He reached out and tugged on Rose's ear, making her pull back in a fit of giggles. Even though Rose was fourteen and about to enter high school, her dad still had the ability to make her giggle like she was a small child. He used to be able to make her mom giggle the same way, too, but that had ended years ago.

"Mornin'," Rose replied, shoving a forkful of eggs into her mouth. "Guess what."

"What?" Dad asked, giving her a sideways glance that pulled his attention away from the TV. Behind him, Rose could see her mom walking down the stairs, looking indecisive about whether she wanted to join the rest of them at the table.

Around a mouthful of eggs, Rose mumbled, "Yer lookink at the fashe of a high school 'irl!" Rose gleamed with pride. Her dad let out a laugh and she even saw the ghost of a smile form around her mom's lips as she passed the table and began dipping herself a plate of eggs.

"Hey now, don't go breaking my heart!" Dad joked, reaching out and ruffling the top of Rose's hair. "And by the way, you're not quite there yet. Still one full school day to go."

"Fine," Rose said, gulping down her eggs. "I'll say that again as soon as I get home from school."

"And what makes you so sure you'll make it

until the end of the day? What if you keel over and die of a heart attack, old lady?" Dad teased, and Rose was sure she saw her mom crack a smile as she sat at the table. Her heart leapt for joy, as it always did when Dad made Mom smile. Maybe there was a chance...

"Listen, if I'm an old lady, then you must've rode to school on your pet dinosaur," Rose retorted, taking a bite of her floppy, underdone bacon. Dad liked his bacon soft and not crispy.

Dad gasped and put his hand over his heart, feigning shock. Rose laughed again, loving the feeling of all three of them sharing this moment around the breakfast table.

"Oh, Mom, Dad, I wanted to ask you," Rose said, shifting gears. "Lacie was wondering if I could spend this weekend at her house. We wanted to celebrate the start of the summer with a bonfire." She saw the smile fall from her dad's face and her parents exchanged a look that Rose couldn't quite decipher. She decided to add more information in case that would help her case. "We're burning all our schoolwork in a fire! Just the stuff we don't need for high school, of course."

Rose's heart pounded in her chest. She was worried that the awkward glances her parents were giving each other would have something to do with their divorce. Was there a reason their divorce would get in the way of her spending a weekend at her best friend's house? She couldn't think of a reason it would.

"Er—Freckles," Dad stammered. Before he could continue, Mom cut in.

"Rose," she corrected him. She shot Dad a

meaningful look. "This is serious."

With a sigh, Dad started again. "Rose, we have been talking. This summer is going to be—er—difficult. For everyone. And your mother thinks, well, we think, maybe…"

"You're going to stay with Grandma and Grandpa Greenwood this summer," Mom cut in again, an air of finality in her voice.

Rose stared at her parents, confusion clouding her face and thoughts. Stay with Grandma and Grandpa Greenwood? Aside from her one visit a full decade ago, Rose had hardly ever seen her grandparents. They had come to see Rose and her parents a total of two times since the visit, and Rose had never been back to the cabin. The thought of being around the river that almost killed her as a child had terrified her, and apparently her mom, so much that another visit had never been planned. Also, she didn't really like her grandparents all that much. They were okay, for stuffy old people. Her grandpa had a habit of picking his nose while he watched TV and flicking it onto the couches, and her grandma seemed to have forgotten what it's like to be a child or to be around children. She either gave Rose way too explicit and adult-rated information about her personal life that made Rose feel awkward and squeamish, or she tried to interest her in movies or games that Rose had outgrown by at least a solid six years. There was no in-between. Plus, they lived in a *cabin.* In the *woods.* Aside from it probably being haunted, it was also miles away from the nearest neighbor, and probably hundreds of miles from the next person near Rose's age. The more Rose pondered the suggestion, the more she dreaded it.

"You can't be serious," Rose started to argue, but she knew it was useless. Her dad was shooting her warning looks, shaking his head, and widening his eyes. Her mother was looking firm and tightlipped, as though she was just asking Rose to give her a reason to start yelling. Since birth, Rose had always been an obedient child, which led to a very boring life and some very high expectations. Instead of arguing, Rose chose instead to show her disapproval by slumping over in her chair, giving pathetic sighs between every bite of eggs, and looking longingly at her parents as if willing them to change their mind.

When Rose finished her breakfast, she left the table without another word to her parents. She slipped into the outfit she had set out for her last day of school, pulled her hair straight back into a high ponytail that lifted her long, light brown hair away from her face, and brushed her teeth. Once she was ready for school, she lumbered down the stairs, letting out frequent loud sighs, and dragging her backpack down the stairs behind her. It was no use, as her dad was staring adamantly at the TV screen again and her mom was choosing to ignore her.

In a last-ditch effort, Rose decided desperate times called for desperate measures. She cleared her throat and then turned to her dad, pulling out The Voice. The only-child-and-daddy's-girl voice. "Daddy?" Rose chirped. "Can you give me a ride to school today?"

Before her dad could answer, her mom stood up and answered, "I'm dropping you off on my way to work."

Rose knew she had no chance against her mom.

On the ride to school, Rose refused to look at her mom. She stared out the window at the passing houses, up into the bright blue sky and at the fluffy clouds, or at her hands. Mindlessly, she used her left hand to outline the shape of a thin scar that ran down the middle of the fatty part of her palm. The scar had been there for as long as she could remember. When she had asked her parents where the scar had come from, they were unsure. Her mom's best guess was that she may have gotten it from a twig or sharp rock when she fell into the river on that infamous day so many years ago, but her dad was sure her hand had not been bleeding when he pulled her out of the water. Not that he would have really been paying close attention to her hands as he tried to pump air back into her lungs and bring life back into her dying body.

"Are you mad at me?" Mom asked, breaking the silence in the car, and keeping her eyes glued to the road.

"No," Rose answered. *Yes,* she thought.

"I know you want to stay here and be with your friends, Freckles. But—" Her mom broke off, as if not sure what to say.

"I know," Rose replied, even though she had absolutely no clue what her mom was trying to say.

"This has all been really hard," Mom croaked, her voice rising with every word. Rose took a sideways glance at her mom and noticed her blue eyes had filled with tears. Uh, oh. Rose had a sinking feeling her mom wasn't talking about sending Rose away for the summer anymore.

"I know," Rose said again, hoping her mom wouldn't continue talking. She didn't. Instead, she leaned one arm against the car window and chewed on the knuckle of her index finger. Rose gave a sigh of relief. Her mother had never showed any sort of emotions involving the divorce, and it somehow made the entire thing worse when she did. Like, it wasn't something they both *wanted,* but rather something that was necessary to keep moving forward with life.

For the remainder of the car ride, Rose glared out the window, hoping her mom wouldn't try to talk to her again about the divorce, or staying with her grandparents for the summer, or anything. Instead, Rose watched the sky, observing the shapes of the clouds and blinking into the sunlight. When they had nearly reached the school, a cloud lazily rolled over the sun, covering part of it.

The sight of the cloud obscuring the edge of the sunlight that beat down into Rose's eyes made her mind shift to her recurring dream. Thoughts clouded Rose's mind, conjuring the odd shape of the elf-boy she had seen in the dream. Blond, messy hair that looked like it had been grown out just a little too long. Wide, stunningly blue eyes with long, almost girly looking eyelashes. And, what else had she seen? Oh yeah, of course. The ears. The part that had reminded Rose of an elf. They were sharp and pointed rather than a soft curve like her own ears.

Rose mulled over this boy who had appeared in her dreams, wondering why he had been there. Obviously, he hadn't been there when Rose almost drowned in the river behind her grandparents' house, considering there were no children anywhere near that lonely cabin. Rose was also quite certain she had never met a boy who looked like an elf since then. If she had, she would likely have remembered those ears. But, if she had never met a boy like him, and he had certainly not been there the day she almost drowned, who was he? And why was he in her dream?

Although Rose couldn't remember for sure, she felt for some reason that this wasn't the first time the same boy had made an appearance in her river dream. In fact, Rose had a strange, gnawing feeling he had been in the same dream every time, always peering down from Rose on that same boulder, halfway blocking the shape of the sun...

By the time Rose's mom reached the school, Rose was almost entirely in her reverie. She broke out of it instantly, though, as she caught a glimpse of her familiar friend group slouching in a semi-circle around the flagpole, their usual hangout spot. Rose thrashed out of the car, barked a quick goodbye to her mother, and all but broke into a run toward her friends and toward the last day of life as she had previously known it.

Chapter 2

The River

Rose pressed her nose against the rear window of her parent's car. The Juke was rolling along a dirt road, either side of the road lined with a wall of trees. Rose couldn't see anything through the thick of the woods, just trees beyond trees. Her grandparents' cabin loomed up ahead, looking tiny and cozy and like it belonged on a postcard against the backdrop of trees and greenery. Where Rose was perched, she couldn't quite make out the raging river that tore through the woods behind the cabin, but she could hear the roar even over the sound of music pouring from the car radio.

Just hearing the noise of thrashing water made the hair on Rose's arms stand on end. She had been terrified of moving water since the near death. In fact, she had never even learned to swim because of her crippling fear. In hindsight, it may have given Rose some much-needed confidence if she had learned to swim. But Rose never quite got over the thought of her lungs filling up the way they had that day.

As the car rolled up to the cabin, the figures of Rose's grandparents emerged from their doorway. Their pudgy, limping figures waved vigorously, and Rose sighed one last, heartfelt time for her parents so they would feel properly guilty as they sent their daughter away for the summer.

Rose stepped out of the car and took in a deep breath, preparing for the obligatory hugs that were rapidly approaching. Her grandma limped as fast as she could toward Rose, which was not incredibly fast due to her old age. Circling her face and falling to her shoulders were wispy gray curls, which were so old and fragile that it looked like she sported a wig on her old, wrinkly head. She was a bit overweight, causing her skin and fat to hang from her arms like limp, wrinkly bags, and those bags swung dangerously as she limped toward Rose with outstretched hands. Grandpa Greenwood, following close behind, was equally pudgy but in all the different places, sporting a great beer gut that poked out as though he had a pregnant belly. His head was entirely bald, but he had a gray beard and bushy mustache that covered his purple lips.

"Hi, Grandma Shirly," Rose greeted politely as she was engulfed in a saggy, droopy hug. "And hi, Grandpa Roger."

"Oh, look at how big you've grown!" squealed Grandma Shirly, giving the most cliché relative-who-never-bothers-to-be-part-of-your-life response.

Competing with Grandma Shirly for Most Cliché Grandparent Thing to Say Award, Grandpa Roger followed this up with, "I'll bet you break all the boy's hearts at school, eh?"

Rose felt her cheeks coloring a little at the comment as she was released from her grandma's hug and turned to give Grandpa Roger a hug as well. Mom and Dad came to exchange some quick words, thanking them for being willing to take her for the summer. As the adults exchanged words, Rose did a quick survey of the area now that she was out of the car. From here, she could see the raging water. The river looked mean and fierce, ripping through the earth, splaying around jagged rocks, sending a shiver down Rose's spine. Part of her wanted to turn around and jump right back into the safety of the family Juke. On the other hand, there was a little tug deep in the pit of her stomach telling her to draw nearer to the water. She shook this off, forcefully turning back to her grandparents and parents.

Her dad tugged her suitcase out of the backseat of the car and handed it off to Grandpa Roger, deep in a discussion about last Sunday's football game.

Meanwhile, Grandma Shirly was talking Mom's ear off about some animal that keeps rummaging through their garbage at night and waking them up. Rose's heart sank even further as she thought about how far removed the cabin was from the rest of civilization. Animals rummaging through the trash at night? And come to think of it, Rose couldn't remember the last house or cabin they passed on the way up. It could have been miles back for all she knew. Why do her grandparents live out here? And what was she expected to do to pass the time while here?

"Kay, Freckles," Dad said, ending his conversation with Grandpa and turning to face Rose. "Give me a hug goodbye!"

Dad opened his arms wide and Rose dove into them, wanting to cling to her father until he whisked her away and took her back home. She wanted to pull Mom into the hug too so they could both be enveloped in the smell of Dad's herbal, earthy cologne. She wanted to go back home with both parents and continue life together as a little team, a little family.

As her dad began pulling away from the hug, Rose was struck with the realization that the next time she saw her parents, their divorce would be finalized, and they'd be living in different houses. It dawned on Rose that this was probably the reason they were sending her to live with Grandma and Grandpa Greenwood in the first place. They needed to get her out of the way so they could fight over belongings and property and move out. Before her dad could pull away, Rose dove back into his chest and demanded a longer hug. Her dad obliged, wrapping his arms around her head in a tight hug and protecting her from the real world.

Finally, Rose had to let go. She gave her mom an equally long hug, ignoring the look of tears welling in her mom's eyes for the second time that same day. Rose had a feeling her mom had been struck, too, by the realization that this was the last time their family would be together as a family. From now on, it would be weekend visits and double holiday celebrations and having two sets of rooms and everything. Rose's eyes puddled with tears at the thought, which she dabbed away before anyone noticed.

When she had given both her parents a hug goodbye, she followed Grandma and Grandpa Greenwood to the front porch and watched her parents turn the Juke around and drive down the little dirt path. She stayed there, watching the disappearing parents until they were long out of her sight. Finally, she turned to her grandparents and followed them into the cabin that would serve as home for the next couple months.

Upon entering the cabin, Rose realized she had no idea what to expect from the inside. Apparently her one visit had been long ago enough that she didn't even have any fuzzy recollection of decorations or the layout of the home. It only took Rose about thirty seconds inside the cabin to recognize her grandparent's obsession with black bears and moose. Every wooden wall of the cabin was adorned with a picture of a black bear, each with cute captions such as 'Life's a bear!' On every table stood small bear or moose figurines, some wearing little fishermen costumes and holding a fishing pole, some climbing a giant honeybee hive, some laying at the edge of a table with its arms and legs dangling off the end. In the corner of the living room, which was directly to the left of the main entrance, stood a tall lamp being held up by a skinny wooden moose. To the right of the main entrance was the kitchen, which Grandma Shirley assured Rose was well stocked with treats and goodies she was welcome to help herself to. Traveling through the kitchen was the only way to the rest of the cabin. There was an entryway on the opposite end of the kitchen from the main entrance leading to a small television room. Along the back wall of the television room was a wide window watching over the river behind the cabin. To the right of the TV room was where her grandparents' room, bathroom, and laundry room stood. To the left was the guest room, which would be Rose's room during her stay.

That was it. There was nothing else to look at in the cabin. No upstairs, no downstairs, no places for Rose to explore or waste away the hours. If Rose had any fleeting hope before that she might be able to find a fun way to spend her summer vacation, those hopes had now been dashed away. Rose knew she would be facing some of the most boring months of her life during this stay.

After politely declining her grandma's offer of making her a snack, Rose gently closed the door to the guest room and took in her surroundings. There was one wooden desk lining the inside wall of the bedroom. The outside wall was taken up primarily by a window that looked out at the river. Pushed up against the only other wall in the bedroom was a full-sized bed, looking like a hotel bed with the covers pulled and tucked so tightly you could bounce a dime off the surface. Because she was already fearing dying of boredom, Rose wasted no time unpacking her suitcase into her new temporary bedroom. She loaded her clothing into the dresser and set her small number of toiletries on the top of the dresser, deciding to keep it all in her room rather than cluttering her grandparents' bathroom with all her own belongings. Once Rose had finished unpacking her suitcase, she sat on the meticulously made bed and stared out the window at the river.

Once again, Rose felt a chill run down her spine while simultaneously something tugged at the pit of her stomach, begging her to go to the river. She shook her head, hoping to shake the feeling away. Her whole life, she had been so terrified of water that she hadn't even braved it long enough to learn how to swim. Now, unexplainably, Rose had a desire to go step out into the river and feel the chill of the water streaming around her legs. She wanted to run her hands across the mossy, cold rocks along the riverbed. She wanted to…what? Search the riverbed for the little door from her dreams?

Of course, there wasn't a little door in the river.

Chalking the odd feelings up to boredom, Rose decided she needed to find something, anything, to do. First, she burned an hour by sitting with Grandpa Roger and watching ESPN news. Because she had never taken an interest in any sport in her entire life, this didn't hold her attention long. Next, she strolled into her grandparents' room to find her grandma, who was folding laundry and tucking it away into her dresser. She began asking questions about Grandma Shirly's childhood and the Greenwood ancestors, listening, and mindlessly outlining the scar on her palm. After about forty minutes, Rose moved idly to the kitchen and found herself a snack. She found some hostess cakes in the pantry and some milk and chocolate syrup in the fridge. She made herself chocolate milk and sat at the kitchen table, staring absentmindedly at the clock on the stove.

I'm going to die. Rose realized, dropping her head onto her hands, and staring at the clock as it turned from 9:21 to 9:22.

Finally, determining it was late enough and there was nothing better to do, Rose turned in for the night. Perhaps it was because of the proximity to the rushing sound of the river, but Rose's dreams were filled once again with the coldness of a river and the stunning blue eyes of an elf-boy.

***

The next morning, Rose woke to the urgent thought that she needed to go to the river. She shook it off and went about her morning routine, helping herself to breakfast and then a warm shower in her grandparents' bathroom. The entire time, there was a nagging at the back of her mind, reminding her the river was there, only about thirty yards away.

Finally, after another two hours of searching aimlessly for something to do, Rose gave in to the gnawing in her stomach. She stepped out onto the back porch, glaring into the sun and at the raging river.

As she approached, her heart beat faster. The river looked unforgiving, ripping through the woods, creating a frothy white foam at the surface of the water. Rose stopped short of the river, remaining a solid two feet away from the water's edge. After the terrifying and painful dreams, she had no desire to draw closer to the water.

That is, until a familiar looking boulder caught her interest.

Rose turned her attention to a boulder only a couple yards away from where she had stopped. The boulder pushed up against the raging river, blocking part of the pathway and forcing the river to move furiously around its sides. It stood tall enough that one could perch over the water and be safe from the pull of the rapids, yet you could still stick your arms into the water.

Drawing a deep breath, Rose moved to inspect the boulder closer. Every time she ever tried to draw up anything specific from her dream, she had always been left with hazy details and unclear images. At this moment, however, staring at the boulder, Rose was quite certain this was the exact same one that appeared in her dream. The one the boy was perched on, staring down at her, reaching into the water.

Perhaps, Rose thought, carefully moving closer to the boulder until her foot securely stood on it. *Perhaps it isn't a dream, but a memory.*

But as soon as the thought came into her head, she chased it away. No, that's impossible. There had been no elf-boy there the day she drowned. She had already had this thought before.

Rose shifted her weight so she was standing fully on the boulder. She dropped to her knees, then lowered herself on her arms so her belly rested flat against the boulder. She scooted herself forward using her arms until she was able to peer over the edge of the rock and stare down into the river, taking the exact same position the boy in her dreams had been in.

Rose studied the raging waters beneath her, facing her lifelong fear dead in the eye. From her safe perch, the rapidly moving river looked almost relaxing. She bravely scooted forward a little more so her arms were able to dangle over the edge of the rock. She extended her arms down so they dipped into the icy cold of the river, feeling a chill cover her skin. As soon as she emerged them, they seemed to take on a green tint, discoloring to the hue of the river itself. She examined the hairs on her arms, which pulled downstream with the movement of the water.

Perhaps it was the sunlight hitting a rock at the bottom of the river, or maybe a fish swimming by, or some other feasible explanation, but for one split second, Rose was sure she had caught sight of...a *little door?*

Rose gasped in shock, jolting her head in the

direction she had caught the image. Before she was able to confirm or deny the existence of the little door, Rose felt the awful pull of gravity yanking her to the river, her stomach slipping up into her throat. She flipped awkwardly, her legs dropping down to the level of her head before her head moved at all, and there was a loud splash as her body entered the water.

The river thrashed around Rose's body, but it was nothing like the calm chaos of her dream. Instead, her nose and mouth filled with water, sending a burning sensation through her sinuses. Her arms and legs smacked against large rocks and twigs, giving her scratches and pain shooting through every part of her body. She reached out, desperate to find something that would steady her. She was large enough that, if she could get a grip and pull herself upright, she would be able to stand up and climb out of the river. But her body was shocked at the sudden icy cold that had overtaken her and the impact of smacking down against the hard earth and rocks that it took seconds of awkward flailing before Rose was able to register what she was doing.

Rose stretched her arms out to catch any debris she could hang on to, and her right hand found a particularly flimsy feeling twig. Rose used the help of the twig to swing her body around so she was facing upriver instead of downriver, hoping she could fight against the tide better this direction. She was successful in flipping her body around, but the twig she clung to snapped in the process. Rose reached forward, searching for something sturdier.

Then, she saw it. The little door. The same door that appeared in her dreams. Small, wooden, with a dainty black handle. She placed her left hand down on a mossy, slippery rock below her and used the force to lunge her body forward, stretching her right hand toward the handle of the door. Her hand slipped against the moss in the process, and, as her right hand stretched out, her body crippled beneath her and her head slammed fiercely into the edge of a jagged, jutting rock. The last thing she saw before her vision blackened was her hand closing around the handle.

Then, black.

Chapter 3

The Elf-Boy

Rose blinked into the sun. The darkness that had overcome her vision was melting away, and Rose felt warmth baking into her wet skin. As she stared into the glimmering brightness of the sun, her view was partially blocked by the head of a boy. It was hard to make out features at first because her vision was still hazy and the sun shone into her eyes, making the head appear to be a black silhouette in front of Rose's face. The outline of the head showed messy hair and pointy ears that jutted straight out, blocking even more of the sun. The head tilted sideways, shielding the rays from Rose's vision, and she was able to make out the bluest eyes she had ever seen in her life, staring down at her with a combination of terror and confusion. With the rays of sunlight directly behind his head, the boy appeared to be glowing an iridescent yellow.

Rose realized she was just dreaming again. The only funny part was that there were a few differences between this dream and the one she normally had. For example, normally she never gets pulled out of the water by the boy. She always just misses his hand before she wakes up, ending the dream floating in the rapids. Right now, she was perched on the giant boulder in a puddle. Also, the boy looked significantly aged in this dream versus her usual dream. Normally, the boy appeared to be a small child. Now, the boy before her could hardly be called a boy. He was definitely older than Rose, despite the wide and innocent looking eyes staring down at her. And the last difference between the usual dream and the one Rose was currently having was the *pain.* There was a throbbing pain in her head, her body felt as though she had just put herself through a high cycle in the washer and dryer, and there was a burning sensation in her nose and face that seemed to be growing wider and hotter.

Overwhelmed with the painful burning in her face, Rose thrust her body up and onto her elbow, sputtering water from her nose and mouth as she coughed fiercely. It felt like every orifice in her head was leaking water—she was hacking up water out of her lungs, streams were leaking out each nostril, a warm sensation was sloshing around in each ear, and her eyes were pooling with tears—and the elf-boy jumped back as Rose spewed water. He watched with a horrified look on his face, his pointy ears thrust straight back on his head like a scared dog.

After a few minutes of confused hacking, Rose finally started seeing more clearly. The haze that had muddied her vision cleared and her head felt less groggy. With the confusion lifted, Rose eyed the elf-boy, realizing why this felt so different from her usual dream. Was it possible this...*wasn't a dream?*

"Who—" Rose sputtered, scrambling to sit up. She eyed the boy in front of her curiously as his pointy ears, which had laid straight back against his head during the past few minutes, shot up straight like a trained hunting dog listening for sounds in the distance. He was dressed from head to toe in all greens or browns in what appeared to be a scratchy fabric. Rose corrected herself. "*What a*re you?"

"Excuse me?" the boy asked, shocking Rose even further. In all the times he had appeared in her dreams, Rose had never considered what his voice would sound like. Now that he had spoken, she realized she had imagined his voice to be squeaky the way she imagined elf voices to sound. His voice was not at all squeaky, though not necessarily deep either. It was somewhere in the tenor range but was entirely ordinary and human-like.

"What are you?" Rose repeated, pulling herself to her feet to stand, feeling extremely vulnerable.

Somewhere deep inside herself, she knew she should feel afraid of this strange creature. For some reason, though, she just felt insanely curious. "Some kind of elf?"

"*Elf?!*" the boy yelled, the pointy tips of his ears turning red. He looked angry at the words. "I'm not an *elf*. I'm a Wood Dweller. And what exactly are *you?*"

He eyed her suspiciously the same way she had done to him, taking in her soaked red shirt and jeans, her muddy white sneakers, and her extremely rounded, fleshy ears.

"I'm a human, duh," she spat, feeling a twinge of anger at the judgmental tone he had taken up. Of course, he was on the defensive, as she had apparently said something quite offensive when she had asked if he was an elf. But she hadn't meant any harm, unlike him.

"A humanda?" Mr. Elf repeated, combining Rose's words together. She was almost certain he was making fun of her, as it was pretty obvious she was a human and there was no such thing as a humanda. Rose felt her cheeks coloring with heat, but before she was able to correct the boy, he jumped back in shock and terror and yelled, "Whoa! Why is your face doing that?!"

"Doing what?" Rose asked nervously, spinning to face the raging river next to her and peering over the edge of the boulder into her reflection. Her face looked entirely normal, although a little flushed with anger.

"It's—it's," the boy stammered, not sure if he

should be confused or terrified. "It's turning *red*."

Rose blinked, staring at him. Now fully convinced he was making fun of her, Rose turned on her heel and prepared to stomp away from him in a huff and return to her grandparents cabin. She stopped short, however, and gasped. Her grandparents' cabin, which had only been about thirty yards from the river, was gone. Just entirely gone, disappeared into thin air, non-existent, vanished, poof, not there. Rose spun around to see if she was just disoriented or confused and the cabin was somehow on the other side of the river. But no, the giant boulder had been on their side of the river. Rose turned again to stare at the place where her grandparents' cabin should be, hoping it would magically reappear the same way it had disappeared. Instead, all she saw in front of her were trees, more trees, and a little farther in the distance—Rose squinted, doubting the accuracy of her vision—little huts? Yes, she was sure they were little huts, several of them, with people roaming about. It appeared to be a little village in the woods.

"What is this place?" Rose gasped; her voice was nearly inaudible next to the massive thundering of the river. She began taking clumsy steps toward the little village, drawn by curiosity, and paying no attention to the unlevel ground before her. Her legs were unexpectedly pulled out from under her and Rose nosedived, her face slamming into dirt and narrowly missing the giant boulder.

"Hold it right there!" the non-elf demanded, his voice towering above Rose. She pulled herself up to her elbows, looking confused and feeling pain shoot through her already aching body.

"OW! Why did you do that?!" Rose snapped, peering up at the determined face of the boy. His expression was once again clouded in confusion and fear.

"Well, I'm not gonna let you just go strolling up to the village! I don't even know you. You could be a spy for the Other-Side."

"What other side?" Rose spat angrily, pulling herself to her knees gingerly and rubbing her right elbow, which was feeling particularly sore from the beating her body was taking that day.

"*The* Other-Side," the boy explained, as if this answered all of Rose's questions. Again, Rose felt anger bubbling up inside her, threatening to rip through her chest in an explosion of yelling fits. Who does this boy think he is? Why would he rescue her from drowning just to shove her down and call her a spy? And what happened to her grandparents' house, how had it turned into a tiny village? Rose wanted answers, and she was prepared to force this boy to give them to her. She stood to her feet, ready to round on the non-elf until he explained everything to her, but just as she made to do so, she realized the boy towered over her, probably about a half a foot taller than her. And his face wore an expression of pure determination, as though his life goal was to prevent Rose from reaching this village in the woods. Rose took a deep breath, deciding it was time to try a new angle.

"Listen," Rose said, brushing the dirt from her

jeans, noticing they had received a nice rip down the leg from the tumble with the river. "We're getting nowhere with this. I'm sorry I called you an elf. My name is Rose Greenwood."

Rose stuck out her hand in greeting. The boy just stared at it as though he wasn't sure what he was supposed to do with it. Then, the funny idea struck Rose that maybe he didn't know what to do with it. With a sigh, Rose let her hand drop to her side, and the boy eyed her suspiciously. Finally, after a tense and awkward silence, the boy replied, "Rylan. Rylan the Small."

"Rylan the *Small?*" Rose asked dubiously, scrutinizing Rylan's tall and slender figure. Was he joking? Then, seeing the warning look on his face, she rushed to add, "I'm not a spy."

"Which is what a spy would say," Rylan answered. Rose fought the urge to roll her eyes.

"Also what a not-spy would say," she pointed out. Seeing his mouth open to argue, she rushed forward to change the subject. "I just don't know where I am or how I got here."

Rylan stared at her, as if trying to make a decision. Then he asked, "You really don't know this place?" Rose shook her head, and he seemed to be deep in thought with consideration. Finally, he seemed satisfied with her answer. He flopped back toward a tree and leaned up against it, perching one barefoot up against the rough bark and leaving the other on the ground to keep him stable. He crossed his arms and smiled smugly. "So, you don't know how you got here.

I can help you with part of that. You were in the river, dying."

"Yeah," Rose replied, feeling a small blush coming on at the realization that Rylan had pulled her out of the river and saved her. "Thank you. For saving me."

Rylan's smug expression that had crossed his face dropped as fast as it had appeared. "It's happening again. Your face, it's turning red."

This only served to deepen Rose's blush. "It's—it's a blush," she stammered, embarrassed both that he was so openly pointing out her blush and at the realization that he hadn't been teasing her before.

"A blush?" he repeated, looking unsure. The word sounded foreign on his lips.

"Yes, you don't ever turn red when you're mad or hot or—" Rose hesitated on the last word, not wanting to admit how she was feeling, "—embarrassed?"

"Not that I know of. I've never seen it happen before," Rylan answered, sounding unsure. Now that he had let his guard down a little bit, Rose noticed how young he truly was. When not guarded and on the defense, Rylan's features softened around the edges and his face seemed to tug into a natural playful smile. He looked at ease and comfortable in the woods, not seeming bothered at all by his bare feet or the rough bark of the tree he leaned against. Rose was sure he couldn't have been much older than her; he appeared still in his teen years.

"What else is different between Wood Dwellers and humans?" Rose asked, curiosity bubbling inside her chest.

"Wait," Rylan barked, once again looking suspiciously at Rose. "I thought you were a humanda?"

"Human," Rose corrected. "A humanda isn't a thing…"

"You mean to tell me you're a human," Rylan snapped, his face hardening once again. "But you're not from the Other-Side?"

Rose huffed a little, trying to keep her patience with Rylan. "I don't even know what other side you're talking about."

After seeing the flicker of confusion cross Rylan's face, she decided to let it drop. "Anyway, as we were talking about before. I fell into the river, and hit my head…" Rose trailed off, the memory coming back to her. The last thing she saw before waking up to Rylan's face was the little door! "I saw a little door!" Rose shrieked, the memory flooding back to her.

Rylan's foot dropped off the tree in surprise at her sudden outburst, nearly knocking him over. When he had steadied himself, he asked, "You saw a door? In the river?"

Rose nodded excitedly, rushed back to the boulder, and peered over the edge. She searched the riverbed for the familiar wooden door. After a moment, Rose decided the little door was no longer there, but she didn't lose hope. Perhaps the Wood Dwellers knew all about the little door and why it was in the river. Maybe then Rylan could help Rose figure out how to make her grandparents' cabin reappear.

"Have you ever seen it before? The little door?" Rose rushed to ask Rylan, only glancing up for a second as she searched the riverbed. "Maybe the door is my key to getting back home! Maybe if I touch it—yes, that's right, I grabbed the knob right before I blacked out, maybe if I can grab it again then I can go back to my grandparents' cabin!"

Rose looked up at Rylan, hoping he could point her to the little door which would take her home. Her heart deflated when she saw the look of confusion on Rylan's face.

"How could there be a door in the river?" Rylan asked, putting words to the thoughts Rose had experienced her whole life. "It's not possible."

"Then—" Rose said, dropping her face back toward the river, peering through the rippling water at the riverbed. She could see twigs, rocks, and even a fish swimming rapidly past her perch. But Rose did not see any signs of a little door. "Where is my grandparents' cabin? How did I get here?"

Before Rylan could answer either question, Rose hopped down from the boulder and followed the river upstream. Perhaps the force of the tide moved her away from the little door before Rylan found her? Then all she would have to do is follow the river awhile until she found the little door. Rose hurriedly scanned every inch of the riverbed within her eyesight, moving a few inches every couple seconds so she was constantly checking a new area. After a moment of silence, aside from the rushing sound of water, Rose threw a look over her shoulder and saw Rylan awkwardly following her, glancing over his shoulders as though looking for help—or a way to escape.

"Well," Rose snapped, no longer caring about keeping a jovial relationship with Rylan. "Wanna help me or not?"

Rylan shuffled his feet awkwardly. "I don't really think I'm qualified to give you the help you need…" he mumbled. Rose shot him an angry look and he suddenly became extremely interested in a cloud in the sky. Rose continued her search a few more inches before Rylan interrupted, saying, "Look, no offense, but you look crazy inching your way along the river, staring into the water at nothing, sopping wet from top to bottom. Why don't you come into the village with me and clean up?"

Rose shot another dirty look at Rylan.

"Then I'll help you look," Rylan rushed to add.

"Don't call me crazy," Rose snapped, not willing to forgive Rylan just yet. Rylan rolled his eyes.

"I said no offense," he answered hotly. Then, looking increasingly uncomfortable as Rose crossed her arms, refusing to move away from the river, he resorted to pleading. "Come on. Have you ever been to Mavarak before?"

Even though Rose itched to continue her search for the little door in the river and wanted desperately to get back to her grandparents' cabin to change into warm, dry clothes, her curiosity flared at the foreign word.

"Muh-ver-ick?" Rose asked, slowing the word down to hit all the unfamiliar syllables.

"Yeah, Mavarak" Rylan repeated the word, his

blue eyes dancing with excitement. He turned toward the village off in the distance and pointed. "It's my home. You'll love it."

"What makes you think I'll love it?" Rose asked, feeling defiant. She didn't like Rylan assuming he knew anything about her.

"Well—okay, I have no clue if you'll love it, I just said that to get you to follow. But we can't just stand here all day. And you got a nasty gash in your head, we should go clean that up."

Rose reached up to her head and felt the gash Rylan was referring to. She hadn't paid much attention to the throbbing in her head since her whole body was hurting a little from everything she had been through, but now that she was paying attention to it, she realized the pain in her head was burning ferociously. And, now that she was noticing how bad everything hurt, a shooting pain was going through her hand as well. Rose inspected the pain on her hand and saw a wide cut going along her palm. She hoped she wouldn't have a second scar to match the one on her right hand. Perhaps it was all in her head, but it felt as though her hands and legs were riddled with scratches and bruises as well. And she would really love to get out of the wet clothes—which were now drying unevenly, leaving her jeans stiff and uncomfortable and her shirt smelling of fish and dirty river—hanging off her body in unflattering folds.

"You promise you'll help me look after?" Rose asked, looking uncertainly at Rylan. She had only just met him, and so far, she wasn't super impressed with him, so she wasn't sure how much trust he deserved just yet.

"Promise," Rylan hurriedly agreed.

"Pinky promise?" Rose asked, sticking out her pinky. Rylan tilted one ear back in a questioning look.

"What's a pinky promise?" he asked. Rose opened her mouth to speak but gave up and instead let out a long sigh, gesturing for him to forget it and lead the way.

Rylan turned and practically bounced as he led Rose to Mavarak. He clearly knew the woods like the back of his hands, because he was able to expertly hop each large rock and duck every jutting branch with ease, continuing conversation as though he were going on a leisurely stroll through a park. Meanwhile, Rose tripped in several places and added a few new cuts to her cheeks and arms by walking into branches that Rylan oh-so-courteously let go with a *smack!*

After a few minutes of walking through the thick of the woods, the trees opened to a grassy clearing. Based on the expanse of grass Rose could make out, she assumed the clearing could probably fit about one football field in it with a little bit of extra wiggle room. Or, in this case, a small village. The village was nestled into the woods, almost blending in with natural colors of brown, green, and gray. Around the outskirts of the clearing were several small huts that used the earth itself as building material. The first hut Rose passed was so well camouflaged into the woods, in fact, that she was only about two feet away from the entrance when a large Wood Dweller crashed through what Rose had taken to be the bark of a tree and sent Rose spiraling sideways into Rylan, who caught her easily and with a loud laugh as though he had planned for it all to happen. Rose squinted at him suspiciously, wondering if he had, in fact, led them so close to the hut on purpose, but he continued right along forward on the path without noticing her look.

Once they entered the heart of the village, though, Rose was taken with how loud the villagers were. She hadn't heard a single sound when they were standing at the river. Now, however, the village was alive with hooting, hollering, calling out to friends, and the sound of life. It was as though Rose and Rylan had stepped over a threshold and all the sound had burst forward. Since Rose had absolutely no clue what Wood Dwellers could do—did they have magical abilities? —she didn't entirely rule it out as a possibility.

The huts were almost more like little caves growing directly out of the ground or, more popularly, the trees. Each hut stood only about ten feet high and was made out of wood, seemingly held up by rocks and glued together by mud. There were perfectly shaped windows cut out of the walls and doors in every hut, and Rose could hear the chattering voices of the Wood Dwellers inside. Leaves adorned the front doors of every home like little wreaths, some spelling out words ('Welcome!' or 'Woods sweet woods,'), some lined up to form simple shapes. The doorknobs appeared to be acorns. There were no gates blocking off certain huts from the others, and the Wood Dwellers seemed to all know each other personally. Rose saw no signs of normal neighborhood items such as mailboxes, bikes, trailers, neighbors walking dogs on leashes. She did, however, pass someone who seemed to be feeding berries to a horse…with wings? Rose stared as she walked by, witnessing the horse creature spit into the Wood Dwellers eyes.

"No!" the Wood Dweller gasped. "Bebes, I'm not ready for a—" the Wood Dweller let out a giant yawn, rubbing his eyes sleepily. "Well, maybe just a little one." And he crumpled to the grass, snoring. Other Wood Dwellers continued past, simply stepping over the sleeping body, and the winged horse casually bent down and continued eating the berries out of the Wood Dweller's hand.

Rose was still watching the now sleeping Wood Dweller when she ran directly into the back of Rylan.

"Oof!" Rose gasped, the air whooshing out of her with the sudden impact. "What gives?"

"This is my home!" Rylan exclaimed, turning his smiling face to Rose. She looked up past him at the hut that stood before him. This hut was built out of two trees, one at either back corner, and it was a bit shorter than all the rest of the huts, standing about 8 feet tall. On the front door—which appeared to be made of tree bark and was jagged and uneven along both the top and the bottom—tiny leaves were arranged in the words 'It's the Small things in life.' There was one small window directly to the right of the door and wafting from the opening was the sweet smell of fresh berries. "Mmm, you came on the perfect day. Mom's making jam!"

For some reason Rose couldn't explain, it slightly annoyed her that Rylan said she had *come* on the perfect day, as though she had chosen to do so. Before she had a chance to give him any sort of sassy remark, however, Rylan twisted the acorn doorknob and shoved the door open to the hut. Rose stepped in, amazed at the sight before her. The front door opened to a living room tastefully decorated and furnished with all entirely natural materials. There were rocks stacked up on top of each other to create a coat hanger directly next to the front door, leaves twisted around each other and glued together with mud to form a couch that lined the left wall of the room. An animal pelt of a creature Rose didn't recognize spanned the floor, covering the mud and dirt below. The color of the animal pelt was so bizarre Rose bent down to examine it closer, noticing the fur of the animal was such a deep shade of black that the gleam was a tint of dark blue. Hanging from the ceiling in an arch, like the way Rose's best friend back home decorated her bedroom with Christmas lights, were several acorns strung together on a thin string. Long leaves cascaded from the ceiling over the window opening, acting as blinds, and were tied off to either side of the window with a sharp blade of grass.

Along the wall opposite the front door were the two trees Rose had seen from the outside of the hut. Each tree fused into the wall, and there was an opening in each tree.

"Mom!" Rylan yelled, closing the front door to the hut behind Rose.

"In the kitchen!" a sweet voice chirped from the opening of the tree on the right, reminding Rose of a songbird. Rylan led Rose, who was wonderstruck by the beauty of the hut, through the living room, over the strange animal pelt, and to the opening in the tree trunk. When Rose passed through the opening, she stopped in her tracks and gasped.

If she had thought the living room was amazing, she was absolutely blown away by the kitchen.

From the outside, Rose had been sure the tree was an entirely average sized tree, being only about a foot wide at best. From the inside, the tree opened into a full-sized kitchen, with all kitchen appliances and furniture seeming to have been grown from the tree itself. Everything was wood, and not the rough, sharp bark found on the outside of a tree, but the soft, smooth flesh of a tree. There was a window on the far side of the kitchen, again just an opening cut straight into the tree, that let natural light flow into the tree kitchen. The earthy, herbal smell of the tree mixed harmoniously with the smell of berries, filling Rose's nostrils with warmth. Bending over a wooden table in the center of the kitchen was a beautiful Wood Dweller crushing bright, cheerful berries in a stone bowl with a stone tool. There were several jar-shaped slabs of wood filled with the same purple substance lined along the table.

The second the beautiful Wood Dweller's eyes fell upon Rose, she gasped and jumped back, covering her mouth with her hands and launching the stone bowl filled with half crushed berries to the ground.

Rose noticed the Wood Dweller had the same bright, stunningly blue eyes as her son. They caught the light as she stared at Rose, giving her eyes a shimmer. She had full blonde hair that fell in soft curls around her pointed ears, which were now pointed straight up in surprise. The Wood Dweller was shorter than Rylan by several inches, closer to Rose's height, but otherwise looked incredibly like him.

"Mom," Rylan greeted, moving in toward his mother and enclosing her with a soft hug. "This is Rose. Rose, this is my mom, Robin the Small."

If Rose had expected anything from Robin, it wasn't what came next. The next thing Rose knew, she had been swooped into a tight hug that caught her off guard and almost knocked her off balance, pinning her arms down to her sides as Robin wrapped her own arms tightly around Rose's middle.

"Rosalie," Robin said, using Rose's full name as though she were a family member. "My love, how have you been?"

Rose was confused by the familiar greeting, as though she were some sort of long-lost relation or an old friend.

Rose looked past the locks of blonde waves and over Robin's shoulder and was relieved, yet more confused, to see Rylan looked just as shocked by the reaction.

"Nice to meet you," Rose said, squirming awkwardly in Robin's arms. As if hurt by the lack of warmth in Rose's response, Robin yanked herself back from Rose and grabbed each of her arms, keeping them pinned at her side. She looked deep into Rose's eyes with her wide, blue saucers of eyes, as if searching her soul for something.

"Ah, yes," Robin murmured. As if she had just remembered the proper way to meet someone for the first time, she stepped back from Rose and gave her a pleasant smile. "It is my pleasure."

"Mom," Rylan said deliberately, as though he wasn't sure she was feeling okay. "Rose fell in the river. Her clothes got soaked and she got hurt, I told her we could help her."

"Yes of course!" Robin cried without hesitation. She had the classic protective mama bear thing going, with urgency trickling into her voice. She stepped to the side of the kitchen and bent out another opening on the right-side wall of the kitchen that Rose hadn't noticed. "Drew! Will you please bring down the herbal medicine kit!"

"Yeah, Mom!" a voice responded, and Robin pulled her head back into the opening. With this one simple task for Robin, Rose was filled instantaneously with more questions. Had the voice just called from an upstairs? If so, where is the upstairs? The hut itself had not been tall enough for a second story, since it was on the shorter side of most of the huts in Mavarak. Was the upstairs...*inside the tree?* Also, an herbal medicine kit? Was that supposed to be like a first aid kit?

Before Rose could pose any of these questions, Robin marched over to what appeared to be a sink embedded in the tree kitchen and pulled a sopping wet leaf out of the basin.

"You," Robin said, directing her words to Rylan now as she scurried back over to Rose with the wet leaf. She softly dabbed the leaf along Rose's forehead, cheeks, nose, and chin. The coolness of the leaf felt soothing against the cuts on Rose's face, and she could feel the grit and dirt being lifted from her skin. "Take Rosalie to my room and help her pick out fresh clothes. Then take her to your room and let her change, she'll have more privacy there."

Then Robin stepped back from Rose and Rose could see the leaf was now soiled with dirt and blood. She felt a pang of embarrassment. It hadn't occurred to her quite how dirty she had gotten from falling in the river.

Rylan obediently led Rose out of the tree, across the living room, and into the opening in the tree on the other side of the hut. When they stepped into the tree on the other side of the hut, Rose saw this room was similar to the kitchen, with the furniture seeming to have been carved directly out of the inside of the tree itself. This room was clearly a bedroom, with a wooden dresser along one wall and a leaf-made bed in the center of the room. Rylan led Rose to the dresser in the room and opened the top drawer. There were several blouses, all of which were different shades of green or brown. Rose picked out a dark green shirt and matched it with the smallest pair of dark brown pants, hoping they would fit her comfortably and wouldn't hang off her body like a potato sack, which is what the material seemed to be made of.

Then, Rylan directed Rose to the window opening along the outside wall of the bedroom. Rose went to it and popped her head out of the opening as Robin had done when calling for Drew, who Rose assumed was Rylan's brother. Rose felt silly sticking her head out the window and looking down at the grass below, having no clue what Rylan had meant for her to do.

"You gonna just sit there and watch the grass grow, or are you gonna go upstairs?" Rylan taunted from behind her. Rose glanced to the side of the window and saw there were clearly steps etched into the side of the tree leading straight up. Rose followed the rungs built into the tree until they reached what Rose could only describe as a tree house, hidden by a mess of leaves and branches in the tree above.

By the time Rose had awkwardly climbed up the tree (which Rylan had annoyingly assured her was the slowest he had ever seen anyone climb a tree), changed into the green and brown clothes—which were oddly soft and brushed gently against her skin, seeming to shrink when on her body so as to fit her exactly right—and allowed Robin to wipe away all the dirt from her arms and legs and rub an earthy smelling medicine on each cut on her beaten body, night had fallen over the village and the villagers were beginning to quiet down.

Robin politely offered the spare tree to Rose. At first, Rose refused the offer, insisting she needed to get back to her grandparents' and they would be worried sick about her. Then, with a heavy feeling in her stomach, Rose realized she had no way of getting back home anyways, and Robin's home felt safe, secure, and oddly familiar to Rose.

As she nestled into her leaf bed in the spare tree of Robin's hut, staring up into the treetop roof, Rose's thoughts turned to her mom and dad. By now, her grandparents would have told her parents she had gone missing. What would they think? Would they wonder if she had purposely run away, or would they fear the same river that had nearly taken her life before? Would they already have driven back to the cabin to search for her? Or would the divorce paperwork be taking up too much of their time?

With thoughts of her mom and dad swirling around her head, and ultimately the wish that she could be snuggled up warm and close to her parents, together again as one happy family, Rose drifted into sleep. Rose dreamt that night, but for the first time in months, she did not dream of falling into the raging river. This time, Rose dreamt of flying on the back of a winged horse.

Chapter 4

The Other-Side

The sound of chirping birds and the smell of sweet berries woke Rose the next morning. When she first groggily opened her sleepy eyes, she had nearly forgotten where she was. Spending one single night in her grandparents' spare room and then the next night in Robin's spare tree was messing with her mind, and she was confused when she lifted her head off the leaf-pillow in a room that was not at all her room in a home that was not at all her parents' house.

The memories of the day before rushed back to

Rose and hit her like a truck, sending her sprawling off her bed in excitement. She needed to get an early start on getting to the bottom of the disappearing door in the river so she could return home before her grandparents worried too much.

Actually, Rose realized it was probably too late for that. She had been missing for at least twelve hours and likely closer to 24 hours. By now, her grandparents had probably called the police. She imagined her parents were back in the woods, searching for her. Hopefully working together, maybe reigniting their love, but probably not.

Rose had never heard it, but apparently at some point in the night Robin had brought in a new fresh pair of clothes. Rose eyed the ones she had been wearing overnight. They didn't appear to be night clothes, but she wasn't sure if the Wood Dwellers had night clothes. Whichever way, Robin had clearly thought Rose would want to change into new clothes for the day, so she obeyed, slipping into a grass green blouse and light brown shorts.

When she arrived in the kitchen, Rylan and Robin were already sitting at the wooden table and eating what appeared to be bread smeared with Robin's berry jam, along with another young boy who looked like an exact replica of Rylan but significantly shorter and, according to the round face that still clung to its baby fat, much younger. Rose guessed he was about ten years old, but she wasn't exactly sure since Rylan's face seemed to grow younger and older depending entirely on how playful he was feeling at that exact moment.

"Merry to see you," Rylan greeted Rose through a mouthful of berries and bread.

"Rylan, manners," Robin snapped, scowling at her eldest son before turning a bright smile toward Rose. "Merry to see you!"

"Good morn—er, merry to see you," Rose murmured back.

"This is Rylan's brother, Drew," Robin introduced, gesturing toward the young boy who had just taken such a large bite of his breakfast that berry jam smeared across both of his cheeks. "As you can see, he does occasionally come out of his tree."

"And, as you can see, we have good reason for keeping him up there so much," Rylan teased, swiping his own bread across Drew's face to cover even more of his cheeks with berry jam.

"Merry to see you," Drew said, dropping his bread and using the back of his hand to wipe up some of the sticky jam. His face looked only slightly better afterward.

"Why don't you have some breakfast," Robin offered sweetly, holding up a basketful of fresh-smelling bread. The warmth radiated out of the basket and wrapped around Rose's face as she took a seat.

"It's the most delicious bread in the woods," Rylan mumbled through another mouthful of bread and berries, ignoring the dirty look Robin was shooting him. "Even the Other-Side doesn't have bread like it!"

Rose picked up a piece of warm bread from the

basket and pulled a wooden knife out of a jam jar, spreading a thin layer of the purple goo. She silently wondered what Rylan meant about the Other-Side. He had mentioned it the day before, too, when he had accused her of being a spy for the Other-Side. Rose's cheeks heated up at the memory. She had woken up in a good mood and had nearly forgotten she didn't much care for Rylan, but upon remembering their first meeting, she shot Rylan a sour look for no good reason. He seemed confused and glanced over his shoulder, as if he thought the look may have been for someone else.

Rose let her teeth sink into the doughy, sticky goodness and was filled in an instant with the warmest, happiest sensation she had ever felt. The sweet tartness of the berries matched perfectly with the soft, flaky bread that melted in her mouth, and she was overwhelmed with a desire to stuff the whole piece of bread into her face the way Drew had done. Chunks of berry dripped onto Rose's fingers, but she ignored the stickiness entirely and sunk her teeth into another bite of bread.

"—fhis is fmtastic," Rose mumbled through a mouthful of bread. Instantly she remembered the dirty look Robin had given to Rylan for talking with his mouth full and felt her face heat up with a blush.

"See, look!" Rylan nearly shouted, making Robin and Drew jump with the sudden explosion. He nudged Drew and then pointed at Rose's face with a piece of bread. "It turns red sometimes!"

"Whoa!" Drew gasped, his mouth dropping

open and exposing half-chewed bread and jam. "How do you do that?!"

"Boys, enough!" Robin snapped, giving both of her sons a warning look. Then she turned and smiled at Rose. "So, what are your plans for today, sweetie?"

Rose didn't like the way Robin had asked, as though she were here in Mavarak on vacation and not stuck against her will. If it had been Rylan who had asked the question, she would have probably shot him a dirty look or given him a sassy reply. As it was Robin, who had so far been nothing but sweet to her, albeit weird during their introduction, she couldn't help but push the annoyance to the side and answer respectfully.

"Rylan promised me he would help me look for, er—" Rose hesitated, remembering the look Rylan had given her the day before when she had mentioned the little door in the river. Wood Dwellers don't find it any more normal than humans do to see little doors at the bottom of rivers. "—something. I'm hoping to go home as soon as possible."

Rose hoped she hadn't sounded rude or ungrateful toward her hosts (except maybe to Rylan), but she also wanted to make it extremely clear she had no intentions of staying in Mavarak for another night. She couldn't stand the thought of so many of her loved ones searching through the woods aimlessly, worried sick about her. Plus, Rose didn't want to spend any more time with Rylan than necessary. He had already accused her of being a spy, called her crazy, and spoken to her in a sassy and accusing manner. She was ready to be rid of him.

When Rose had scarfed down three more pieces of bread with berry jam, her and Rylan set out the way they had come, toward the river. Although Rose had insisted to Robin she wouldn't be returning that night, Robin waved her off, refused to say a final goodbye, and ensured Rose she would be welcome to stay the night again if she needed. It was as though, Rose thought, she didn't believe Rose would be leaving that day.

Rose shook the thought away and followed Rylan out the front door and through the chaotic, grassy clearing that was Mavarak.

The Wood Dwellers—Mavarakites, as Rylan had called them—bustled around the same way as the day before. This time, Rose noticed, it seemed as though each person had some sort of job they were doing. For example, Rose passed three young Mavarakites who were climbing up trees and dropping strange fruits into a basket. Another Mavarkite was corralling several very young Mavarakites and playing games with them, with multiple teenaged Mavarakites helping with classroom management. Then there was a small group of Wood Dwellers standing in a shady corner of the village clearing chopping wood into small pieces. And Rose and Rylan passed a tent with several fierce looking Mavarakites sharpening the blades on arrows, bows sitting at their feet.

"Do all Mavarakites have jobs?" Rose asked as Rylan lead her past the bow and arrow tent, eyeing a ginormous pile of arrows that must have been already sharpened and were looking particularly lethal.

"Well yeah, what else do you think we do all day?" Rylan remarked, not even slowing his pace. He seemed to want to get rid of Rose as bad as Rose wanted to rid herself of him. "Except the ones that are too young. They usually just learn about all the different jobs and then do stuff like play, sing, act in plays, you know. That sort of thing."

Rose scurried to catch up with Rylan, as her observations of the village were slowing her down. "Do you have a job?"

"Yeah, of course," Rylan tossed over his shoulder. "I care for the Trusks."

"The *Trusks?*" Rose repeated, wondering if she had heard correctly.

"The Trusks," Rylan said in a matter-of-fact voice, as though Rose were being stupid. "You know..." he finally slowed down, coming to a full stop so he could scan the village in search of the so-called Trusk he was referring to. Finally, he pointed in a direction back toward his hut and Rose followed his gaze, her eyes landing on one of the magical beasts she had seen the day before with a giant horse's body and head, giant wings, and magical spit which makes people fall asleep. Several of the strange creatures roamed through a large Trusk pen that was gated by wooden posts and vines. The pen was kept just along the outskirts of the village clearing, so one side of the pen ran along the thicker part of the woods. Trees from the woods cast shadows along the grassy Trusk pen, and many of the winged animals lounged under the shade to avoid the hot sun. The pen was nearby the Small's hut, which meant Rylan had a short walk to work every day.

"You take care of those things?!" Rose shrieked, watching as one of the roaming creatures reared back onto its hindlegs, looking deadly. Several of the Mavarakites near the penned creature scampered away, looking afraid for their lives. Rose was glad it was across the village from her.

"Yep! They're not as bad as they look. I have one, she's beautiful and a total sweetheart," Rylan gloated with a smile and faraway look in his eyes. "There is nothing, I repeat, nothing as wonderful as taking flight on one of those things."

Rose turned to look at Rylan, her eyes wide as saucers, wondering if he were kidding. Before either of them could say a word, Rose saw a tall Mavarakite sidling up behind Rylan, approaching the pair. He was a full head taller than Rylan and sported short, choppy brown hair. He was good looking, but he had a stern expression and wore what appeared to be armor. Contrasting against the majority of the Mavarakites Rose had seen, he sported almost exclusively brown and black colors, making him stick out even more than his height.

"Rylan," the Mavarakite said, his voice surprisingly jovial considering the stern and serious expression he sported. When Rylan turned in response to his name being called, his entire face brightened at the sight of the Mavarakite.

"Max, merry to see you! What are you doing

roaming the village? Are you doing work away from the hut today?" Rylan asked.

"Yes," Max answered, his brown eyes darkening. "Last night Jordan the Quiet was on watch in the Tower and witnessed several Other-Siders roaming the woods only about three yards from our border. We don't know if they have been tipped off, but we are checking to see that our Guardians are still standing and the village is still hidden."

Rylan nodded along to the news, seeming to understand everything he had just been informed of, but Rose was confused about several parts of what Max had just said. First, the Other-Side had again been mentioned, and Rose couldn't help but wonder who exactly these Other-Siders were. Based on conversations with Rylan and this comment Max had just made, Rose was gathering the Mavarakites were not particularly fond of the Other-Siders. But the part Rose was really intrigued by was this mention of the Guardians. What Guardians are protecting the village? How are they keeping the village hidden?

Rose pondered which of these questions she wanted to know most, and finally landed on, "What are the Guardians?"

Max looked fiercely at her, and she could clearly see his dark eyes flicker to her ears. The tip of his pointy ears began turning a deep red.

"Rylan," Max said, not taking his eyes off Rose. He noticed the round, fleshy ears protruding from her flat brown hair. "Who is this—this—*what is this creature?*"

"I'm a human," Rose answered confidently, taking care to not call herself a humanda again.

Max's nostrils flared in anger. "You brought a human into Mavarak?!"

"Don't worry," Rylan rushed to assure Max, stepping toward Rose and slightly in front of her, as if to protect her from Max. Or hide her. "This is Rose. She couldn't have been with the Other-Siders. She was with me and my family all night last night."

Max still eyed Rose intensely, but his anger seemed to dissolve into curiosity as his eyes scanned her, taking in the Mavarakite clothing she sported.

"I see," Max said. "Merry to see you, then. I'm Max the Warrior."

The Warrior, Rose thought, taking in the armor and all brown and black clothing Max sported. He certainly looked like a warrior.

"I'm Rose," Rose stated, then remembered Rylan had already told Max her name and she felt her cheeks warming with a blush. She hoped Rylan and Max wouldn't be able to see the blush, especially since Rylan never failed to make the blush deepen by pointing it out. To cover her embarrassment and the blush in her cheeks, Rose stuck her hand out toward Max to shake hands. Beside her, she could hear an audible sigh come from Rylan as he shook his head and covered his face with his hand in embarrassment. Meanwhile, Max stared at Rose's extended hand in bewilderment. Rose remembered Rylan's confusion when she had attempted to shake his hand the day before.

"What are you doing?" Max asked, staring at Rose's hand. She dropped her arm and whispered for them to forget it, but she could feel the blush in her cheeks growing darker.

"We better be going," Rylan said hurriedly, seizing Rose's arm and dragging her away from Max. "We have a lot to be doing today. Good luck checking on the Guardians! I'm sure it was nothing, those dopes on the Other-Side probably just got lucky."

Max tilted his head, not saying anything as Rylan dragged Rose away in embarrassment.

"Really? You have to act like that in front of *Max the Warrior* of all people?" Rylan asked, not letting go of Rose and not slowing his pace one bit as he stormed away from Max and toward the outskirts of the village. Rose stumbled over the unfamiliar terrain, not able to keep up with Rylan's pace. As they fled past other Mavarakites, Rose noticed a few curious glances following them.

"Let go! You're hurting me!" Rose snapped, yanking her arm out of Rylan's grip. Rylan shot her a dirty look but continued scurrying toward the edge of the village clearing. Rose scrambled to keep up. "And by the way, where I'm from it is incredibly polite and a show of respect to shake hands when meeting someone new!"

"*Shake hands?*" Rylan repeated, still not slowing his pace. Rose was practically jogging to keep up.

"Yes, shake hands! WOULD YOU SLOW DOWN?!" Rose shrieked. A clump of Mavarakites gathering fruits from a tree nearby turned to look at

Rose and Rylan. Rylan stopped walking through the clearing and sighed, turning on Rose to face her.

"Sorry. I just wanted to put some space between us and Max before he started asking more questions. He is an incredible warrior, and he is very protective and suspicious. And you showing up the day the Other-Siders appear near the border of the village does not look good," Rylan explained, lowering his voice with every word until he was in a low whisper and Rose had to lean her head in to hear. "Then you go and act weird, for all we know Max has already called the order to have you inspected and questioned."

"I wasn't acting weird!" Rose huffed, glaring at Rylan. "I was acting like a normal human! Normal humans shake hands when they meet, I already told you."

"What is shaking hands?" Rylan snapped, looking irritated. In response, Rose stuck out her hand toward Rylan.

"Put your hand out like this," Rose explained. Rylan followed instructions, and Rose clasped her hand around his and shook it. "It's our way of greeting someone new."

Rose dropped Rylan's hand, and he lifted his hand up to inspect it. "I don't think I did it right. It didn't do anything." He turned his palm toward Rose so she could see his bare hand.

Rose rolled her eyes. "It's not supposed to do anything. You just shake hands and then let go, that's all."

"But *why?*" Rylan asked, scrunching up his nose

in confusion.

Rose floundered, searching for words. "You just —it's just—you just do!"

"Hmm. Seems pointless to me," Rylan said, folding his arms over his chest.

"Well, you Mavarakites do pointless things, too!" Rose snapped, feeling anger bubble in her chest. "Like, why do you all wear only green and brown all the time?!"

"So we blend in, in case the Other-Siders find us," Rylan answered, raising an eyebrow at Rose. Rose scrambled to think of another thing she had seen the Mavarakites do that seemed pointless. She couldn't think of anything.

"And who are the Other-Siders you keep talking about?!" Rose snapped, changing the subject instead.

Rylan sighed, as though he were trying to calm down a small child throwing a fit. This aggravated Rose further. "Okay, okay, fair question. I'll show you the Other-Side and tell you about it when we get to the river. Let's just get out of here before you draw any more attention to yourself or the fact you don't belong here."

Rylan turned on his feet to continue their journey to the river, which shouldn't have taken nearly this long if it weren't for all the pauses and Rose finding reasons to yell at Rylan. As Rylan turned on the balls of his feet, however, he ran directly into a Mavarakite who had appeared unnoticed behind him.

"Oof—Lyla!" Rylan stammered, and Rose saw the tips of Rylan's ears turn red and his eyes pop open wide. Standing in front of Rylan was the most beautiful Mavarakite Rose had ever seen. Her beauty outshone even the most beautiful celebrities. She had a stunning waterfall of blonde hair cascading down her back in soft curls, reaching the small of her back, with soft flowers and vines woven into her hair in streaks. She had one small dimple on her right cheek and a beautiful, soft smile resting easily on her face. Her ears, like all the other Mavarakites, were pointed and poked through her blonde hair so just the tips were seen. She had blue eyes which, unlike Rylan's bright blue eyes, were deep like the depths of the ocean. Lyla was wrapped in a light green shirt and dark green shorts, and tiny pink flowers were woven into her clothing in the same way they were twisted into her hair.

"H-hi Lyla," Rylan stammered, and Rose thought she saw beads of sweat popping up on Rylan's forehead. For some reason Rose couldn't explain, Rylan's stuttering and stammering in front of this beautiful Mavarakite irritated Rose even more than anything else Rylan had said or done.

"Hello, Rylan," Lyla greeted sweetly, her voice a sing-song melodic sound. "Who is your friend?"

Lyla noticed Rose much sooner than Max had, which brought a blush back to Rose's face. Rose wanted to kick herself for blushing every time she met another new Mavarakite, especially this beautiful one who seemed to exude confidence in every blink of an eye or twinkle of a smile.

"My friend?" Rylan asked, apparently forgetting Rose's existence. Rose huffed and Rylan turned to her as though just remembering she existed. "Oh, right! This is Rose. Rose, this is Lyla. Lyla the Beautiful."

Rose stifled a laugh. Lyla the Beautiful? Who decided to call her that? Rose was seriously considering calling herself Rose the Stunningly Gorgeous and Amazing to the next Mavarakite Rylan introduced her to. As she considered this, Lyla interrupted her thoughts with yet another mention of the Other-Side.

"I assume you've heard the Other-Siders have been wandering around near the village?" Lyla asked Rylan, not even acknowledging Rose's existence. Rose decided she didn't like Lyla one bit. As Rylan nodded in confirmation, Rose tugged on his arm and took a step in the direction of the river.

"Rylan, we need to go," Rose urged, suddenly keen on leaving Lyla at that exact moment in time and searching the river for the little door.

Rylan waved a goodbye toward Lyla as Rose took her turn to drag Rylan across the woods. Lyla watched with a suspicious look in her eye as the pair headed in the direction of the river. "You're not going to do anything stupid are you?" she called after Rylan. "You know the Other-Siders are wicked, don't mess with them!"

"We won't!" Rylan called back as Rose dragged him past the village line, past the small hut on the edge of the village she almost hadn't noticed the day before, and into the thicker part of the woods.

Once they were out of ear shot of Lyla or any

of the other Mavarakites, Rylan ripped his arm from Rose's grasp and glared at her. "What was that all about?!" he demanded.

Rose widened her eyes in an innocent manner. "What do you mean? I just want to go back home."

When the words first left her mouth, she was mostly trying to cover up her odd and unexplainable dislike for Lyla. Now that she said it, though, she realized how true the words were. Her heart ached for her family, and she knew by now her parents were deep in the woods behind her grandparents' cabin, scouring every inch in hopes of a sign that would reveal where she was hidden. For a fleeting moment, Rose wondered if her parents would stumble upon the little door in the riverbed. Then her heart sank as she realized that, if they were checking the riverbed, they likely thought her drowned and dead. Her parents would be so worried. They might even be enthralled in another fight over the last time she drowned. Yes, if anything, this latest disappearance would be causing an even greater rift in her parent's relationship. Her heart panged in her chest with a longing to return to her parents and be together, all three of them, once again.

With the newfound eagerness and the reminder of how upset her family would be, Rose marched to the river and ignored every trip or stumble over the still unfamiliar woods floor. Even Rylan, who seemed to have memorized the woods by heart and floated over every rock and ditch with ease, struggled to keep up with Rose's pace. When the sound of the roaring river began growing in Rose's ear, she broke out into a full run and stopped only when she reached the muddy edge of the river and peered down into the clear water.

It seemed to have slowed down since the day before. The water Rose had fallen into had been angrily raging through the woods, tearing across the ground in an unforgiving manner and yanking Rose into the depths with ease. Now, it coolly rippled over the mud of the woods, springing over rocks happily. Rose didn't believe it could possibly change this much overnight and glanced at Rylan, wondering if Wood Dwellers had some sort of magic trick to calm the river down. She hadn't seen Wood Dwellers doing many magic tricks, but then again she had only been in the village for a day and wasn't sure what all they were capable of.

"Here we are," Rylan said, leaning grumpily against a giant tree and folding his arms lazily over his chest. "Search away."

"You promised you would help!" Rose snapped.

Rylan rolled his eyes and pushed away from the tree. For the next few hours, the pair worked together to scour the bottom of the riverbed in search of a little door or any other way Rose could have magically entered the water near her grandparents' house and emerged in the village of Mavarak.

After a while, the cool breeze of the morning disappeared and the dew clinging to the green leaves around the river dried as the sun drove higher in the sky and beat down on the earth. With every passing minute, Rylan began complaining more and searching less. He clutched his growling stomach and begged for a lunch break while Rose stuck a long stick into the river and poked holes into every inch of the riverbed, wondering if the mud had shifted to hide the little door. Rylan himself had spent his time fighting against the tide of the river to dig a large hole into the ground next to the boulder, where Rose was convinced the little door would be. Rose refused to join him in standing in the cool river despite his insistence that the pull was not strong enough to drag her into the water.

Eventually, Rylan gave up entirely on searching and sprawled out against the boulder, staring up into the clouds and rubbing his empty stomach.

"This would go faster if you would help," Rose snapped, jabbing a stick into the riverbed several feet upstream.

"I did help," Rylan replied, still staring at the blue sky and puffy clouds that refused to cover the harsh rays of sun. "Yesterday I told you there probably wasn't a door in the river, which was helpful. Today I looked for said non-existent door for hours, and now I can say without a doubt there is no door in the river."

"Well then how do you explain my grandparents' cabin *disappearing into thin air?!*" Rose's voice grew louder in frustration as her stick broke into the thick mud and she threw the half she still held into the tide. It sailed downstream and out of sight.

Rylan pointed at a cloud. "Look, that cloud is shaped like a Trusk!"

Rose glanced into the sky but couldn't spot the cloud Rylan referred to.

"Look," Rylan said, dropping his hand back behind his head to rest on as a pillow. "You were unconscious when I found you. You probably floated downstream for a while before I pulled you out."

"No," Rose argued, shaking her head and folding her arms over her chest in defiance. If she were being perfectly honest, the thought had crossed her mind already, but now that Rylan said it, she wanted to make sure he knew how stupid of a thought it was. "That's impossible. I know for a fact the boulder you are on right now is the same one I was on when I fell in. Besides, if I had been unconscious underwater for so long that my grandparents' cabin is now out of sight, then I would be dead."

Rylan bolted upright and looked at Rose in surprise in response to this. "Humans die if they're underwater for a long time?"

Rose blinked at him. "Yes."

"Hm," Rylan murmured in response, as though this were interesting news. Then he flopped back down against the boulder to look at the sky again.

"Don't Wood Dwellers?" Rose asked, wondering once again exactly what powers these creatures had.

"Of course, we do," Rylan said matter-of-factly.

"What about Other-Siders?" Rose asked, sitting down on the grass near the side of the river, a safe distance away from where she could get pulled in. She didn't want to admit this to Rylan, but she was starting to give up on the thought that there was a little door in the river. She poked the riverbed with a stick for hours and found nothing, and Rylan dug a giant hole right where Rose had sworn she saw the door. She was beginning to wonder if she had been seeing things.

Rylan sat up once more and gave Rose an intense look, as though she were finally asking an interesting question. "We don't really know what the Other-Side is capable of. They're really secretive. That's part of what makes them so hard to beat."

"So…" Rose hesitated to ask another question, trying to figure out how to best find out about the Other-Siders without sounding dumb. "Who exactly *are* they?"

Rylan's face turned dark. He glanced around the woods, as though worried someone might be listening. Then he stood from the boulder, beckoned for Rose to follow him, and began stalking into the woods upstream. He treaded lightly over the ground, as though trying to make as little noise as possible and put a finger over his lips to direct Rose to do the same. She did her best, but her steps were noisy compared to Rylan's light step. She swore a branch or stick somehow made its way under her foot with each step, even if she had been sure to check the ground before putting her weight down. Rylan shot her several dirty looks for being so noisy, but he led her through the woods regardless. They didn't walk far, only a few feet away from the river, but Rylan led her into the deepest and thickest part of the woods. Through the trees, the water seemed hushed and faraway even though Rose knew they were just a few steps away.

Rylan led Rose to what seemed to be the biggest tree in the woods. The tree looked different from any other she had ever seen before. The bark seemed rough and jagged, jutting out in odd places, and it was thicker and larger than the trees Rose was used to seeing. When Rylan reached the tree, he placed a foot directly onto a jutted part of the bark and began swiftly climbing with ease. He scaled the side, looking like a squirrel scrambling up a tree, his arms and legs grasping each hold in rapid succession. He had made it nearly halfway up when he glanced down and realized Rose was still safely perched on the ground.

"What are you doing?!" Rylan hissed, trying to keep his voice low while still calling from a great distance. "Follow me!"

"I—" Rose hesitated, looking at the rough bark and observing how far the branches were from each other. There were definitely several places where Rylan was using just the jutted areas of bark instead of grasping onto a branch. There was no way Rose could do that. She had never been big on climbing trees. The roughness hurt her soft hands and she always felt like the tree was too weak to hold up her weight. She wasn't exactly afraid of heights, but she didn't trust herself holding onto nothing but some frail bark and climbing up twenty feet into the sky. "I can't..."

"What do you mean?!" Rylan snapped, staring down at her incredulously. He huffed angrily and began descending back toward the ground. When he got there, he shot a look of frustration toward Rose and pointed at a pokey part of the tree. "Put your foot there."

Rose hesitated but eventually complied, sticking her barefoot (none of the Mavarakites wore shoes, so she ditched them to fit in a little better) against the rough bark in the foothold. Rylan came up so close behind her she could feel the heat of his body against her back, which caused her face to grow warm and she was glad she was facing the tree so he couldn't see her blush. He directed her hand into another hold in the bark of the tree and then commanded her to pull her weight off the ground. She did so slowly, feeling her arms begin to shake. The rough bark cut into her hands and her foot felt as though it would slip out of the shallow hold at any second. She knew she wasn't even a foot off the ground, but when she looked down she felt the earth stretch farther below her body.

"I'll help you," Rylan insisted, keeping his hands firmly against the small of Rose's back. "You can do it."

"I can't," Rose repeated, dropping from the tree and refusing to look Rylan in the eye. She folded her arms over her chest, indicating she would not be attempting to climb the tree again. After some prodding and begging, Rylan gave up.

"Fine," Rylan snapped, beckoning for Rose to follow him. "This is, by far, the best tree to climb to see the Other-Side. But I know another, *much shorter—*" Rylan gave Rose a pointed look, "—tree with so many branches even *you* would be able to climb."

Rylan led Rose a little deeper into the woods,

further from the giant boulder that was the only landmark Rose recognized, and to a small clearing which opened to a stubby green tree with a lot of branches that looked like nothing Rose had ever seen before. It resembled a pinecone, only covered with large leaves on every fat branch.

Rylan was right. Even Rose was able to climb the stubby, fat branches of the pinecone-looking tree. She followed Rylan up the side of the tree, moving carefully from branch to branch and awkwardly shifting her weight around the large leaves. The branch of this tree was far rougher than the giant tree, leaving imprints against Rose's tender skin and scraping her hands and knees. Even so, with the many fat branches Rose trusted to hold her weight, she still made it easily up the tree. When she finally joined Rylan at the top of the tree ("Oh, nice of you to finally show up!"), her hands were red with anger and screaming in pain, but there was a nice breeze that rustled through the leaves and cooled her skin.

Rylan waited patiently while Rose caught her breath and blew gentle, cool air against her irritated skin. The scar on her palm stood out against the redness of her skin. When Rose finally stopped whining and rubbing her irritated skin, Rylan pointed in the direction opposite of Mavarak.

"That," Rylan said, his eyes focused on the direction he pointed, "is the Other-Side. The people who want to kill us."

Rose followed Rylan's pointed finger and saw, with a small amount of shock, what appeared to be a full-blown city in the midst of the woods. Tall, dark skyscrapers stood eerily against the backdrop of nature, looking odd and out of place and making the trees look small. From their perch, Rose and Rylan could clearly see through the dark windows of the closest buildings. If there had been any Other-Siders on the other side of the windows, Rose would have been able to just make out their silhouettes. However, there were no Other-Siders moving within the building Rose could see.

At the center of the mass of tall buildings stood the tallest, darkest building. All the buildings were entirely gray, but this building seemed to be the darkest and dingiest gray. It also had more windows than any of the other buildings. In fact, almost the entire building was made of dark, reflective windows.

As if reading her mind, Rylan said, "That's the House with the Many Windows. It's the powerhouse of the Other-Side, where all the evil happens."

Rose stared at the House with the Many Windows, wondering what exactly Rylan meant by all the evil. She didn't ask, however. Instead, she asked, "If they are so evil and want to attack Mavarak, why do you stay so close to their community? Wouldn't it make more sense to move the village?"

Rylan guffawed, looking shocked at the suggestion. "We can't just move Mavarak. We have children and elders in our village. They wouldn't be able to make it. Plus, the flesh of the trees in Mavarak are the softest and most supple of any in all the woods, which is why we're able to make our homes inside the trees."

"That makes no sense, Rylan," Rose insisted, shifting her weight against the wide branch she had rested on so she could look at him. "They want you dead, and you live so close it would take ten minutes to travel between the communities. How have they not killed you all?"

"Oh, that," Rylan said, leaning back against the tree and putting his hands behind his head, as though this were the most relaxed he had been in his life. "They can't find us."

"Why not?" Rose asked, turning again to the Other-Side and staring inquisitively at the House with the Many Windows.

"Because," Rylan explained, "we are under a spell. A protective spell."

Then something Max had mentioned when they ran into him in the village flashed through Rose's mind. "The Guardians," she repeated out loud.

"Yeah," Rylan agreed, smiling proudly. "A long time ago, when I was only 5 years old, two of the bravest Mavarakites gave a sacrifice, becoming the Keepers of the Guardians. Since then, the village has been entirely invisible to anyone who is not a true Mavarakite!"

Rose could feel her mind racing with this new information. Several questions came to her mind and she wanted to blurt all her questions out at once. Instead, she asked the one clawing at her mind the most. "If the village is invisible to anyone who is not a Mavarakite, how was I able to see it?"

Rylan's proud smile faltered, and it seemed as

though he had wondered that himself. "Er, well, that's kind of why Max is checking on the Guardians. No one is sure how that is possible, and it's really weird you showed up on the same night the Other-Siders were wandering near the border of the village...I don't see how the Guardians could have fallen...the Mavarakites who gave a sacrifice would never..."

Rylan's voice trailed off, and it seemed as though his response had become more for him to think out loud than it was for Rose to understand. She decided to ask her next question in hopes of making more sense of the bizarre story. "So then, who are the Guardians?"

"Oh!" Rylan exclaimed, his confused and dark face brightening instantly. Rose saw a twinkle in his eye, and he was clearly proud of the Mavarakites once again. "That's the brilliant part of it. The Guardians aren't a who, but a what!"

Rose blinked. "What?"

"Yes exactly, a what!"

"No, no. I mean...what do you mean?"

Rylan swung a leg around the branch he was perched on so he was straddling it, which made Rose's heart skip a beat as she imagined him swaying right off the tree and falling to his death. Meanwhile, while he swung his legs around precariously, Rose realized she had a death grip against the branch on either side of her perch, her knuckles turning white with the tightness of the grip. Now aware of how uncomfortable she must appear to Rylan, Rose attempted to relax her grip a bit and lean against the trunk of the tree.

"Well," Rylan exclaimed. Rose was sure she heard a groan from the branch she had her weight on, causing her to shoot upright and tighten her grip once again. "The Guardians are two stone statues, one at the entrance of either pathway to the village. One is a snail, to represent the Keeper who was not born into the village but rather slowly learned to become one with our people. The other Guardian is an owl, to represent the Mavarakite who was born into the village and yearns to leave, but whose loyalty to the village keeps him here!"

Rose detected a slight change to Rylan's face as he finished this description. His features, which were bright with pride and excitement, seemed to fall a bit. It was so slight Rose wasn't sure it had actually happened. When he spoke again, though, his voice also sounded slightly crestfallen, and Rose was sure she was correct. "I know how that Keeper feels. When you've lived your whole life in this tiny village, it's easy to want to leave."

"Where are the Keepers now?" Rose asked.

Rylan shook his head, staring deep into Rose's eyes. "The Keeper of the Snail fled Mavarak, terrified of becoming the one to break the Guardian's spell. To protect the village, the Keeper thought it safest to leave. As for the Keeper of the Owl," Rylan sighed, "he's still trapped here, still wanting to leave."

Rose thought about that, then finally asked the question she had been thinking since the conversation first turned to the Guardians. "What kind of a sacrifice did the Keepers have to make to create the spell?"

Rylan waved the question off nonchalantly. "Just a blood sacrifice. No big deal. Nothing compared to what they'll have to do if they *break* the spell."

Rose shivered. She was about to ask Rylan what exactly that meant, but just as she opened her mouth to speak a loud gurgle erupted from Rylan's stomach.

"Now can we take a lunch break?!" Rylan asked, clutching a hand to his growling stomach.

"Fine," Rose said, looking down toward the ground and knowing it would be a while before she made it to the bottom. "But after we eat, we have to go back and check the river one more time."

It took Rose such a long time to reach the safety of the ground that Rylan had time to return fully to the village, retrieve some meat and fresh bread for lunch, leave the basket of lunch at the base of the pine-cone-looking tree, pick some berries to go with lunch, and begin assembling sandwiches at the base of the tree before Rose made it all the way down. When she finally reached the safety of the grass and sank to the ground to begin eating, Rylan was already finished with his first sandwich and was making a second.

"What kind of meat is this?" Rose asked as she folded the bread open to peer at the unfamiliar white meat. It looked like turkey but had a distinct sweet smell.

"Holken," Rylan mumbled around a mouthful of sandwich.

"Holken?" Rose repeated, still scrutinizing the sandwich. "Wait, did you put the berries on the sandwich?! Gross!"

"Try it," Rylan insisted, taking a giant second bite. Rose tentatively took a bite of the sandwich, small enough to not waste food if she didn't like it but large enough to get bread, meat, and berries all in the same bite. A sweet juice burst into her mouth, coating her tongue with sweetness that countered the salty meat. "Good, huh?"

Rose didn't want to admit Rylan was right, so instead she sunk her teeth into a giant second bite of Holken and Sweet Berry sandwich.

***

After a long morning of scouring the riverbed with a stick, climbing the rough pinecone-looking tree and holding on to the branch for dear life during a long conversation about the history of Mavarak, a brief lunch break and then another half hour bent over the river and poking into the riverbed with a new stick, Rose was feeling exhausted and frustrated. Upon returning to the riverside, Rylan spent a good two minutes walking through the river and half-heartedly searching for a little door. Since then, he had been climbing the nearest tree and swinging upside down, sideways, and dangling from branches using nothing but his legs.

"I'm so glad you're helping me," Rose said bitterly as she stretched her arms above her head and heard a loud pop from her tight back muscles.

Rylan, hanging upside down from a low tree branch with his legs, laughed. "Do you still believe you actually saw a door in the river?"

"How else did I get here?" Rose snapped, jabbing her stick into the same spot she had already checked six times.

"I've been wondering that myself," Rylan mused, pulling a sweet berry leftover from lunch out of his pocket and popping it into his mouth, still dangling upside down. "How did a small, useless, pathetic creature with apparently no gifts or abilities whatsoever stumble upon a magical door hidden in the river that allowed her access to the beautiful hidden village of Mavarak?"

Rose felt anger ripple through her stomach and, in an instant, reached down into the river and scooped water into her cupped hand, splashing it at Rylan's upside-down figure.

"Hey! Watch it!" Rylan shrieked, using his hands to grab onto the branch and swing himself back onto the ground.

The anger that had flared inside Rose's chest soon melted into sadness. "How am I ever going to get back home?!" Rose asked. The heat of the day beating on Rose's back combined with her already aching body and Rylan's offensive comment all worked together to bring a single tear to Rose's eye, which she dabbed away in hopes Rylan hadn't seen. She was apparently not so lucky, though, as she could tell Rylan was now staring intently on the eye that had just teared up.

"Hey," Rylan said, his voice now gentle. He stepped toward Rose and lightly reached out a hand to touch her arm. "It's not a big deal. Mavarak is a magical place. If there is a little door—" he was careful not to reveal how unlikely that possibility was, "—and it revealed itself to you once, then it will reveal itself to you again. When it's time."

His sudden kindness only served to further aggravate Rose. She yanked her arm away from his hand and snapped, "If the tables were turned and you were the one who needed to get back home, you wouldn't be so casual about it!"

Rylan returned to his former snide and nonchalant behavior. "If the tables were turned, *I* wouldn't have fallen face first into a river and lost my home. *I* wouldn't leave home for anything."

Rose's voice rose with every word until she was yelling in Rylan's face. "*You're* the one who said you know how the Keeper of the Owl feels! I bet you wish you could run away like that other Keeper did. And guess what?! I wish you would go away, too!"

"If there was such a thing as a stupid door in the river, I would have found it by now just so I could get rid of you!" Rylan yelled back, his ears turning a dark red and his face twisting with anger.

"Then help me find it and get home!" Rose yelled, loud enough that a small part of her brain feared the Mavarakites in the village would hear and come to investigate.

"I told you, the door DOESN'T EXIST!!!" Rylan screamed and Rose was sure someone in the village would have heard. The same thought seemed to have occurred to Rylan, too, as he took a deep breath and, when he spoke again, his voice had lowered significantly. "Look. I can't help you find this door you claim exists. I have no clue where it would be. But I do know someone who might be able to help us. The smartest Mavarakite who ever lived."

"And who might that be?" Rose asked, her voice also lowered to a speaking voice, but with a note of irritation.

Rylan smiled mischievously. "Whitney the Wise."

Chapter 5

Whitney the Wise

"Whitney the Wise?" Rose asked, repeating the name. "Who is—"

But she trailed off before finishing the question because Rylan, who had previously been angrily yelling in her face, seemed to have dropped all anger and spun on his heels, walking with newfound purpose toward the village.

Rose looked back at the riverbed pathetically one last time, wishing a little door would be sitting there next to the large boulder as if it had never disappeared. With a sigh, Rose turned and hurried to catch up to Rylan.

"Who is—" Rose began to repeat the question she hadn't been able to finish before. Once again, however, her question was cut short as Rylan, without pausing his long strides, answered the question she had never finished asking.

"Whitney the Wise is the most brilliant Wood Dweller who ever lived," he explained, glancing over his shoulder just long enough for Rose to catch his words. "He knows just about everything there is to know. But, fair warning, he's also a bit nutty."

"As opposed to the rest of the Wood Dwellers I've met…" Rose said, purposely loud enough for Rylan to hear. He shot her a snide look over his shoulder. Then, without warning, Rylan peeled off the usual trail to the village and cut across Rose's path, bumping hard into her shoulder on the way.

"Ow!" Rose yelped, rubbing where Rylan had bumped into her.

"My mistake!" Rylan said smugly, and Rose had the sneaking suspicion it had not at all been a mistake. He continued merrily on his way into the thick of the trees, but Rose stopped. The clearing toward the village was directly ahead, but Rylan had turned into the woods and was continuing south. She could see the outlines of several Wood Dwellers bustling away at their daily jobs just up ahead.

"You're going the wrong way," Rose informed.

"Oh," Rylan said, slowing down and turning to face Rose. He continued to walk backward, expertly dodging the rocks and somehow managing to walk more smoothly on the uneven terrain backward than Rose could do while walking the correct direction. "Whitney doesn't live with the rest of us in the clearing. He lives just along the outskirts, barely within the border of the Guardians."

"Why?" Rose asked, crossing her arms across her chest. She felt defiance bubbling up inside her, annoyed at Rylan's insistence on hurrying off to get rid of Rose. Of course, Rose wanted to get out of Mavarak and return to her grandparent's home just as much. She just didn't like that Rylan couldn't even stop for a second to talk to her.

"Ugh," Rylan grunted, rolling his head back and looking to the sky in exasperation. Grudgingly, he stopped his impressive backward walking, which gave Rose a small amount of pleasure. "One minute, you're screaming at me to help you get home. The next, you're demanding I stop helping you and talk. I thought you wanted to find the stupid door?"

Rose kept her arms folded firmly over her chest. "I do want to find the door, go home, and *get away from you*—" she gave him a sharp look, "—but I also want to know who it is you're about to introduce me to. Especially because I have a funny feeling you're planning on telling this guy about the little door. Which makes me sound nuts."

A smile crept across Rylan's face. "Trust me. You do not have to worry about Whitney thinking you're nuts. You'll see."

With that, Rylan once again spun around to

lead Rose through the trees.

"Wait!" Rose called after him. Dropping her stubborn pretense, she desperately chased after Rylan. "You never answered me! Why doesn't Whitney live with the rest of the Wood Dwellers?"

"Oh, not all Mavarakites live in the clearing," Rylan explained, slowing enough for Rose to catch up and keep his pace. As if he had planned it, Rylan gestured to a tree they were passing just as a door etched into the wood swung open. Rose gasped and jumped to the side. Just like the hut at the opening of the clearing, Rose hadn't even noticed the little home disguised in the woods. Now that she knew it was there, however, the features of the home came to life and Rose felt a little embarrassed she hadn't noticed it right away.

"It's not the location of Whitney's home that makes it so bizarre," Rylan explained, leading Rose still farther into the thick of the trees. Rose now scanned the trees around her for hidden huts and was surprised to find there were several along the way.

"So, what makes it so bizarre?" Rose asked. Her mind flashed to the flying horse-like creatures that spit in eyes, the rooms in Rylan's hut that couldn't be reached without climbing up the outside of the tree, and the pointy ears all Mavarakites sported. She couldn't imagine what constituted 'bizarre' to a Wood Dweller.

"That," Rylan said, coming to a sudden halt.

Rose slammed into his back, unable to stop her momentum in time to avoid a crash. Rylan was entirely unaffected, however. Instead, he was now pointing to the top of a particularly tall and narrow tree. Rose followed his gaze. Nestled comfortably among several narrow trees was the largest treehouse Rose had ever seen in her life. Surrounding the treehouse was about a dozen swarming, giant beehives and sweeping vines adorning the walls of the hut. Unlike the tree Rose had climbed to get to Rylan's room, this treehouse did not seem to have any detectable entrance. There also appeared to be no doors and only one single, tiny circular window that faced the direction of the village center. It was the least welcoming of all the huts Rose had seen from a Wood Dweller so far. *Of course,* this would be the place Rylan brought her. Rose was just beginning to wonder if this was somehow a trick or cruel joke on Rylan's part when he interrupted her thoughts.

"Isn't it weird?" he asked, looking sideways at her to see her reaction.

"It's a treehouse," Rose answered, still taking in the looming home before her. "What's so weird about that?"

Rylan looked stunned and thoroughly disappointed at Rose's response.

"Well, yeah. It's a treehouse. Like, *in the tree!*" he said, exasperated. Then, when Rose still didn't seem impressed, he added, *"In the sky!"*

"So?" Rose asked, partly because she really didn't understand, and partly because she was rather enjoying Rylan's frustration.

"So, only a true dingbat would live in a tree!"

Rylan answered in an exasperated voice, clearly becoming frustrated.

Rose giggled a little, finally tearing her eyes away from the giant treehouse to look at Rylan's bewildered face. "Rylan, isn't your room in a tree?"

The tips of Rylan's ears began turning crimson, which only made Rose giggle more. After a moment of shocked embarrassment, Rylan began stammering out a response. "Well—*yeah,* but—I mean, *I guess.* But that's different because, I mean…the whole house isn't in the tree!"

Rose giggled more, cherishing every second of Rylan's embarrassment and confusion. "Seems the same to me!"

Rylan's mouth flopped open like a fish, searching for a response, ears red as an apple. Before he could stammer any other lame excuses out, Rose heard a bang and then a strange whooshing sound, as though something were cutting through the air. Rylan and Rose both turned their attention back to the treehouse before them just as a rope ladder came tumbling to the ground. At the top of the ladder, a small opening in the bottom of the treehouse had appeared. Rose and Rylan exchanged a look and then stepped forward so they could peer directly into the opening.

"The stars told me I would be receiving visitors soon!" said a knowing voice. Then a wide, smiling face appeared in the opening. A small Wood Dweller with snowy white hair stared down at Rose as she stared back up at him. "Come, as it is destined you should!"

Rylan shot a told-you-so smirk at Rose. Ignoring his smugness, Rose took hold of the swinging rope ladder and began her trek up. It took her longer than she had expected, as the rungs of the ladder seemed to be a type of marble and were extremely slippery. Plus, Rose had never climbed a ladder while it swayed in the wind before. With every jerky step she took, the ladder shifted beneath her, making her feel like she could topple off at any given time. As if determined to be the most unhelpful person to ever help Rose, Rylan frequently muttered as he waited for her. Rose attempted to block it out, but she frequently caught snippets of words such as "my rotten luck," and *"trying to* go slow just to infuriate me?"

Eventually, Rose emerged from the opening in the bottom of the treehouse and entered the home of Whitney the Wise. Without meaning to, a small "whoa," slipped out of her mouth as she took in her surroundings. The first thing Rose noticed was the peculiar roof. To make up for the lack of windows around the walls of the hut—save for the one measly window that overlooked the woods surrounding the village—there were uneven openings cut into the slanting roof that allowed light to filter in. The light jutted through the hut in odd shapes because of the shadows of branches and leaves that supported the little home.

Between the floor Rose emerged from and the odd roof was the oddest clutter Rose had ever laid eyes on. The entire treehouse seemed to open into just one room, and there was no apparent organization to the mess of items Whitney owned. On one side of the open room, there was a giant globe, which appeared to have several purple marks scattered in a seemingly random pattern. Directly next to the globe was a tall podium with an ancient looking book propped open and, oddly, a small jar of purple berries. Rose squinted toward the purple marks and began to have a creeping suspicion the purple marks all over the globe were made with smashed berries. The placement of the smashed berries seemed entirely random, and Rose wondered what Whitney was keeping track of.

On the opposite end of the room was a giant, traditional looking green chalkboard, like the ones used in classrooms back in the olden days. The chalkboard was marked with several odd shapes and scrawled words naming different constellations. Next to the filled chalkboard was a dirty little table littered with tubes and flasks, reminding Rose of a typical high school chemistry classroom. There was also a little scale weighing out some unrecognizable spice, or fruit, or herb, or something. Just a bit off-center and facing a crooked angle in the room was an unmade bed. And, to top the whole bizarre scene off, it seemed as though every square inch of the entire room was coated in a thin layer of dust, as if the treehouse hadn't been lived in for several years.

As Rose peered around the entire cluttered hut, she began to get the creeping feeling up her neck that only comes when being watched. She turned in the direction she could feel Whitney's gaze and saw him sitting calmly on a tiny, dingy couch placed directly in front of her and facing the opening in the floor. Rose felt her cheeks turn red as she realized Whitney had been staring wide-eyed at her the entire time she had been taking in the sight of his home.

"Curious little creatures, yes, and the fleshiest looking ears," Whitney mumbled. He was staring directly at her, but his words were clearly not meant for her.

"Even you can't possibly be this bad of a climber!" Rose heard a shout from below her. "What on earth is taking so long?!"

Rose felt the beginning of a blush spread across her cheek. She hurriedly pulled herself up onto the dusty floor and stepped to the side so Rylan could pull himself through the opening as well. As she stepped to the side, she took a closer look at the tubes and flasks splayed across the dirty table she had seen before.

"No interest in alchemy, yet she stares at the tubes and flasks intently. Mere curiosity, then?" Whitney continued to mumble.

"Sorry, did you say something?" Rylan asked as he stepped away from the little opening.

"She is right, you know," Whitney said, this time clearly speaking toward his new company. Rylan glanced curiously at Rose, who shrugged to show her mutual lack of understanding. Whitney added, "It is the same."

Rylan still looked as confused as Rose felt. She wracked her brain to think of what Whitney could possibly mean. Finally, Whitney continued.

"Our homes in the trees." Suddenly, a bizarre, toothy grin spread across Whitney's wide face. "You are too, as you have said, a dingbat."

Whitney sat with his insane, toothy grin and stared at Rylan, who looked horrified. Rose, on the other hand, couldn't help but snort out a laugh.

Her laugh was short-lived, however, because Whitney's smile evaporated from his face and he jumped to his feet. He absentmindedly began scratching at his chin as he briskly walked to his chalkboard.

"Yes, the Trusks are restless today," Whitney mumbled, and Rose knew he had returned once again to talking to himself. "Curious."

Rose looked at Rylan. At this rate, she would be stuck in Mavarak another year before Whitney told either of them any more about the little door.

"They are both marked. Yes, yes, the bond is clear," Whitney continued his senseless rambling, scratching still at his reddening chin. "And it is in the stars, it is time, the warrior has returned."

Rose gave Rylan a desperate look, begging him with her eyes to interrupt Whitney. Even though he wasn't a particularly large Wood Dweller and seemed absolutely harmless, something about him still made Rose feel a bit tentative. However, it seemed as though Whitney's rambling was unimportant, even to him. All of it came out fragmented, like his mind was darting around like a young child's.

Rylan loudly cleared his throat, but to no avail. Whitney didn't even pause in his mutterings. "The Farcriers shall come, yes. But it will take more."

Rylan cleared his throat a second time. "Excuse me, sir, we don't mean to disturb you, but…"

Whitney did not seem one bit disturbed, though. Instead, he spun on his heel, the insane smile returning to his face. "Yes, the stars did tell me, you are here for guidance."

"Sir—" Rylan began again, but he couldn't get another word in before Whitney cut him off a second time.

"But alas, it is not your time," Whitney said, raising a hand toward Rylan to stop him from continuing. "For it is Rosalie's story, not yours. Proceed."

Whitney's eyes were focused on Rose. She was shocked and, according to his eyes as wide as saucers, so was Rylan. For an instant, Rose floundered, unable to remember why they had come to Whitney's house. How did he know her name? And, like Robin, he had addressed her by her given name like a family member or an old friend. But she had never met him before, and even her closest friends didn't call her by her full name. Rose considered the possibility that it was part of an adult Wood Dweller's abilities to intuitively know someone's name. But that wouldn't explain the equally confused look on Rylan's face.

Somehow, Rose finally managed to find her voice and remember the reason she was here. "Whitney, er, the Wise, we had a question. We, um, well, I'm not from here, and I actually ended up here by, well, it sounds weird, and I don't normally say things like this…"

Rylan jammed his elbow into Rose's side to get her to quit mumbling.

"Sorry. What I'm trying to ask is whether or not

you've ever heard of a little door appearing to certain people in the river?" Rose hurried to spit the question out before she started mumbling again.

Rose wondered if Whitney had heard the question. Instead of answering, he continued to stare into Rose's eyes for a moment or two after the question had been asked. Then he closed his eyes and took a deep breath in, a hint of a smile still lingering. Once again, Rose shot a look at Rylan, begging for his help. Rylan opened his mouth to repeat Rose's question just as Whitney's eyes dreamily drifted open and he peered into her eyes once again. Rose felt as though he was studying her soul.

"You are experiencing a time of unrest," Whitney said, extremely unhelpfully. Rose couldn't help but feel the beginning of anger prickling her ears. *Yes, I am feeling quite unrestful being stuck here talking to you instead of getting home to my family!*

"Yes," Whitney smiled knowingly. "Even now your mind drifts to those who cause it. A bond has been broken. A bond of love between two people. You wish to fix the bond, as you feel you are somehow the cause of it."

Rose didn't even attempt to hide the blush furiously covering her freckled face. How did he know? How could he possibly know this? Had he somehow been stalking Rose? And, if he was somehow following her, if he knew all this…could it be his fault she was stuck here?

"The stars wish you to know you did not cause it, nor could you possibly mend it. The only heart you can stop from hurting is your own, child," Whitney proceeded.

"How did you know?" Rose asked. Her voice came out a low growl, and she could see out of the corner of her eyes Rylan shifting uncomfortably as his gaze darted back and forth between Rose and Whitney.

"The stars, the stars, it is all told in the stars," Whitney said dreamily, a ghost of a smile still haunting his face.

"The stars?" Rose asked, her voice still coming out as a low growl. She was about to snap, demanding Whitney explain himself, but before she could Whitney pressed on.

"Yes, the stars in yours eyes, child," he said, flashing that same knowing smile and then turning his back to the pair. As if it were perfectly normal at this point in the conversation, Whitney stepped again to his chalkboard and picked up a piece of chalk. He scribbled something on the board. Rose attempted to decipher the scrawl, but it was entirely illegible. She wasn't sure if it was some separate form of writing, or if his writing was simply too messy to read.

"There is also the beginning of love in your eyes," Whitney added nonchalantly, fiercely jotting a period at the end of the word he had just added to the board. He dusted off his hands and peered over his shoulders. "Perhaps you have met a handsome young man—or Wood Dweller—recently?"

To Rose's horror, Whitney clearly glanced at Rylan as he asked this. Rose felt her cheeks burning now with both anger and embarrassment. Meanwhile, Rylan, who had been watching the scene with confusion and interest, now broke into a wide smile and laughed out loud.

Rose shifted uncomfortably, well-aware of the bright red in her face and the awkward way she stood in the middle of the room next to Rylan. She wanted to shift away, or simply turn around and full on run from the entire scene, but still had received no answers from Whitney.

"Ah, yes," Whitney said, still smiling knowingly. He turned his mysterious gaze to Rylan. "And in your eyes, it is revealed you are far past the beginning stages of love."

That cut Rylan's laughter short. Instead, he clenched his jaw shut and began shifting awkwardly. The point of his ear turned a crimson red, and he suddenly became extremely interested in scrutinizing the berries in the jar on the podium Rose had noticed earlier. Rather than feeling less embarrassed by this most recent progression in the conversation, Rose felt herself growing redder, if possible.

"Anyway, we were wondering if you knew anything about the little door. In the river. The one I mentioned earlier." Rose hurried to shift the subject back to the original question. She realized how long Rose and Rylan had been standing stiffly at the entrance to the treehouse. It felt like hours ago since they had been eating the delicious Holken and Sweet Berry sandwiches.

"Ah, right. The little door." Whitney nodded.

He turned and walked crisply to the couch he had been sitting on when Rose first appeared in the opening through the floor. He sat but did not offer Rose or Rylan a seat. There were several wooden chairs scattered throughout the cluttered room, but Rose and Rylan continued to stand stiffly and awkwardly at the entranceway as though they might need to hurriedly escape at any given time. If, for example, Whitney found himself back on the topic of love, Rose felt like she might just forget the ladder and jump straight through the hole and hope the landing wasn't too bad.

"You say the door appeared to you in the river?" Whitney asked, a slight smile still playing on his lips. Rose nodded. Though he was smiling, Rose didn't feel as though he was making fun of her. In fact, she had a sneaking suspicion he somehow knew exactly what she was talking about. Regardless, his answer was in the negative. "It is quite strange. I have never heard of such an appearance."

Rose's heart sank. She was sure he was lying. The knowing look in his eyes doubled with the small smile convinced her. He had been her last hope of seeing her family again.

"There it is again," Whitney said, the smile fading from his face. "They are troubling your thoughts, aren't they?"

Rose didn't answer. It was a question, as though he was only guessing. She wondered how he could possibly know what she was thinking about. He didn't appear to be a mind reader in any other scenario, but he knew whenever her family came creeping into her head.

"And you are similarly troubled," Whitney guessed again, turning on Rylan. "But not with any sort of broken bonds of love. No, you are troubled... with your loyalties."

The statement seemed vague, and Rose was plagued with memories of going to Chinese restaurants and reading the lousy fortune cookies. She glanced at Rylan, ready to share a look of incredulity. Instead, she noticed Rylan's face had changed. His expression had darkened, and there was a brooding behind his eyes. Somehow, the stunning blue had even seemed to darken to match the rest of his face.

"Don't you ever question my loyalty to this place," Rylan growled. Rose's heart skipped a beat. His voice sounded the exact same as Rose's had when Whitney had first discussed her troubling times. And, just as he had been oblivious to Rose's anger, Whitney proceeded in his same carefree manner, unbothered by the darkness in Rylan's demeanor.

"You hope to experience greater adventure. But you are bound by the rope around your neck," Whitney said, the smile returned to his face. "If you feel such way...you could simply cut it..."

Rylan took a step forward, as though he were going to hit Whitney. Instinctively, Rose reached out and put a warning hand on Rylan's arm. He didn't acknowledge it, nor did the darkness leave from his face, but he did stop in his tracks. He continued to glare at Whitney, who was as oblivious as ever.

"We should go," Rose whispered. She took a

small step toward the opening, ready to leave the buzz of bees and the musty smell of dust. More than anything, she was ready to be rid of Whitney's strange mutterings and odd words.

"Yes, we should," Rylan agreed, not lifting his gaze from Whitney. In a flash, he turned and stepped down through the hole in the ground, his foot quickly finding the first rung on the rope ladder.

"But before you go," Whitney said, once again scratching his chin. While he seemed entirely unscathed by Rylan's daunting attitude toward him, Whitney now seemed deeply troubled as he stared intently at the chalkboard. It was as though something had appeared on the board that hadn't previously been written there.

"You have attempted to dig into the earth. If you are not having luck with this approach, perhaps you should try a new direction," Whitney suggested. Then, as quickly as the troubled expression appeared, it left, and Whitney returned to his knowing smile.

"New direction?" Rylan snapped. The darkness had lifted a little, but he definitely seemed less fond of Whitney now than he had an hour ago. Which was saying a lot, since he hadn't seemed particularly fond of Whitney an hour ago. "What new direction?"

Whitney smiled, peering straight into Rylan's eyes. "I think it safe to say us Wood Dwellers know more directions than just into the earth. Just look at us dingbats and you will see!"

Rylan sneered and disappeared through the hole without another word. Apparently, this last bit had done it for him, and he had had enough of Whitney the Wise. Rose was pretty much in the same boat and was just about to slip through the hole in the ground to follow him when Whitney interrupted one last time.

"And, Rosalie," Whitney chirped, his voice sounding distracted, as though several thoughts were occurring to him all at once. "I must give you one warning before we part. Some things in life require sacrifice. The important part is knowing which of these is *worth* the sacrifice. And it seems as though the bees are a bit more aggressive today as well. It is in the stars they should be."

Somewhere in Whitney's warning, he slipped instead into another rambling like when Rose had first arrived. She listened for a short amount of time, wondering if he would return to the warning he had been giving her and explain what he meant, but he never did. She waited for an opportunity to thank him, but he never did pause in his mumblings again. Finally, after a moment of listening to the buzzing of the bees and the muttering of Whitney the Wise, Rose gave up and began her long trek down the slippery rope ladder.

After a long time of Rose clinging for her life to the ladder and moving down the rungs inch by pathetic inch, Rose finally made it safely to the ground. She sprawled across the grass, her bones and joints aching and stiff from the work she had done that morning paired with the excruciatingly long trip down the rope ladder.

When Rose had finally stretched her muscles out and her heartbeat had returned to normal from being safely perched on the ground long enough, Rose sat up and peered around. Rylan was sitting on a boulder nearby, mindlessly ripping apart a long blade of grass and staring furiously into space.

"Rylan?" Rose said, pulling herself to her feet and rubbing her still aching joints.

"Well, that was a total bust. Complete waste of time. I have never in my life met someone as utterly clueless—incompetent..." Rylan seemed too angry to string along words to complete a sentence. He continued ripping apart the blade of grass.

"Well," Rose answered hesitantly, taking a careful step toward Rylan. She was searching for something to say to make Rylan feel better about the way they had spent their afternoon. The morning hadn't been too great either. The whole day was turning out to be a waste. "He did give us some advice."

"Yeah, *try a new direction,* what does that mean?!" Rylan snapped, throwing the shredded grass on the ground and angrily ripping up some more. He began angrily mimicking Whitney's jovial yet mystified voice. *"You have attempted to dig into the earth,* yeah maybe because we're LOOKING FOR SOMETHING IN THE EARTH!"

Rose opened her mouth, searching for something to say to calm Rylan down. Before she could utter a word, Rylan continued with his rampage. *"I think it safe to say us Wood Dwellers know more directions,* WELL OBVIOUSLY! There's up, down, left, right, you don't think I know that?! I'm only the best Trusk rider of any Wood Dweller in all of Mavarak, of course I know—"

Rylan stopped in his tracks, his mouth flopping open. Confused by his sudden pause in the middle of a rant, Rose peered into the woods where Rylan was staring, wondering if he had seen something. Then, Rylan jumped up, and a giant smile spread across his face.

"Of course! Rose, a new direction! I'm the best Trusk rider in all of Mavarak!" Rylan repeated, excitement exuding from him. He grabbed Rose by each arm, pinning them to her sides and shaking her with excitement. "I'm the best Trusk rider in all of Mavarak!"

"So?" Rose asked, not understanding his excitement.

"So, Whitney is telling us we need to try *flying!*"

Chapter 6

Meeting the Trusks

"*Flying?*" Rose repeated, looking at Rylan quizzically. "We need to try…*flying?*"

Rylan let out a shriek of laughter, released Rose's pinned arms, and jumped around in a 180-degree circle, looking positively giddy. When he landed, his back now facing Rose, he set off into the woods with purpose, as if on a mission.

"Rylan, what does that even mean?" Rose called after him. As was becoming habit, he didn't slow his stride, nor did he turn around to answer her question.

Rose watched the back of his head intently as he disappeared into the woods. "Rylan?! I'm not going to chase after you through the woods again! If you think I'm about to run after you right now—"

Rylan still never faltered, and his bobbing blond head became hard to detect amongst the trees. His brown and green outfit had faded into the background, matching its surroundings almost perfectly.

"Rylan?!" Rose shrieked, her heart beginning to pound. Normally, she would prove stubborn enough to plop right back down on a rock and wait for Rylan to return to her. However, she wasn't familiar enough with these woods to feel comfortable doing so. Plus, she couldn't help but notice it had become darker since they first ventured to find Whitney's hut. Rose tipped back her head and peered into the sky. Through the blanket of trees, Rose could detect a lovely shade of pink, which meant the sun was setting and it would be dark soon. With an irritated huff, Rose dropped her eyes back to the bobbing blond head now far in the thick of trees.

"Rylan, wait for me!" Rose called, running to catch up with him and somehow managing to trip or stumble over every root or branch on the ground. By the time she caught up with him, the two were almost back to the clearing. "You left me! I could have gotten lost, you know?" Rose clutched at a stitch in her side and panted, trying to slow her breathing.

"You also could have followed me instead of standing around," Rylan retorted, giving Rose a sly sideways glance. She noticed, however, that he slowed his pace a little bit to help Rose catch her breath.

"What exactly do you mean, we're going to try flying?" Rose asked, finally slowing her breathing. The two rounded a fat tree and the land opened to the familiar clearing of Mavarak. The bustling little village was less busy this time of day. Rose could see several huts were lit from the inside by the flickering light of a candle. There were a few young Mavarakites chasing after each other across the clearing, and Rose noticed a couple snuggled close together in a leafy hammock she hadn't noticed the first several times walking past the hut.

"I mean, the Trusks are winged creatures. They fly. We're going to ride Kearn—my Trusk—and see if we—" Before Rylan could finish, Rose cut him off.

"And what exactly do you expect me to do while you are flying your Trusk?" Rose demanded. She tried to use her most threatening voice so Rylan would take her seriously, but he seemed genuinely unconcerned as he marched up to the wooden fence which encased the herd of Trusks Rose had seen earlier.

"I expect you to come with me," Rylan answered, stepping up onto a slant of wood and swinging one leg over the fence, then the other, and dropping himself onto the other side. Rose had been actively trying to ignore the giant creatures staring at her and focus only on talking to Rylan. Now, however, Rylan's shoulder was gently tousled by one of the animals, and Rose felt a pang in her chest as she turned her attention to the looming horse-like creature standing before Rylan, only three feet away from Rose herself.

Now that Rose was up close to one of the Trusks, she could see they were far larger than a horse, although they looked a lot like them. The eyes of the creatures were more bulging and darker than a horse, and their legs appeared leaner. In fact, in every way these creatures seemed like the upgraded, more powerful, more dangerous version of a horse. Not to mention the giant, furry wings sprouting from the back of the Trusk. Rose glanced around at all the beasts and noticed the wings of each creature were uniquely patterned and none quite matched the color of the Trusk's fur.

Rylan was affectionately patting the snout of the Trusk that had tousled his shoulder. "Hiya, Dawn," Rylan said, reaching out and roughly scratching the giant shoulder of the creature. The creature tossed its giant head back, shaking out its stringy mane, and bopped its snout hard against Rylan's shoulder. His whole body flung back from the impact, but he seemed to be in no pain and even let out a hardy laugh.

Rylan noticed another approaching creature and gave this one an award-winning smile. "Awe, Kutcher, are you coming to say hi?" Rylan asked the new Trusk. This creature's fur was far lighter than the first one, but its wings were golden. Kutcher the Trusk also bopped its snout against Rylan's shoulder, then made a deep gurgling noise from the back of his throat.

"Kutcher, no!" Rylan shouted in response to the

noise, slapping both hands to his eyes. Rose watched in bewilderment as the gurgling noise from the back of the throat turned distinctly into the sound of the creature spitting. Rylan's hands were both covered in the creature's slobber.

"What on earth is going on?!" Rose asked, her voice coming out high-pitched and terrified. She cowered on the safe side of the fence, not daring to approach any closer to the strange creatures.

Rylan let out a goodhearted laugh and uncovered his eyes, flinging the slime off the back of his hands. "It's the Trusk's main job and power," he explained as Kutcher the Trusk lazily trotted away. "If they spit in your eyes, it puts you to sleep almost immediately."

"Ew!" Rose gasped, instinctively reaching up to cover her eyes as though one of the creatures were spitting its venomous spit at her. "Does it hurt?"

Rylan busied himself with pouring an unidentifiable slop into a trough as he answered. "No, it doesn't hurt at all. It's actually really good for your eyes, too. A lot of Wood Dwellers use Trusk spit as eye drops to clear their tear ducts and improve their vision!" Rylan flashed a smile toward Rose as he added, "They just make sure to use the drops right before bed."

Rylan jumped out of the way just as several of the Trusks began surrounding the trough. They began noisily slurping at the slop, eating it messily. Meanwhile, Rylan came back to the wooden fence Rose stood safely behind, slid his legs through the open slats, and sat comfortably on the fence facing Rose. He looked as comfortable sitting on the wooden fence enclosed with the giant beasts as he had looked swinging from the tree branches in the woods. Rose could tell he had been doing this a long time.

"What else do these things do?" Rose asked, peering sideways at the mass of Trusks eating from the trough. One of the Trusks lifted its head to peer its beady black eyes into her soul, and Rose thought she heard a quiet gurgling sound. She gave the Trusk a warning look.

"Absolutely nothing. They fly, they spit, and they eat a lot," Rylan laughed. "They come in handy though, especially against enemies. Somebody is swinging a sword in your face? Bam! It's bedtime!"

Rylan continued to laugh, looking admiringly at the creatures. Rose continued to peer cautiously between Rylan and the Trusks.

"I'm not riding one of those things," Rose said, eyeing the creatures suspiciously as they ate.

"What?!" Rylan snapped, turning his attention away from the Trusks and back to Rose. "Why not?"

"Well," Rose snapped back, folding her arms stubbornly across her chest. "First of all, I could fall off and die." Rylan opened his mouth, clearly about to disagree, but Rose pressed on before he could cut her off. "Secondly, it's getting dark out. We won't be able to see anything. Thirdly, what good will it do to fly anyway? We're trying to find a tiny door at the bottom of a river. Not exactly going to help us to be up in the sky, will it?"

By this point, Rylan looked a bit deflated, as though he realized Rose was probably right. "And lastly," Rose added, to make sure she won this argument. "I'm starving. We need to eat dinner. And it's been a long day. I'm exhausted."

Although Rose had clearly won the argument, her heart sunk at this last point. A full day had slipped by. Her grandparents must be worried sick. Rose wondered how many people were out looking for her. And were her parents fighting again? Would they blame each other for her disappearance? Rose could imagine it, her mother's rising, whispered voice saying, 'You just had to send her back to the same place she almost died before! Do you *ever* take *anything* seriously?!'

Rylan seemed to detect Rose's changed demeanor, because he didn't fight back at all about riding the Trusks. Instead, his pointy ears laid back against his head and he clambered over the fence swiftly.

"Hey, it's okay," he blurted, stepping toward Rose. His bright blue eyes peered down at Rose gently. He placed a comforting hand on her shoulder. "We'll have more luck tomorrow. We'll go home, eat some food, get some sleep, and then tomorrow morning we'll come out and fly a Trusk. Maybe we can travel farther upriver and see if we can find your grandparent's cabin or—sure, a little door in the river—maybe the reason we had no luck today is because we were looking in the wrong place. Yeah, I bet you anything you were blacked out for a while and didn't even know how far downriver you travelled. Tomorrow everything will go back to normal."

Rose peered up into Rylan's soft blue eyes and let out a defeated sigh. She didn't bother reminding him the boulder next to the river was the same one she had fallen off. She didn't bother insisting she hadn't travelled downriver at all. She didn't even bother reiterating that she was *sure* there had been a little door in the river. Instead, she let Rylan put a comforting arm around her as he led her back to his hut.

The entire walk back, and even at various points through their dinner, Rylan repeated his mantra of "Don't worry, tomorrow everything will be better."

***

Robin didn't seem one bit surprised to see Rose return for dinner that night. Even though Rose had already said her goodbyes and insisted she wouldn't be staying another night, it was as if Robin never quite believed her.

Drew and Rylan stuffed themselves with the Sweet Meat and Nickleberry Salad Robin had so delicately prepared for dinner. Rylan was so hungry from their long day that he didn't even bother wiping away the trickle of Nickleberry juice dribbling down his chin. Meanwhile, Robin continued polite conversation with Rose, who had to really focus her attention on not scarfing her food down with the same velocity as the two growing boys at the table.

"So, Rosalie—erm, Rose—how much longer do you expect to stay here?" Robin asked politely as she dabbed some Nickleberry juice from her chin with a leaf.

"Oh, not much longer at all," Rose blurted around a mouthful of Sweet Meat. The flavor of the Sweet Meat was the most delectable sweet and salty flavor Rose had ever tasted, and the juices from the meat warmed the back of her throat in a way that made her feel oddly nostalgic for a place she had never known.

"Do you think you'll stay for the harvest festival?" Robin asked casually, as though she thought Rose should be aware of what the harvest festival was.

"Oh yeah!" Rylan shouted, his bright eyes flashing. "With all that's going on between getting Rose back home and the odd behavior of the Other-Siders, I almost forgot about the harvest festival!"

"What's the harvest festival?" Rose asked, looking between Robin and Rylan. Unexpectedly, though, it was Drew who answered.

"The harvest festival is the best part of the year every year!" he answered, swallowing a bite of his dinner. "It's a celebration of the Great Crusades of the Other-Siders!"

"It's a celebration of our *win* against the Other-Siders," Rylan corrected pointedly.

Drew didn't miss a beat even with Rylan's interjection. He continued explaining, his eyes wide with excitement. "After the Keeper's blood sacrifice, everything in Mavarak went back to normal, and we celebrated with a huge feast and celebration. All the Mavarakites came out, even the ones who had gone into hiding in the woods. It was the first time little Wood Dwellers came out to play. All Mavarakites worked together to harvest the fruits we had so long neglected because of the Crusades. As a village, we ate Narcott pies, Sweet Meat, Honeysickles, Holken and Sweet Berries, even Trusk meat—which is a delicacy in Mavarak because the Trusks are so valuable to us, we almost never slaughter one! It was the greatest celebration the Mavarakites had ever seen!"

"Not that Drew would know," Rylan said, giving his younger brother a pointed look. "He was too little to remember. Even I can barely remember the first harvest festival."

"But they do a retelling of the Crusades every year at the festival and remind us all why we celebrate. It's in two days. You should come, they can do a much better job at explaining it all than we can," Drew finished off his story with a large bite of his salad.

"Yeah, you should come," Rylan automatically agreed. Then, as suddenly as he had said it, Rylan's eyes widened a little and Rose saw the tips of his ears turn crimson. Rose felt her cheeks begin to turn red as well. *Rylan wanted her to stay?*

"Well," Rose said, picking up her wooden mug and bringing it to her face, in hopes of hiding her red cheeks. "I guess we'll have to see."

Rose tossed her head back and let the sweet juice in the cup fill her mouth. From behind the cup, she saw Rylan's ears turn a darker shade of red as Drew jabbed a teasing elbow into Rylan's side and Robin gave a knowing smile.

***

The morning had brought a fresh vigor in Rose to get back home to her parents. Thoughts of staying an entire day for the harvest festival had entirely dissolved, especially as Rylan's former comforting, sympathetic air had gone away and was replaced with the snippy, argumentative Rylan that Rose had come to know so well.

"You can't cover your eyes every time she looks at you, you're making her nervous!" Rylan snapped, glaring at Rose through the sun blaring down over the Trusk field. Rose peered through the cracks between her fingers to look at the towering Trusk that stood before her. Kearn, Rylan's Trusk, had initially seemed more likeable to Rose since this Trusk stood a full head shorter than every other full grown Trusk Rose had seen so far. Kearn was such a light color of brown that she simply could have been a dirty white Trusk, and her wings faded into a darker color until the tips reached a deep black. Her eyes were larger than the Trusk Rose had examined the day before, and they were a slightly lighter color of black, more like a dark brown. Rose had yet to hear a gurgling sound of gathering spit emitting from Kearn's throat, but nevertheless she would shield her eyes every few seconds in case the creature decided to sneak attack.

Rose tentatively lowered her hands but kept them just below her chin for easy access. Kearn tossed her head back and shook her mane, and Rose yelped and slapped her hands back over her eyes again.

"You're making her angry!" Rylan snapped, exasperatedly stroking Kearn's long neck to calm her down yet again.

"She's already angry, she hates me!" Rose shrieked from behind her hands.

Rylan gave a soft chuckle. "She gets a little jealous when I bring girls around. You should have seen her when she first met Lyla, she tried to spit in her eyes before Lyla even entered the gates!"

Rose felt her heart twinge a little as she remembered Lyla the Beautiful, the Mavarakite she had met the day before with the waterfall of blonde curls and the cute little dimple in her cheek. Rose lowered her hands and shot a dirty look at Rylan.

"What?!" Rylan snapped defensively, his ears tucking themselves against his head. "What did I do?!"

"Nothing! I just—this is stupid. Kearn isn't going to let me fly her, and even if she does, we're not going to find anything. I already told you, I came out of the river exactly where I fell in. We're not going to find anything upriver," Rose snapped. Kearn lifted her eyes to Rose, who hurriedly hid behind her hands once more.

"Come here," Rose heard Rylan's voice from the other side of her shielding hands. She felt a tug on her wrist, where Rylan was pulling on her gently to follow him. "How about this. I'll mount Kearn so she feels safe, and you can ride with me. She'll let you do that; she just doesn't trust new riders very much. Especially ones who are so—erm—*inexperienced* with Trusks..."

Rose sighed but went along with Rylan. Kearn wasn't pleased with it, but she did eventually allow

Rose to climb on her back with Rylan as the rider. Rose didn't feel any better about the plan even after successfully climbing on Kearn's back. She felt awkward and uncomfortable, as she had never even ridden horseback much less on the back of a winged horse-like creature. Kearn took a small step forward, which almost sent Rose flying off the back of the Trusk. She wrapped her arms tightly around Rylan, feeling her entire body shake with fear. And this was before they had even taken to the sky.

"Oof—you don't need to squeeze so tight," Rylan struggled to get out, as Rose squeezed tighter around Rylan's gut. "Kearn is a smooth flyer, you'll be fine!"

And with that, Rose watched as the two black-tipped wings stretched out on either side of her and gave one strong, thick *whoosh.*

"Wait, I don't know if I'm ready yet!" Rose gasped, clasping Rylan even tighter and digging her nails into his sides.

"Ow!" Rylan yelped just as Kearn bent down low on her hind legs, kicked her front legs high into the air, and let out a loud gurgle sound like the one they made when preparing to spit. The wings gave another, harder bound and Rose felt a gush of powerful wind push her hair straight back into the air.

"Holy crap, Rylan forget it I don't want to—" Before Rose could finish her exclamation, Kearn kicked off the ground with her powerful legs. She bound forward, as if she were a happy dog frolicking through tall grass. She gave another bound coupled with a flap, and another, and finally on the fourth time her strong wings picked up speed and she took to the air.

Rose felt the sensation of her stomach falling to the ground as the rest of her body went up, up, up into the air. As the ground fell away from her, Rose buried her face into Rylan's back and closed her eyes as tightly as they would shut. She could feel the wind in her hair as the Trusk picked up speed, and she instinctively knew with every bound of the wings that the ground was falling farther below.

"I think I'm going to be sick!" Rose yelled into Rylan's back. She wasn't sure, but she thought she heard Rylan give a shriek of laughter in response. The sick feeling lingered in Rose's throat for a full two minutes as the creature's body lunged with every flap of its hardy wings. Eventually, however, the sick feeling gave way to the pulse of Rose's adrenaline, and Rose began to feel courage mounting in her chest. In a moment of bravery, Rose pulled her head away from Rylan's back and opened her eyes, peering downward to see how far they had taken to the sky. She snapped her eyes shut and again shoved her face into Rylan's back, digging her fingernails deeper into his shirt.

"Rose, loosen your grip a little, you're going to leave scars!" Rylan shouted over the roaring sound of the wind. Rose didn't listen right away, but after another minute of burying her face, she felt the bravery return again. She loosened her grip on Rylan by a fraction and opened her eyes once more. She refused to look down this time, but she did keep her eyes open and looked straightforward to the glorious mountains up ahead.

"There you go," Rylan laughed a little, peering over his shoulder at Rose as she loosened her grip a bit more. "Now you're getting the hang of it. Soon you might even start having fun for the first time in your life!"

Rose shot a dirty look at Rylan, but he didn't notice. He was busy guiding Kearn through the sky, higher and higher from the tall trees that buried Mavarak in their wake.

"Isn't it beautiful?" Rylan asked, and for the first time Rose realized Rylan was entirely captivated by the beauty of the world beneath him. Rose couldn't even brave a peek at the world below, and meanwhile Rylan was enthralled by the beauty of it. Seeing the glow of Rylan's face as he took in the world, Rose decided it was time. She sucked in a deep breath and turned her face so she could see the woods below.

Rylan was right, it was beautiful.

The treetops glistened with a green glow, and the world of Mavarak was entirely concealed. The trees rustled slightly in the wind. The river tore through the valley and glittered in places where the sun glistened in the reflection. It was glorious. But the beauty of the woods paled in comparison to the ugliness of the Other-Side. It was as if the world below was split perfectly in half. On the right side, the world was captured with grace and nature. The trees were voluminous, the green shone from a mile away. On the left side, the world was dark. Tall buildings stretched their ugly arms toward Rose, the grayness dark and dirty next to the beautiful trees. The grass was dark, brown in patches and dead. The House with the Many Windows loomed above the rest of the Other-Side, the world shut out around the building.

"What did they do to all the trees?" Rose asked, her heart heavy with sadness. It was stark, the difference between the two sides of the river. She didn't need to explain who she was talking about to Rylan. He knew.

"They're killing the earth," his answer came darkly, angrily. Rose peered at Rylan from behind and could see he was glaring down at the House with the Many Windows. "They don't even care. They want to keep killing the earth. That's why they hate us...we don't just live in the woods; we live *with* the woods. We embrace the woods like a loved one. They don't think we should. They think we're savages. Well, they would think that anyway, but..."

Rylan trailed off. Rose thought he continued talking, but she couldn't tell over the sound of the beating wings and the wind whistling through her hair.

"Why would they think that anyway?" Rose asked, raising her voice as if to remind Rylan he needed to speak over the wind for her to hear.

"It doesn't matter," Rylan answered, his voice firm and resolute. "Let's get closer to the river and head upstream, see if we can find your grandparents."

Rose didn't push him right away. For a while, she allowed the only sound to be the beating of Kearn's large wings against the air to keep them afloat.

After long minutes passed away and the trio searched the earth on either side of the river upstream from Mavarak, Rose couldn't help the itch she had to find out more about the bad blood between the Other-Siders and the Mavarakites.

"Rylan," Rose asked cautiously, watching his ears to see if they would give away anything as to how he was feeling. "Will you please tell me why the Other-Siders hate the Mavarakites?"

"It's not just the Mavarakites," Rylan answered, intently searching the river and refusing to look back at Rose. "They hate all Wood Dwellers."

This took Rose by surprise. "There are more Wood Dwellers out there, aside from the Mavarakites?"

"Of course," Rylan said, finally breaking and turning over his shoulder to peer back at Rose. "There are tons of villages hidden through the woods. Tons of them! Some we don't even know about. Some villages that are too small and weak to fight the Other-Siders, so they stay hidden and unknown to the world instead. But then there are also our sisters in war, such as the Farcriers. If the Other-Siders attack, we know we can count on the Farcriers to join us in battle. If it weren't for them, we likely would have lost the Crusades."

"So then…" Rose tried again at asking the question, feeling as though Rylan was avoiding it. "Why do the Other-Siders hate all Wood Dwellers?"

"Besides the fact we celebrate the earth while they destroy it?" Rylan spat out vehemently. Rose waited patiently, knowing he was just looking for her to give him an excuse to talk about something else. Finally, Rylan sighed and directed Kearn to drop to the ground so Rylan and Rose wouldn't have to scream over her beating wings. With the newfound quiet of the woods, Rylan continued. "They think we're disgusting creatures. Because of our history."

Rose had about a million questions pop into her head at this, but she voiced none of them. Instead, she waited in silence while Rylan went on. "You see, we come from…well, you might think we're disgusting too. Wood Dwellers are the offspring between an elf and a human."

"What?!" The word slipped out of Rose's mouth before she could contain herself. She remembered Rylan's offended look when she had called him an elf the day they met.

"Yep, and pretty much all humans have the same disgusted reaction you just had," Rylan snapped, and Rose watched his ears turn red. He shifted his weight so he faced straightforward, watching intently as Kearn passed gracefully through the gentle, swaying trees. Rose couldn't see the look on Rylan's face, but she felt his body tense beneath her grip. "When word got out there were these disgusting hybrids between human and elf, everyone wanted to kill us. I mean it, everyone. The humans and the elves all thought we were a disgrace."

"I didn't know elves exist," Rose admitted sheepishly. Even after meeting Rylan and seeing the strange, magical world he came from, she had never considered elves might be real, too.

"They don't," Rylan snapped. He paused for a beat, then added, "Not anymore. The humans killed them all in anger for creating the Wood Dwellers. Don't get me wrong, it's not like the humans are evil or anything. The elves tried to kill the humans too. A lot of humans died. It was kind of a war between species. The humans insisted the elves had taken advantage of their woman, which didn't make sense because the elf woman gave birth to Wood Dwellers as well. It didn't matter, anyway. The humans killed off the elf species—or at least that we Wood Dwellers know about. When the species was almost entirely extinct, some elves went into hiding like the Wood Dwellers did. Maybe some survived. It's impossible to know for sure. Anyway, the humans went on pretending the elves never existed, and most humans, like you, think of them as made-up fairytale things. Some humans, like the Other-Siders, go on hating the Wood Dwellers with a passion. They still try to kill us to this day."

Rose listened intently, shocked about the anger and resentment that could still live on in the hearts of the Other-Siders. "But the Wood Dwellers never did anything to them. Why are they still so angry?"

"Well, a lot of people believe the ancestors of the Other-Siders are the ones who birthed the first of the Wood Dwellers. If that's the case, then the Wood Dwellers just remind the Other-Siders of what they did. It makes them angry, knowing we still exist. Especially because we refuse to live like they do. We take care of the trees and the river; we don't live to pollute and destroy like them. To this day, they deny our history. They refuse to believe their ancestors could possibly have created such monsters as us, half human and half elf. Neither species, truly."

"So, the Wood Dwellers remain in hiding?" Rose asked.

"Yep," Rylan answered, finally turning to look at Rose again. He looked angry, but Rose was relieved to see it didn't appear as though his anger was targeted at her. "And in fear. None of us can leave. If we did, we risk outing our entire village. If any of us ever left Mavarak, we could put everyone we love at risk."

"You wish you could leave?" Rose asked. She watched Rylan's eyes become dark instantly, just as they had when Whitney mentioned Rylan's loyalties. Abruptly, Rylan whistled, and Kearn came to a halt and swooped around, shifting directions so suddenly that Rose nearly toppled off.

"I'm not seeing anything, and there's no way you could have travelled this far in the river and survived. Also, we're not protected by the Guardians here. Let's go back," Rylan said. He dug his heel into Kearn's side, and she once again took to the sky. His voice sounded cold, faraway. Rose racked her brain for something to say, but nothing came to mind. Instead, she listened to the sound of the wind hitting her face from either side as the three made their way back to Rylan's home.

***

By the time Rose and Rylan had returned Kearn to the Trusk pen and were headed back to the hut for lunch, Rylan's dark mood had mostly dissolved into mild irritation. This was good, because when Rylan opened the door to the hut, they were met with the sound of Robin shrieking commands at Drew and a house full of chaos and clutter.

"I don't know what step you're missing but you are obviously not following the instructions correctly!" Rose could hear Robin's voice from somewhere buried in the kitchen. On the bright side, the hut was filled with the strong scent of another sweet-smelling berry Rose didn't recognize. "It clearly says the jam should reach the consistency of melted butter, but yours has reached the consistency of snot. Toss it out and try it again. Be careful this time!"

Rose and Rylan stepped into the hut cautiously, and Rylan carefully shut the door behind them. Despite their attempt at being quiet, and despite her shrieking, Robin still somehow managed to hear them. "Rylan, is that you? I need your help!"

Rylan and Rose exchanged nervous glances before obediently trekking to the kitchen. Upon entering the opening in the tree, Rose noticed Robin furiously mixing a bowl of delicious smelling purple sauce, jam smeared on her face, while Drew was grumpily dumping a lumpy and suspicious looking substance into the sink.

"What on earth is going on here?" Rylan asked, staring incredulously at the mess. Drew was giving him warning looks, but it was too late. Robin had been triggered.

"What's going on here is *Leslie the Gatherer*

—" Robin snapped the name in such a manner that Rose got the distinct sense of dislike. "—has entirely dropped the ball on the harvest festival this year. Apparently, she told the Committee she would bring Sweet Berries, Sweet Berry Jam, and Sweet Berry sauce to the festival, but waited until today to inform them her Sweet Berries haven't fully ripened this year and are bitter. So now—"

At this point in the story, Robin dumped the bowl of purple sauce she was stirring into a jar, slopping a large amount onto the kitchen table in her rush. "Oh, for the love of—anyway, now they have asked me at the last minute to provide the Sweet Berries, because every Wood Dweller knows it wouldn't be harvest festival without Sweet Berries!

"But do they expect me to go out and pick the Sweet Berries and somehow also make the jam and the sauce all at the same time with only one day to prepare for the festival? There is only one of me!" Her voice sounded desperate and exasperated.

"Rose and I can help!" Rylan offered, much to the dismay of Rose. She had no idea how to make jam or sauce, and she had no knowledge or skill in the kitchen whatsoever. Now did not seem like the time to let Robin discover how unhelpful Rose could be.

"Oh, Rylan, that would be great," Robin replied in such a heartfelt way that Rose couldn't back out. "Could you please gather more berries from our tree?"

As Rylan led Rose back out of the hut and to the Small family orchard—which was just around the hut and hidden from view if you were looking from the inside of the village clearing—Rylan informed Rose he would be doing the tree climbing and she could catch the berries in a basket as they fell. Rose looked at Rylan confusedly, as she had never heard of berries growing on trees before. Didn't berries grow on bushes?

Just as Rose opened her mouth to ask about the berry trees, she was practically knocked over by a hunched, short Wood Dweller who was scurrying past the two so fast they didn't have time to jump out of the way. Rose watched the figure continue to scurry by, noticing the figure was wearing a brown, patchy hood covering her head. The figure disappeared between the Small's home and the neighboring hut, heading toward the village clearing. Rose turned to ask Rylan about the Wood Dweller, but before she could ask the question, she noticed a peculiar look on Rylan's face as he, too, stared after the hunched over figure.

"Who is that?" Rose asked, even more curious because of the look on Rylan's face.

"That," Rylan said, "is Cecily the Witch."

"The Witch?" Rose repeated, turning her gaze once again to the bustling, hooded figure that had almost entirely disappeared into the thick of the crowded clearing.

"Yes. She is famous for her potion making. And she may just have something that could be your ticket back home…"

Chapter 7

The Potion

    Rylan and Rose spent the next few hours in the orchard, Rylan scrambling like an ant up the trees and shaking the branches to knock berries down. Meanwhile, Rose stood below the branches, catching as many berries as she could before they hit the ground. Several berries would bounce off her head, arms, and face, and some would smack her with a swift *splat*, leaving little blotches of berry juice all over her body. Rylan got a good laugh out of it, which first made Rose quite angry, until Rylan nearly knocked himself out of a tree during one laughing fit. Eventually, however, it became a game of Rylan attempting to hit Rose with as many berries as possible, which in turn inspired Rose to launch berries at Rylan as he climbed up each new tree. By the end, the pair were covered in patches of berry juice, but were generally in good moods and had spent much of the time laughing at the other's pain.

Meanwhile, Rylan had filled Rose in a bit on Cecily the Witch. Unlike the stereotypical witch Rose had come to know in the human world, witches were quite accepted in Wood Dweller's lives. In fact, Rylan talked about Cecily's magic as though it were a home remedy for whatever issue you may run into. However, he had not initially considered going to Cecily for a potion to take Rose home because, apparently, due to Cecily's high volume of customers, she is unable to make an entire potion from scratch without the customer paying an arm and a leg for it. For a reasonable price of Holken meat (which Rylan, in unusually high spirits, helpfully offered to cover), Cecily will provide ominous directions to make a potion, with absolutely no guarantee it will work.

Given the circumstances and the limited options Rose had left, she was willing to agree to the less-than-reliable terms.

Eventually, Rylan and Rose finished gathering the berries for the harvest festival. While it appeared as though Robin was still stressing over finishing the preparations with only Drew's help, she didn't ask for Rylan and Rose's help in the kitchen, which came as a relief to Rose. After they dropped off the berries and rinsed the berry juice off their arms and faces, Rylan led Rose once again into the heart of the Mavarak clearing.

This time, the walk through the clearing went entirely uninterrupted (Lyla the Beautiful spotted Rylan from across the clearing and had called a quick "Merry to see you," but, to Rose's relief, hadn't approached the pair). Cecily's hut was easy to spot. It was one of the huts surrounding the clearing of Mavarak and was just about dead center. Like many of the other huts Rose had identified, this hut was built directly into one large tree. Unlike the other huts, however, this one was adorned with a line of customers waiting outside the hut. In Rose's head, she had imagined Cecily's hut to be mysterious, maybe surrounded by a cloud of mist, and in the outskirts of the village. Much to her surprise, it appeared more like a small business. The hut was entirely average, if not plainer than some of the others, and there was no mystical smoke or other bizarre trinkets setting the place apart from other huts Rose had seen.

As Rose and Rylan waited in line, Rose listened in on the conversations happening all around her.

"Last time I came to see Cecily, I had a poppy infestation," said a Wood Dweller who appeared around Robin's age to a much taller Wood Dweller with a large nose, "I spent half the day gathering jelly seeds, a blade of red grass, a small pebble, and all sorts of other supplies. I set out the potion just like Cecily said but the poppies didn't go away. A week later I had to hire someone to take the poppies out for me. This time, I'm giving Cecily all the Honeydews she wants to just make the potion herself!"

Rose's palms began to sweat listening to the conversation. Jelly seeds? Poppies? Honeydews? The potion didn't even work? How is Rose supposed to be able to gather ingredients she's never even heard of? And what if she goes through all that and drinks the potion and it doesn't do a single thing?

To distract herself from the disconcerting thoughts, Rose turned instead to Rylan and finally asked a question she had long wondered but never asked out loud. "Rylan, is Cecily the only magical Wood Dweller?"

Rylan, who had been picking at what appeared to be a scar on his hand, glanced up at Rose. "Well, depends on what you mean by magical. She's the only one who sells potions if that's what you consider magic."

Rose didn't feel satisfied one bit by that answer. "Well then, what even is the difference between a human and a Wood Dweller? I mean, aside from living in the trees and having pointy ears…"

"Humans change color a lot more than Wood Dwellers," Rylan answered. As if on cue, Rose felt a blush rise to her face in embarrassment at the response.

"Rylan," Rose snapped. "I'm serious. I know you know what I'm asking. What are Wood Dwellers capable of? Do you have any powers?"

Rylan gave out a sigh and answered, "Yeah, I get

what you're asking. It's hard to explain though. Wood Dwellers have...subtle powers."

"Subtle?" Rose asked, shifting forward in line as another customer entered Cecily's hut.

"Yeah. We can't, like, move things with our minds or cast magic spells or anything like that. But, we have, erm...gifts," Rylan searched for the right words to explain. "It's sort of like a talent, but an extension of that. Does that make sense?"

Rose blinked. "Not at all."

"Okay," Rylan said, busying himself with scanning the number of Wood Dwellers left ahead of them. There were only a few. "It's like this. Some humans are born and they're just really good at singing, right?"

"Right," Rose nodded along.

"Right. So, a Wood Dweller might be born with a similar talent. Except, they aren't just really good at singing. They have such a beautiful, glorious singing voice that it can, say, calm a fight, or put a fussy baby to sleep. It's like an extension of a talent."

"Oh..." Rose murmured, taking another step forward as another Wood Dweller disappeared into the hut before them. "So, instead of just being really good at taking care of Trusks, you can..."

"Talk to them, yeah." Rylan finished the sentence for Rose.

"Wait," Rose exclaimed, surprised. "You can *talk* to the Trusks?!"

Rylan's ears shot up straight, as though surprised, and turned a little red at the ends. "Oh, I mean, yeah, kinda...they don't answer back or anything!

They just really seem to be soothed by me. It's like they understand me better than other Wood Dwellers."

"And Robin..." Rose considered the ways Robin seemed gifted.

"When you take a bite of her cooking, you're transported to a different place. Sometimes I'll take a bite of her Sweet Berry Jam, and I can remember times from childhood I didn't even realize happened!"

Rose laughed, realizing she too had been transported every time she ate some of Robin's cooking. The Wood Dweller who had talked about the poppies disappeared into Cecily's hut, leaving Rylan and Rose next in line.

"And Drew?" Rose asked, thoroughly enjoying learning this new part of Wood Dwellers she had never known about before.

"We actually don't know about him yet," Rylan answered, shifting awkwardly and looking away from Rose. "I mean, he's still pretty young. Some Wood Dwellers show early signs of their gifts, like me. I started playing with Trusks when I could barely walk. But Drew is a late bloomer. He hasn't really shown any signs yet..."

Rylan trailed off, keeping his eyes glued to the hut, prepared to step in as soon as the poppy Wood Dweller left.

"Do all Wood Dwellers have a gift?" Rose gently pressed, still curious about the scope of Wood Dweller's abilities.

"Most of them do..." Rylan answered, finally meeting Rose's eyes. "The ones who don't develop any kind of a gift really struggle. To fit in, to find a job, to be useful to the community. They're called Noids. It's short for a humanoid, and most Noids end up being homeless. Or a financial strain on the family..."

Before Rose could ask more about Noids, or comfort Rylan with the reminder that Drew is still young and might develop his gift soon, the poppy Wood Dweller stepped out of the hut. Rylan gave Rose a look, and the two stepped into the tree together.

Once again, Rose had been expecting the hut to appear magical. She was expecting mist, or perhaps shrunken heads hanging from the ceiling, or some sign that this was the hut of a magical being. Instead, Rose stepped into a living room nearly identical to the Small's. Just like the Small's living room, there was a leaf couch, a wooden table, and a window cut into the side of the room. There was no animal rug, unlike the Small's, but there was an opening leading to another room on the far-right side of the living room. Sitting on the couch facing Rose and Rylan was the small, hooded figure that ran into Rose before, the one Rylan had called Cecily the Witch. Cecily gestured toward a smaller couch placed adjacent to the couch she was perched on.

As Rose took her place on the couch next to Rylan, she was able to get a closer look at the face behind the hood. Cecily had scratchy, straw-like black hair dropping over her eyes, her pointed ears were entirely covered, and her lips looked dry and cracked. She didn't smile, nor did she seem to enjoy her job at all. In fact, from the second Rose entered the room, she got the distinct feeling Cecily wanted to get her out as fast as possible.

"What issue are you facing?" Cecily the Witch demanded icily, not bothering at all with introductions or greetings.

Rose and Rylan exchanged glances, both unsure who should speak next. Rose began to feel her face flush. They should have practiced explaining the problem before meeting Cecily.

"Today, please," Cecily croaked impatiently, her eyes boring a hole into Rose.

"Well," Rose and Rylan both started at the same time. Rose snapped her mouth closed at the same time as Rylan.

"I will make it easier on you," Cecily barked, clearly already reaching the end of her rope. "The one with the problem, please come forward and explain."

Rose gulped. That would be her.

"Well," Rose tried again, and this time Rylan remained silent next to her. "I accidentally got lost here, and I can't find my way back home. Er—to my grandparents' cabin."

"A potion to return home," Cecily snapped. Rose was shocked, as she had expected to explain the dilemma further—she had been prepared to explain the little door and Whitney the Wise and the Trusks and everything—but apparently Cecily had heard all she needed to hear. "That will require a cup of pond water mixed with half a cup of pond scum, the juice from three sweet tree berries of a moon tree, a drop of sweat from an enemy, and the tail feather of a Trusk.

Stir three times to the right and twice to the left. Do not over stir the mixture. Do you need me to repeat the directions?"

Rose blinked and Rylan muttered stupidly, "Er—"

"Very well then," Cecily snapped, then repeated the directions. This time, Rose committed each step of directions to memory. When she finished repeating the steps, Cecily asked, "Anything else?"

"Er—" was Rylan's only reply, once again.

"Great. Roger the Collector will be around to collect payment within one week's time. Where can he find your Holken meat?" Cecily asked.

"At my hut. Er, I mean, at the Small's hut. Which is my hut," Rylan stammered.

"Thank you for your business," Cecily responded. Without a smile or a shift in her perch, she extended an arm toward the door, excusing Rose and Rylan. Rylan hurried to his feet, and Rose followed close behind him.

Once they were safely in the village clearing and several paces away from Cecily's hut, Rylan let out a loud sigh.

"I didn't even realize I was holding my breath," Rylan said. Rose too let out a sigh of relief, then the two exchanged a look. Simultaneously, they both burst into a fit of laughter.

"You should have heard yourself! Er—er—you couldn't say anything else!" Rose laughed.

"Did you hear her, though?!" Rylan laughed. He forced a serious face to fall over his smiling features and snapped in a rushed, flat voice, "Today, please."

"And did you hear how fast she went through all the ingredients for the potion? It's a good thing she repeated them, because if she hadn't, we would be wasting an entire Holken for literally nothing. I don't think I remembered one word she said the first time."

"Agreed," Rylan said, nodding his head as if to show how much in agreement he was. "We better get started if we want to collect all the ingredients by the end of the day. We should probably split up to make it go faster—"

"Split up?!" Rose interrupted Rylan's planning. There was no chance she was venturing through Mavarak in search of the sweat of an enemy without him by her side. "I can't do this without you!"

"Oh, right," Rylan said, the tips of his ears growing red. Rose realized what she said and felt herself blush a little. To save both of them from further embarrassment, she feigned turning to look around the clearing.

"Do you know of any nearby ponds? Two of our ingredients are there."

Rylan seemed pleased she had changed the subject.

"Yeah, those will be the easiest ingredient to get. Let's stop by the hut to get some jam jars, then we can start collecting stuff!" Rylan instructed. With that, he headed off in the direction of the hut.

***

Rylan was right. Retrieving the pond water and scum was by far the easiest part of the potion ingredients. Unfortunately for Rose, as Rylan stepped on a slippery looking rock to retrieve some scum, he slipped straight into the pond, sending Rose straight into a laughing fit and aggravating Rylan.

"You could help me instead of standing there laughing!" Rylan griped as Rose doubled over in laughter. She tried to pull herself together and help Rylan out of the pond, but with one glance at his reddening pointy ears and his soaking wet clothing, Rose snorted again.

"It isn't funny! Pretty brave of you to make fun of the one person helping you find the ingredients you need to get out of here!" Rylan snapped, angrily scooping up the pond scum off the slippery rock that had sent him flying into the water. At this thought, Rose stifled a laugh and straightened up quickly. Rylan seemed to notice the fear that had struck Rose at the thought, and he got a suspiciously mischievous look.

"You're right," Rose said apologetically, hoping it wasn't too little too late. "It wasn't one bit funny. Do you need help?"

Rylan stepped carefully out of the pond, avoiding Rose's extended helpful hand, and shook out his hair and clothes like a dog, sending dirty pond water flying all over Rose.

"Hey, watch it!" Rose screeched, shielding herself.

"Come on, we better go find the moon tree!" Rylan chirped, still smiling his mischievous smile. "You better get climbing soon, it's gonna take you a while!"

Rose stood stock-still. "Did you say *I* better start climbing soon?"

Rylan sent a devious smile over his shoulder and beckoned for Rose to follow him into the woods.

Rose scurried to catch up with Rylan and match his pace. "Rylan, I can't climb the tree. It will take me twice as long as you!"

"Twice as long? Don't be ridiculous," Rylan said, rolling his eyes, a mischievous gleam still lighting his features. "It will take way longer than that."

"Rylan!" Rose whined. She regretted that second and third laughing fit now. She continued to plead as she followed Rylan up to a looming white tree. The white bark stood out against the greenery of the forest.

Upon reaching the tree, Rylan comfortably leaned against the white tree, perched one foot against the smooth bark, and folded his arms lightly across his chest. "Better get on it. I'd say Mom will be expecting us back home for dinner in about four hours, and we still have two other ingredients to get after this one."

Rose huffed indignantly. Rylan clearly had no intention of helping her retrieve the sweet berries of the moon tree. Rose looked at the white bark and scanned the tree for the nearest branch. It was easily three feet above her head. She scanned higher, hoping the berries were near the bottom. They weren't. She would need to work her way up at least five branches before she reached the lowest hanging berries.

With one more loud huff in the direction of

Rylan, who was letting out an obnoxiously loud yawn, Rose stepped up to the white tree he perched against, purposely elbowing him as she reached for the nearest branch.

Clutching the rough wood of the branch for dear life, Rose scrambled her feet in search of a hold on the trunk. She couldn't find one and slipped off the branch, thudding back onto the ground. She shot a dirty look at Rylan, who was snickering behind his hands. Wiping off her palms, she prepared for a second try, planning a running head start this time. She launched herself up the tree, scrambling up as fast as she could. With the running head start, she was able to gain enough momentum to throw her elbow over the branch and pull herself up. Once she had her entire body safely on the lowest branch, she triumphantly smiled down at Rylan. Meanwhile, he was sliding himself down to a sitting position and stretching his arms above his head, as though ready to take a nap.

Angrily, Rose peered above her head to spot her next branch. Carefully, she brought her body up to a standing position. This branch was not nearly as high as the first one, and she easily wrapped her body around it and flung her leg over, putting her in a position where she was straddling the tree. Feeling a little too brave with her success, Rose stood up precariously and nearly slipped off the branch, sending her sprawling to a sitting position and clinging to the trunk of the tree for dear life.

After several more slips, near falls, and mishaps, including one long and angry scrape up her arm,

Rose finally reached a branch that, when she stood carefully on tiptoes, was within arms-length of the sweet berries. They were dangling gloriously above Rose, shining such a deep maroon color that they were nearly purple. Rose stretched one arm as high as she could, lifting herself carefully onto tippy-toes and clinging with her free arm to the base of the tree. Her fingertips just brushed the berries, but not enough to be able to pick them off. She shifted carefully on the branch she stood on, loosening her grip slightly on the trunk so she could reach higher.

With a distinct *plunk!*, Rose picked a stem that contained several berries.

"Yes!" Rose shouted, shooting her handful of berries into the air victoriously. With the sudden movement, she began to sway dangerously on the branch.

"Congratulations," Rylan said from several feet below Rose, his voice flat and non-congratulatory. "Now climb back down."

Rose angrily threw the berries down toward Rylan for safe-keeping ("Ow! You purposely aimed for my head!") and began her trek down the tree. The climb out of the tree was significantly faster than the climb up ("You aren't climbing down, you're *falling* down!"), and Rose made it out of the tree and onto the ground with only two more scrapes than the journey up!

Once she was safely on the ground, she shot a triumphant look at Rylan and clapped her hands, bouncing with excitement. "I did it! I climbed the tree, no thanks to you, and I got the berries!!!"

Rose was positively giddy, until she noticed Rylan still glowed with mischief. He popped a single berry into his mouth and smiled slyly up at Rose. She stopped celebrating and looked at him suspiciously. "What are you smiling about?"

"Nothing," Rylan replied, plopping the berries on the ground next to his leg and crossing his arms behind his head as a pillow. "You did a great job collecting the sweet berries of a *blood* tree."

"Yes, I did," Rose snapped, crossing her arms defiantly. "I collected the berries of a...wait, did you say a blood tree? No, it's a moon tree. I remember Cecily saying..."

Rose trailed off as Rylan smugly popped another single berry into his mouth. "Yep, Cecily did say a moon tree. Which would be that one right there," Rylan pointed sharply at the murky brown tree directly next to the shiny white tree Rose had just conquered.

Rose studied the tree Rylan was pointing at, then the tree she had just climbed, then finally quizzically looked at Rylan. "You can't be serious..."

Rylan smiled proudly.

Rose burst with anger. "But you leaned against that tree! You did that on purpose just so I would climb up the wrong tree! You—you—"

"Brilliant genius?" Rylan finished for her.

"You jerk! How can you be so immature?! We just wasted so much time—"

"Because you're slow," Rylan interrupted.

"—and I could have gotten seriously hurt—"

"It's a miracle you didn't, really…"

"And I just want to go home!" Rose screeched, stomping her foot angrily. As soon as she said it, an image of her parents floated through her head. She could imagine them searching through the woods, calling her name. She knew her dad's brow would be furrowed in concern; her mom would make passive aggressive comments about Dad sending her off to the same place she had almost died years ago. Or maybe this time it was Mom's idea, and Dad would huff and say 'And yet somehow this is all *my* fault…'

A single tear formed a puddle in Rose's eye, threatening to spill over and reveal the pain Rose really felt. She whirred around, hoping to hide her feelings from Rylan. But it was too late. Even before she had spun to face the other way, she could see Rylan's ears tuck back against his head.

"Whoa, Rose, I'm sorry…" Rylan apologized, and she could hear him rustling to his feet. Soon, she felt his warmth behind her. "That was stupid, I was just messing around. I shouldn't have—"

Before he could finish his apology, Rose cut him off. "No, it isn't your fault. I'm just worried about my parents."

The single tear that had formed in Rose's eye fell down her cheek. As much as she wanted to wipe the tear away and tease Rylan right back, her mind was in a different place. Images of her mom and dad floated through her head. On the one hand, she could so clearly see them laughing together, Dad making a goofy remark and Mom rolling her eyes but not being able to stop a giggle from slipping out. On the other hand, she could imagine Mom's scolding look that told Dad to quit joking around, her sigh that said she was so over having to be a mom for him, too.

"You think they're worried sick about you, huh?" Rylan guessed, his warmth still informing Rose of his close proximity behind her.

"It's not that. I mean it kind of is. But," Rose let out a deep sigh, then spilled the contents of her heart, "my parents are getting a divorce. It's my fault. I almost died when I was little, and my mom blames my dad for letting me out of sight long enough to get hurt. If I had just stayed where I was supposed to..." Rose trailed off. She was crying now, and it was becoming difficult to talk through it. Rylan circled around her so he could see her face, which embarrassed her. She closed her eyes as the warm tears trailed down her cheeks. Surprisingly, it wasn't long before she felt Rylan's arms wrap around her body and pull her in tightly. Instead of pushing away as she would normally have done, Rose leaned her face into Rylan's shoulder and let go of all the pain she had been holding on to.

When the tears finally dried and Rose entered the hiccupping stage of crying, she took a step away from Rylan and wiped her face clean. For a short while, the two of them stood facing each other in an awkward silence. Then, without another word, Rylan turned on his heels and stepped up to the real moon tree. In less than a minute, he had scaled the side of the tree, retrieved a small branch filled with berries, placed the twig securely between his sharp teeth, and scaled back down the tree. He pocketed the branch, picked up the jam jar filled with pond water and scum, and looked at Rose. The moment they had shared had entirely vanished, and it was back to business for Rylan.

"Alright, three ingredients down, two to go. Do you remember what else we need?" Rylan asked.

Rose sniffled, still trying to pull herself together from her break down. "Um, yeah, it was…oh, the sweat of an enemy!"

"Right," Rylan said, nodding. "Do you have any enemies?"

"Besides you?" Rose asked. Rylan looked surprised at first, but Rose smiled softly so he knew she was teasing him.

"Oh! We could get sweat from an Other-Sider! They are the enemies of all Mavarakites!" Rylan exclaimed.

Rose glanced nervously in the direction of the Other-Side, thinking about the Crusades where the Other-Siders had attempted to wipe out the entire species of Wood Dwellers single-handedly. Taking them on seemed a bit dangerous.

"What about…" Rose considered her options. As if a lightbulb had appeared above Rose's head, she was struck with an idea. "Oh, I got it! We can get sweat from Lyla!"

As soon as she said it, Rose felt herself begin to blush. Rylan looked at her confused, one of his ears perking up and the other lying flat in confusion. "Lyla the Beautiful? Why would she be your enemy?"

Rose suddenly became extremely interested in the scar on her palm, avoiding the prying eyes of the confused Rylan. "Don't worry about it. I just get the feeling her sweat will work…"

During the walk back to the clearing, Rylan attempted several times to find out why Lyla would work as an enemy, which Rose would casually change the subject or entirely ignore the questions all together. Lyla was certainly weirded out by the request, but Rylan was able to awkwardly stammer out some lame excuse about a science project and she willingly did some jumping jacks until she worked up a sweat. Meanwhile, Rose did her best to avoid all eye contact with Lyla during the entire exchange.

Finally, the pair were down to one ingredient, and luckily Rylan happened to be just about the best Mavarkite around to help Rose get the tailfeather of a Trusk. Despite almost being trampled to death by Kearn when Rylan yanked the tailfeather out, Rose would ultimately rather have to pull out 50 more tailfeathers before asking Lyla for another bead of sweat.

"Alright, we've got them all!" Rylan exclaimed as they stepped out of the Trusk enclosure and sat down together on a nearby tree stump. "The sweat is already in the jar with the pond water and the scum. I'll rip up the tailfeather a little so it's easier to mix into the other ingredients, and you squeeze the juice out of the three berries," Rylan directed.

"Wait, you already put the sweat into the jar?"

Rose asked, looking at Rylan with wide eyes. "We're supposed to mix the scum and pond water together first before we add the other ingredients!"

"What? No, Cecily didn't say that. She just said to stir the ingredients together at the end, three times to the left and twice to the right," Rylan insisted, grabbing the jar away from Rose as if she were purposely conspiring against him.

"No, she said the potion needed pond water and scum mixed, then all the other stuff, then stir three times to the *right* and twice to the *left*," Rose corrected, reaching out and pulling the jar away from Rylan. "We need to get fresh pond water and scum. And more of Lyla's sweat."

Rose intended on letting Rylan deal with the sweat.

Rylan seemed deep in thought. Finally, he reached out for the jar and said, "Okay, you might be right about the directions to stir. But I'm sure she didn't mean to stir the ingredients together before adding them all into the jar. When she said to mix them, she just meant to put them in the same bowl."

"But that's not what mixing means!" Rose argued. "If you mix ingredients, it means to stir them together!"

"Then why wouldn't she have just said stir the pond water and scum together?!" Rylan snapped, yanking the jar out of Rose's hand. "You don't know anything about Wood Dwellers, you don't know what she meant when she said to mix them."

"I don't need to know about Wood Dwellers

to know what it means to mix something!" Rose snapped, yanking the potion back toward herself.

"It's going to work fine! And even if it doesn't, we'll just get all the stuff again and try it your way. It won't take all day long if I get the berries next time," Rylan reasoned. Finally, Rose nodded and allowed Rylan to rip the tailfeather into the mixture. One by one, she squeezed the juice of each sweet berry into the mixture. Once all the ingredients were in the jar, Rylan retrieved a stick from the ground to stir the ingredients together. Obediently, he stirred three times to the right, twice to the left. Then, he handed the potion over to Rose.

"Bottom's up," Rylan said. Rose looked down at the barely stirred mixture. She could still clearly see parts of a Trusk tailfeather sticking up. The scum and pond water reeked, and she could distinctly smell bacteria mixed with a few drops of something sweet. She wrinkled her nose.

"This looks and smells disgusting," Rose whined.

"It's a potion, it's not supposed to taste good! Just gulp it down really fast!" Rylan commanded.

"Am I just going to disappear as soon as I drink it?" Rose wondered, partially nervous about being sick from the potion and partially wanting to stall.

"Oh," Rylan mumbled, his ears lowering on his head. "I didn't think about that. I guess this is goodbye..."

Rose looked up into Rylan's captivating blue eyes and, with a pang in her chest, realized they held a deep sadness in them. He didn't want her to leave. And, with another pang in her chest, Rose thought about what was waiting for her back home. If this potion worked, she would be whisked away from Rylan forever. She would never see those pointy ears, or those big blue eyes, or that mischievous smile ever again. Instead, she would be met with parents who hate each other, a summer of boredom with her grandparents, and a million questions about the Wood Dwellers that would never be answered...

Rose lowered the potion decidedly. "Well, the potion doesn't have an expiration date, right? I have to at least stay for the harvest festival..."

Rylan's ears perked up, and Rose couldn't stop a smile from spreading over her face.

Chapter 8

The Harvest Festival

The morning of the harvest festival was a whirlwind in the Small's hut. Robin was absolutely anxious with all the preparations in providing the Sweet Berries, Sweet Berry Jam, and Sweet Berry sauce. She loaded Drew, Rylan, and Rose up with basketfuls of delicious smelling berries an hour before the festival began because she didn't want to chance being late. Rose wondered how it was possible the group could arrive late to an event being held right outside the door, but she thought it best not to argue with Robin.

As soon as Rose stepped out the door of the tiny hut, arms full of jam jars, she realized Robin was not the only Mavarakite who was anxious about the day's festivities. The town center was bustling with Mavarakites all preparing for the day in their own way. Rose spotted Max the Warrior along with several other iron-clad warriors sharpening short sticks into knives outside the weaponry hut. Lyla the beautiful sat in a field of wildflowers styling young Wood Dweller's hair into braided fashions woven with flowers like her own hair. Several other very young Wood Dweller's—who, according to their beautifully fashioned hair, had already visited with Lyla—were running around the village placing gorgeous flowers in decorative patterns in various places.

With a quick glance around the clearing of the village, Rose noticed many activities had been set up overnight. It reminded her of the fair she had gone to when she was 7 years old with her parents, but without the rides that had been set up. There was an obstacle course that ran directly through the Trusk pen which the creatures lazily walked around. There was a giant crate filled with crispy looking leaves and an engraved wooden sign that said, 'Find the berry in the leaf stack!' Nearby Cecily's hut was a leaf-fort and a sign that read, 'Glimpse into the future with Talia the Seer!' At the center of the clearing was a long, oval-shaped wooden table and an elderly Wood Dweller who appeared to be rearranging different Mavarkite foods along the table. Robin led the basket-carrying group toward that very wooden table and directed each of them to unload their goods in a certain order along the table.

"Robin, it all looks delicious!" an older Mavarakite appeared behind the group, dropping a plate of bread directly next to Robin's jam. Even though both Drew and Rylan stood between Rose and the bread, she could still distinctly smell the warmth of freshly baked dough wafting in the air, and her stomach growled.

Rylan, who could apparently hear her stomach, turned to Rose and flashed a twinkling smile at her. "We can eat as soon as Bryce the Leader announces the festivities have begun. Once we finish eating, we should go over to the obstacle course. I want to see if you set a record for all-time slowest completion!"

Rose shot a dirty look at Rylan, and he responded with a kind-hearted laugh that told Rose he was in an exceptionally good mood that day. She couldn't help but feel a bit bubbly as well being surrounded by Mavarakites who all excitedly celebrated their success in the Crusades.

Once they had set up the Sweet Berries as Robin had directed, her anxiety lifted and they were all able to look around at all the activities that had been set up before the festivities officially began. Rose was most excited to play Shoot the Other-Sider, a game that involved throwing a variety of small fruits at whittled figures of evil-looking Other-Siders on pegs to knock them down. Stab the Fruit also looked fun. This game involved knocking berries out of some trees near the clearing using the wooden knives thar Rose had noticed Max the Warrior crafting earlier. While she was looking forward to several of those activities, she intended on keeping far away from the Trusk pen with the 'Groom and Ride a Trusk!' sign nearby.

The group had just about circled the entire clearing and were coming up on the last section of unexplored activities when she heard a deep and booming voice call from the center of the village, "Merry to see you all! Merry to see you all!"

Rose, Drew, Robin, and Rylan all stopped and turned their attention toward the voice, along with all the other Wood Dwellers that filled up the bustling clearing. It was easy to spot where the voice was coming from, as a tall Wood Dweller with particularly large, pointy ears and a bald head was raised above the shoulders of the other Mavarakites on a wooden platform placed directly next to the table of food.

"I would just like to remind you all that we celebrate today a glorious occasion," the Mavarakite, presumably Bryce the Leader, said with a warm smile reaching from ear to ear. Before he was able to continue his opening statement, there was an uproar of cheering coming from all the Wood Dwellers. "On this day exactly ten years ago, the Keepers of Mavarakite completed a successful blood sacrifice. Since then, our Guardians have kept us safe and hidden, ending the Crusades of the Other-Siders for good!"

Bryce the Leader paused as the Wood Dwellers erupted into another rousing cheer. When they quieted down, Bryce continued once more. "Today, we eat some of our finest delicacies, we celebrate a day of no work, and we come together to have some fun as a tribute to the great magic of Whitney the Wise and Cecily the Witch, who worked together to create the magical bond that has kept us safe for all these years. And, as a tribute to the Keepers, who gave their blood and have stayed loyal to Mavarak all this time!

"In honor and thanks to those who gave their lives, gave their magic, and gave their blood to protect our species. Together we live!" Bryce shouted gloriously.

"Together we live!" Drew, Rylan, Robin, and every other Mavarakite chanted.

Immediately, the woods came alive with the buzzing and chattering of Mavarakites.

"Rylan," Rose leaned over to Rylan, not wanting Robin or Drew to hear, "what exactly did the Keepers of the Guardians have to do for their blood sacrifice?"

"Oh," Rylan said, seeming caught off guard by the question, as though he had forgotten Rose wasn't a Mavarakite and didn't fully understand the history of Mavarak. "Well, first they both had to cut open their hand and drop some of their blood into a potion made by Cecily. Then they had to drink the potion, which was pretty nasty. But the greatest sacrifice they gave was their promise to always remain loyal to the village. If either of them betrays Mavarak, then the bond will be broken and the spell will fall, instantly revealing the pathway of Mavarak to the Other-Siders."

"So—" Rose opened her mouth to ask more questions about the Guardians. Before she was able to,

Rylan interrupted.

"It will all be explained way better during the reenactment. I mean, the reenactment is always put on by the young Wood Dwellers of Mavarak, so the acting isn't exactly great, but it does explain the history of the Crusades and the Guardians. It's at the end of the festival," Rylan said. Rose nodded her agreement to hold all questions until after the reenactment, and with that, Rylan and Rose ran to join Drew and Robin for a rousing game of Swat the Berry.

Eventually, Max the Warrior and Lyla the Beautiful joined Rose and the Smalls. At first, Rose was annoyed to see Lyla join the group, especially when she caught a glimpse of Rylan's puppy dog face as he watched Lyla swat an Orangeberry out of the sky. However, there was so much giddiness and positive energy that it was difficult to stay in a bad mood for long. Plus, Lyla gave Rose her Orangeberry Muffin when they ran out, insisting she had eaten hundreds in her life and Rose had to try one while she was in Mavarak.

The warm, sweet and salty, delicious food, the endless games and activities offered at the festival, and the weight of finding her way home lifted by the knowledge of the potion sitting in Rylan's hut put Rose in such a great mood that her and Rylan didn't get into a single fight during the entirety of the festival. In fact, when the group found their way to the obstacle course, Rylan even willingly chose Rose as his partner! Despite the kindness of the Orangeberry Muffin, Rose couldn't help but give Lyla a smug look when Rylan wasn't looking.

Max, who Rose had only ever had one awkward exchange with, turned out to be a lot of fun when off duty. His stone-cold face didn't often light up with a smile, but when it did, he would let out a deep and silky laugh that Rose couldn't help but laugh along with. Rose even caught a hint of playfulness from Max when he held Rylan back by the neck of his shirt so Lyla could catch a lead during the obstacle course. When Rylan protested, Max gave him the most wonderfully innocent puppy-dog eyes and asked, "Do you have no chivalry?" Though he hid behind a hardened exterior, Rose learned that Max was only serious all the time because his family had been severely damaged during the war that took place between the Wood Dwellers and the Other-Siders. Rose learned this information during dinner, when Rylan and Drew were sent back to the hut by a disgruntled Robin ("No one brought the jars of Sweet Berry and Honey jam I put out?!") and Rose was left to awkwardly sit on the grassy clearing between Lyla and Max.

"So Rose," Lyla asked, flipping her beautiful hair over her shoulder. Rose caught a whiff of a delectable flower scent emitting from Lyla's golden waves. It took a lot of self-control to keep from glaring at her. "Will you tell me what the human world is like?"

Rose coughed, buying herself more time. She had no idea where to even begin explaining the human world to creatures who had only ever known life in the woods.

"Well," Rose said, growing nervous as she

looked at her expectant audience members. Lyla sat peacefully with her legs crossed, a permanent gentle smile glued to her face. Meanwhile, Max sprawled on the ground laying down, his head perched on one bent arm and the other picking through the fruits adorning his wooden plate. Rose felt like she was sitting at the popular table at school and was trying to prove her worth.

"Perhaps you could tell us a bit about your friends," Max added helpfully, popping a purple berry into his mouth. Rose smiled at him gratefully.

"Well, my best friend is Lacie. She's great, she can always make me laugh. I have other friends, but none I really hang out with outside of school," Rose answered.

"School?" Lyla asked, tilting her head. One of her ears laid down and the other perked up just as Rose had seen Rylan's do when he became curious.

"Oh yeah, human kids and teenagers have to go every day. We learn about things like English, math, science, history…" Rose explained.

"Oh yes, just like our daily lessons!" Max exclaimed, seeming excited to brag about the Wood Dweller's version of school. Rose had learned Max was extremely proud of Mavarak's accomplishments. He talked about the village with gushing admiration every chance he got, which was fun for Rose since she liked learning about the Mavarakites.

Max continued to explain. "We have daily lessons on Alchemy, Astronomy, Numbers, Words, Harvesting, and Wood Dweller History. Only the very young participate, though. By the time Mavarakites recognize their Gift and begin to work, they no longer have to go to daily lessons."

"When did you recognize your Gift as a Warrior, Max?" Rose asked, picking up a Honeysickle and nibbling on the end of it. A Honeysickle, Rose had learned, was semi-hardened honey on a stick and coated with a special berry sauce. It melted in Rose's mouth, and she instantly wanted to load five more Honeysickles onto her plate.

"When I was three," Max informed casually. Rose was shocked. He became a warrior at the age of three? Max, who was a man of few words unless speaking proudly of his people, apparently felt this statement alone was enough information. Rose had to press for him to go on, but eventually he continued. "My father was killed by the Other-Siders during the Crusades when I was three. My mom was taken hostage, so I was taken as an orphan by my father's best friend, Killian the Warrior. Killian was the leader of the Mavarakite warriors. He didn't know much about raising a young Wood Dweller, but he knew a lot about being a war hero. So, he began training me at the age of three to fight in the war.

"By the time I was 7, Killian too was taken by the Other-Siders. I was distraught, as Killian was the only caretaker I had ever known. I vowed to avenge his death and begged to go to war with the other Mavarakites. By this time, the war had been going on many years, and many of our Wood Dwellers had fallen. I was drafted to fight for our people, which I did so proudly. It was then the other warriors began to realize I was a powerful fighter even at my ripe age. I was bestowed the honor of a powerful name: Max the Warrior. At the age of 8, I was set apart as the Chief of War. It has been such for the last ten years, and it will continue to be so until the day I die."

Rose was shocked, and she had to stop herself from gaping incredulously at Max. He began training for war at the age of 3? He was drafted into the war by 7, and a leader by the age of 8?

"You lost everything…" Rose said, her heart swelling with pain for Max. Then she snapped her mouth shut and glanced at Max, realizing the cruelty of the words she had just said. She didn't need to remind him of how much he had lost.

Rose half expected Max to lash out in anger as Rylan would have. But Max was patient and calm, unlike the wild-spirited Rylan, and he didn't seem angered by her comment at all. Instead, he gently shook his head and corrected Rose. "I didn't lose everything. My people still stand, and I will continue to protect them until the day I die."

Lyla, who Rose had nearly forgotten was still around, reached out a comforting hand and placed it on Max's shoulder. But Max looked far from needing comfort. His face was stoic and void of emotion. He had the countenance of someone who was simply doing their duty.

Before Rose could poke and prod any further into Max's personal life, Rylan and Drew returned with the Sweet Berry and Honey jam. From there, the conversation turned lighter, as Rylan and Drew were in high spirits and had apparently spent their time discussing the exciting activities the group had yet to do rather than war and death as Rose, Max, and Lyla had done.

When Rose and Rylan each finished their second helpings of Holken Meat and Honeysickles, Rylan energetically dragged Rose to a Bow and Arrow station. He excitedly informed Rose he had been looking forward to teaching her because he had the distinct feeling she would be awful at it. Rose initially defended herself, but soon found he was correct. Luckily, Rylan was still in high spirits, enough to inform Rose that he wasn't a great shot either, but he still had a ton of fun doing it.

Eventually, after Rylan showed Rose proper form and gave her several tips and tricks, Rose was able to aim an arrow that bounced off the tree where her target was posted. Though she hadn't hit her target successfully, this was the first time the arrow had gone in the vicinity of Rose's aim, and her and Rylan happily celebrated the improvement.

It wasn't until the sky turned pink and orange with the beginnings of a sunset when the crowd gathered around the center of the clearing. Where the table had previously stood bearing all the delicacies known to Wood Dweller-kind, there now stood a platform wide enough to be used as a small stage. Small, clearly mobile wood stumps surrounded the platform like seats in an auditorium. Before all the seats could fill up, Rylan snatched Rose's hand and dragged her to one of the open stumps near the front.

"This is your first time ever seeing the show and learning about Mavarak history, you need a good seat," Rylan exclaimed as he and Rose took their places on a tree stump, which was surprisingly soft and springy.

"I'm so excited," Rose said, looking around nervously as the tree stumps around her filled up. Drew and Robin found tree stumps just one row back from Rylan and Rose. Meanwhile, Max politely offered an open tree stump further back for Lyla to sit in. He stayed standing himself, holding a spear in one hand as though he were standing guard over the village. Which, the more Rose thought about it, the more she decided that was exactly what he was doing.

"Once everyone is seated, they'll begin," Rylan explained, his voice a low hum, as the village was growing quiet. The sky above the trees cast a perfect backdrop for the play, as it lit a gorgeous shade of hazy pink and burnt orange. At each far corner of the platform were blazing torches to provide light for the play once the sun set behind the trees.

Finally, everyone seemed to find themselves wood stumps in the audience. The quiet hum of conversation died out as an adolescent Mavarak boy stepped onto the platform and walked directly into the middle. He squirmed a bit, as though nervous. But once he spoke, his voice was calm and clearly well-rehearsed.

"Long ago, before the dawn of Wood Dwellers, the earth was filled with humans and elves who lived in harmony."

As the narrator said this, the stage filled with several other young Wood Dwellers, all who seemed around the age of 9 or 10. The shorter Wood Dwellers were all dressed in dark shades of green and had pointy green hats covering most of their hair, showing off their long, pointy ears. The taller Wood Dwellers all wore white shirts and tan pants, with their pointy ears covered. Rose had never seen a Wood Dweller wear white before, and she felt these actors must be representing the humans of the earth.

"Not only did the elves and humans coexist. Some of them even developed great friendships."

At this time, several of the pointy hat Wood Dwellers joined hands with the white-clothed ones.

"Some of these friendships even turned into love. And thus, the first Wood Dwellers were born!"

At this, a Wood Dweller who looked about Rose's age walked onto stage, holding hands with a noticeably young Wood Dweller, maybe only 4 or 5. Following this young Wood Dweller was a line of other pre-school aged Wood Dwellers. As the line of young actors stepped onstage, one of them looked out at the crowd of watchful audience members and began crying. Another only wanted to wave at an audience member that was clearly the tiny Wood Dweller's mother. Once the entire line had all made it onstage, still holding hands, the teenager stepped to the side and several of the handholding 'elves' and 'humans' stepped forward and took each hand of the tiny Wood Dwellers. This created little families of one elf, one human, and one baby Wood Dweller.

"The new species began to grow," the narrator said, and the teenager returned, taking the first preschool aged Wood Dweller's hand and leading the line back off the stage. Another teenaged Mavarakite had to come rescue the crying Wood Dweller, who was paralyzed with fear. Once the babies were off the stage, the older kids transformed onstage from elves and humans into Wood Dwellers by taking off their pointy hats or white shirts—revealing various shades of leafy-green shirts, in true Wood Dweller fashion—and stepped into the middle of the stage.

"And as they did, the humans and elves began to turn on them...and each other." The narrator finished. As he said this, several pre-teen Mavarakites joined the younger ones onstage, surrounding them on all sides. On the left side of the stage, there were several Mavarakites dressed like the 'elves,' complete with a pointy green hat. On the right side were the 'humans,' in white shirts and dark pants. The preteens all wore scowling expressions, some looking at the group across the stage, some looking at the Wood Dwellers, who were shaking with fear in the middle.

"While some of the parents of both species tried to protect their offspring..." with this, some of the elves and humans grabbed Wood Dwellers and pulled them safely behind them, "...most of the Wood Dwellers lived in fear for their lives. Then, a war among species broke out."

For the first time in the play, some of the actors onstage aside from the narrator spoke. One of the humans pointed across the stage to the elves and yelled, "You took our woman by force and created this disgraceful species! Now you all shall die!"

Chaos broke out on stage. Elves and humans paired up, pretending to fight each other—fist-fighting, anyways, which Rose imagined was not entirely historically accurate but slightly less violent for a kids' show. The little kids who were playing the Wood Dwellers began running around in circles, most of them giggling and breaking the façade of a violent genocide on the elf species.

"Soon, all the elves were gone," the narrator said, and the pre-teens who were playing the part of the elves all collapsed. The humans cheered.

"Then they chased the Wood Dwellers into the woods, and the Mavarakite tribe, as well as many others, have lived there since!"

With this, the pre-teens who had been the elves jumped up from their dead positions on stage and ran off stage, while the ones who had played the parts of humans all pulled off their white shirts and revealed different shades of green underneath, just as the younger Wood Dwellers had done before. For a moment, all the Wood Dwellers went around and acted as though they were in a typical day in Mavarak. During this transition, the boy who had been a narrator hurriedly stepped offstage and was replaced by a girl who was slightly younger than him.

"However, the Mavarakites did not live in peace for long before they were found by the Other-Siders," the new narrator said. With this statement, all the elf pre-teens reappeared onstage, this time wearing black armor that appeared slightly too big for them. In their hands, they each held one of the spears Rose had seen Max and the other warriors sharpening earlier. She stifled a giggle thinking about all those tough, scary looking Wood Dwellers sharpening sticks to be used for a skit later in the day.

"For the Mavarakites had the Traitor on their hands. The Traitor sold out our people to gain riches from the leader of the Other-Siders, Black Eyes."

A teenager dressed as a Wood Dweller appeared onstage, holding hands with and apparently leading another teenager who was dressed as an Other-Sider. This Other-Sider, however, had dark circles drawn onto his eyelids, creating the appearance of two black holes for eyes.

The moment Rose's eyes fell upon the boy who was playing Black Eyes, her heart began racing. *Where have I seen him before?* Rose thought. She remembered climbing up the tree with Rylan and looking at the Other-Side and the House with the Many Windows. She hadn't been able to see any Other-Siders from that great distance, and even if she had she couldn't have possibly seen clearly enough to know whether they had dark circles for eyes.

So why was he so familiar to her?

"And that was the day the Crusades began. The Mavarakites tried everything. They ran for many years. They hid for many years. They begged and pleaded and offered compromise. They fought back. But Black Eyes was a cruel leader and was merciless against our people."

As the narrator spoke, the Wood Dwellers all acted out everything she said. Meanwhile, the 'Other-Siders' all performed a dance-like motion where they swung their spears back and forth in their hands.

"The Crusades went on for many years like this. Then one day, a visitor appeared."

All the teenagers acting as the Other-Side turned around and knelt, signifying they were no longer a part of the scene. Meanwhile, the Wood Dwellers all opened a path for a small Wood Dweller, barely older than the preschoolers who had been onstage earlier. This Wood-Dweller had on a white shirt and wore her hair covering her ears, indicating she was a human.

"The visitor was a human, but she came in peace. She lived among the Wood Dwellers for many years, and even learned to fight so she could help protect the tribe."

Somewhere off-stage, a spear was handed up to the human, who took on the same dancing motion the Other-Siders had done before.

"This inspired many Wood Dwellers, including Whitney the Wise and Cecily the Witch!"

For the first time during the play, the audience members broke out in a cheer, hooting and hollering as two pre-teen Wood Dwellers stepped onstage. Rose snickered a little as she recognized the white hair and wide-eyed, smiling face of Whitney and the hooded, hunched over figure of Cecily. The actors did a great job capturing the insanity of Whitney and the fierceness of Cecily.

"There is a magic strong enough to hide the Mavarakites," Cecily said behind her hood.

"But a great sacrifice must be made in order for the magic to work properly!" Whitney added, attempting but not quite recreating the whimsical and mysterious voice of Whitney the Wise.

"There is a deep magic connected to two stone figures. These figures are called the Guardians. One is a snail, to represent the sacrifice given by one who was not our kind, but slowly became one of us," Cecily said. From inside of her hooded coat, she pulled out a stone shaped like a snail.

The female narrator interjected here, explaining, "This sacrifice could only be completed by an outsider who was so loyal to Mavarak she would give her blood to protect our people. The human bravely volunteered herself, doing her part to save us all."

Once again, the audience broke out in a cheer as the small human Wood Dweller stepped forward to stand next to the actor for Cecily. She lifted her hand out, and Cecily took a knife out of her hooded coat. In one swift movement, she acted out slicing the human girl's hand with the knife. The human girl cried out in mock pain, then reached out and placed her hand on the shell of the stone snail.

"Thus, the human became the first Keeper of the Guardians, named such because she was required for life to keep loyal to the Mavarakites. Should she give away our secrets, the Guardians would fall, and the magic would be broken, revealing our village to the Other-Siders!"

The audience cheered wildly. Rose, in shock, turned to Rylan and whispered, "The first Keeper was a human? And a girl? Why didn't you—" But she stopped in the middle of her question. Rose had been so taken into the magic and the story being told before her that she hadn't even noticed Rylan had begun looking sick to his stomach. His brow was furrowed, and his face was stony and serious. His ears laid straight back on his head apprehensively, as though he feared something.

The narrator pressed on, drawing Rose's attention back to the stage.

"However, for the bond to work properly, there needed to be two sacrifices made to the Guardians."

While the human girl and Cecily seemed to have frozen with the human girl's hand rested on the back of the snail shell, Whitney stood next to the pair, pulling the second stone Guardian out of his jacket. He pulled an owl-shaped stone out of his jacket and held it up for the audience to see.

"The second Guardian is an owl," Whitney explained, "to represent the sacrifice given by the one who wished to leave Mavarak but stayed and remained loyal regardless."

A teenaged Wood Dweller stepped forward, holding hands with a very young boy, about the same age as the first Keeper of the Guardians.

"My son would like to prove our loyalties to the Mavarakites," the teenager said, and the boy nodded and stepped forward.

"My family's loyalty has been called into question, but I am here to prove we will never betray Mavarak. I will be the second Keeper."

Just like with the human girl, Whitney pulled out a knife and sliced the hand of the boy. He cried out in pain, then placed the hand over the head of the owl.

"And a bond was created that day between the two Keepers and their Guardians!" the narrator girl shouted with excitement. The audience roared with excitement. Rose couldn't help but clap along with the excited crowd, sneaking a sideways glance at Rylan to see if he had joined in the cheering. Rather, he seemed even more apprehensive than before, his ears tucked so far back against his head they could barely be seen through his messy blond hair.

"From that moment on, the Other-Siders couldn't find our land no matter how hard they searched!"

All the Wood Dwellers hunched down, as though hiding, while the boy who had been playing Black Eyes stood up and turned around in circles, as though looking for the Mavarakites.

"Where did they go? How did we lose them?!" Black Eyes shouted angrily. "Go find them!" he yelled, and all the Other-Siders stood and marched off stage together, Black Eyes following close behind.

All the children Wood Dwellers onstage, Whitney, Cecily, and the two Keepers erupted into cheers, which lead to the audience members following suit and cheering as the Crusades in the reenactment was won by the Mavarakites.

Once the cheering died down, the narrator continued with the story. "However, soon after the war was won and the Other-Siders disappeared into their own city, Whitney gave a warning that scared us all."

The actor for Whitney once again attempted to recreate the whimsical yet scattered voice of Whitney the Wise, still not quite capturing it. "Do not become too comfortable. For it is in the stars, the day will come where one of the Guardians will fall."

All the children Wood Dwellers onstage gasped and looked around.

"The only way for the Guardians to fall and the bond to break is for one of the Keepers to betray Mavarak," Cecily said pointedly to Whitney, and the two Keepers audibly gasped.

"The human Keeper was so terrified she would be the one to break the bond," the narrator said, "that she decided it was best for her to leave Mavarak and go back to the world she came from. To this day, she has not been seen or heard from again. But the bond remains unbroken, and the Guardians protect over our land."

Every actor onstage dropped to one knee and bowed their head except for the two Keepers, who stepped forward and faced each other.

"Goodbye Rylan," the human Keeper said to the Wood Dweller Keeper. "Until we meet again."

And with that, the two Keepers turned to face the audience, wide smiles covering their faces, and they joined hands. On each side of them, Whitney and Cecily joined the line with hands held, and the four actors lifted their hands into the air and then bent into a deep bow. The audience erupted into cheers as the four ran off the stage in one direction. Behind them, the young Wood Dwellers ran forward in a line, joined hands, and bowed. The rest of the actors and actresses took their turns bowing for an applauding audience, but Rose couldn't bring herself to cheer for the play. She sat in complete shock, eyes wide, jaw open, staring in disbelief at Rylan.

Rylan was one of the Keepers?

Rylan was one of the Keepers?

Chapter 9

The Keeper of the Owl

Rylan's ears were still tucked all the way against his head, and Rose could see behind his messy hair that they were glowing red. He refused to meet Rose's prying eyes, but she could tell by the way he awkwardly squirmed on his stump that he felt her eyes on him.

For a second, Rose was sure it had been a misunderstanding. Maybe it was a different Rylan? Or, perhaps she had misheard, and it was actually Ryan? Sure, that was entirely possible!

But then she thought about how nervous Rylan had been during the whole play. Memories flitted through her brain, everything seeming to tick into place. Rylan's dreamy voice as he told Rose about the Keeper of the Owl Guardian. Or the way his face melted as he flew over the woods on Kearn, looking at all the places in the world he longed to explore but couldn't. Or Whitney the Wise saying…what was it he said to Rylan when they had gone to see him? *You are troubled…with your loyalties.*

It was Rylan. Rylan was the Keeper of the Guardian, and he had never mentioned it to Rose!

Finally, the entire cast of the play had all joined hands together and performed a deep bow. All around Rose and Rylan, Wood Dwellers were beginning to stand from their tree stumps and stretch their arms and legs. A low hum of conversation was beginning to break out among the village once again. But Rose and Rylan remained silent, Rose staring intently at Rylan who avoided her accusing look.

Finally, Rose asked, "Why didn't you tell me?"

Rylan let out a deep, sad sigh and brought his twinkling blue eyes to Rose. The look that he gave her was almost as surprising as the discovery that he was one of the two Keepers. For as long as Rose had known Rylan, she had seen him look angry, frustrated, tired, bored, mischievous, happy, excited, nervous, embarrassed, and many other emotions. She had seen his eyes grow dark and determined, she had felt his mood shift to a dark place. But never had she seen him look so…heartbroken.

"I didn't want you to know what everyone else in Mavarak knows…" Rylan whispered. "That I'm nothing but a traitor…"

"What do you mean?" Rose asked, confusedly. "If it wasn't for you, the Mavarakites may have been killed off by the Other-Siders! You saved this village."

"Yes, but did you notice no one treats me like a hero?" Rylan asked. Rose thought back to the events of the festival. The audience had roared for Whitney and Cecily. Even when the human girl gave her blood sacrifice to the Guardian of the Snail, the audience had cheered. But after Rylan's character gave his blood sacrifice, no one clapped until the narrator said the bond was completed. It hadn't been Rylan's character they cheered on…it had been the bond itself. Plus, she had walked through the heart of the village with Rylan while it was bustling with Wood Dwellers, and not once had anyone ever treated Rylan like the war hero he was.

"Why wouldn't they treat you like a hero?" Rose asked gently. She could see Rylan didn't want to talk about it anymore, but she didn't understand the difference between his sacrifice and the little human girl's.

Before Rylan could answer, Drew's head appeared in between Rose and Rylan, scaring her enough to practically send her flying off her tree stump. "Well, what'd ya think?! I thought last year's Whitney was a better actor, and I thought the dance thing they had the soldiers do with the spears looked weird, but besides that it was pretty cool!"

Rylan gave some non-committal mutter in response to Drew then made an excuse to grab Rose's hand and drag her away.

"Come on, if we're going to talk about this, we need to do it in private," Rylan said. He led her to a tree just outside the clearing of the village and climbed the branches swiftly. He had clearly chosen a tree with many footholds for Rose, and she followed him up with no complaint and only one scraped knee. When they reached the highest branch, Rose and Rylan both comfortably straddled the tree in such a way that they were able to look over the village of Mavarak. Rose watched as many of the Mavarakites began collecting tree stumps, collecting the signs, and cleaning up from the festivities of the day.

For possibly the first time since the moment they met, Rose didn't pester Rylan one bit. She waited patiently and observed the village, watching as the sun's last few rays disappeared behind a mountain in the distance.

Rylan seemed to be taking in the village himself, and Rose couldn't help but notice how beautiful his eyes were when they twinkled in the final rays of daylight. His hair so carelessly fell over his face, making him look young and playful. But his facial features, in the moment, had none of their usual playfulness. Instead, he looked deep in thought, troubled by something Rose didn't quite yet understand.

When Rylan's voice did finally cut through the silence of the night, it caught Rose a bit off guard. She hadn't realized how much she had enjoyed the peaceful quiet the two had fallen into. However, she was eager to hear why Rylan had hidden his past from her so carefully.

"Have you ever wondered why my family is called the Small?" Rylan asked, still watching the Wood Dwellers down below. Rose realized that no, she had never even considered it, and was relieved the darkness setting around them disguised her now blushing face.

Luckily, Rylan didn't wait for her to answer the question before he pressed on. "I was born under the name Rylan the Giving. But Mavarakites refuse to honor it as my family name and have refused for decades now. Instead, we have been given the name Small as a punishment. It's a dirty name that refers to my grandfather's betrayal of the Mavarakites to the Other-Siders. He—he's the Traitor, the one who brought Black Eyes to Mavarak in the first place, leading to the Crusades. He's the reason we lived ten years running, hiding, and fighting. He's the reason hundreds of Wood Dwellers were slaughtered."

Rose watched as tears welled in Rylan's eyes. "He sold us out to the Other-Siders because Black Eyes promised him riches. When the Crusades began, he disappeared into the Other-Side, presumably to live there with his riches. A year later, we found his body strung up in a tree. They used him for all the information he had, then they killed him. His family wasn't even allowed to mourn his death. The Mavarakites said he received a traitorous death, one he deserved. For a long time, my mom and dad lived in partial exile. Mavarak granted them a safe haven to hide, but they weren't accepted as part of the community. Eventually, when enough of the warriors died in the Crusades, the Mavarakites allowed my dad to fight in war against the Other-Siders, proving us to be more loyal than our traitor of a grandfather. He died proving our loyalties to our village.

"When word began to spread that Cecily and Whitney were in search of a worthy Keeper, it was my idea to offer myself. It was perfect for the Guardian of the Owl. Someone who wished to leave...our family had been in partial exile and under watchful eye my whole life. Of course I wanted to leave. I wanted to run away with my mom and dad and little brother, to start a new life where no one looked down at us, no one considered us dirty or small. But if I became the second Keeper, it would prove my family was loyal to the Mavarakites. I wasn't exactly everyone's first choice, seeing as how they weren't sure they could trust me. But Whitney, you know, spoke to the stars or whatever, and they told him I was the only Wood Dweller who would work. I was the only one who had a true desire to leave Mavarak. Everyone else leaned on Mavarak to keep them safe, they knew they couldn't survive outside the village. So, I became the Keeper of the Guardians.

"That's why I'm so bent on proving my loyalty. If I fail, I don't just fail myself. I fail my mom. I fail Drew. I fail all the Mavarakites. If I fail, Dad's death was for nothing. I would do *anything* to prove my loyalty to Mavarak...So, I stay." Rylan finished, and with those last words, Rose watched all his soul leave his eyes.

"That's a lot of pressure…" Rose said, her heart aching for Rylan. She had no idea he hid that much pain behind his mischievous, playful smile.

"It's alright. It's not all bad," Rylan murmured, his eyes and face lighting up as he turned toward the direction of the Trusk pen. Rose couldn't help but notice the Mavarakite who had been cleaning the obstacle course that ran through the Trusk pen was now balled up on the ground fast asleep, and an innocent looking Trusk stood nearby his snoozing figure. "There are a lot of beautiful animals here. And it is incredible the way Wood Dwellers live with the land. If I did leave and travel the world, I would probably just spend the whole time angry about people killing the earth. My place is here, among the Mavarakites."

Rylan sounded rather convincing, but he wasn't fooling Rose. She had seen the look of longing and pain in his eyes. She knew what he really wanted.

"So, anyway, here's what I'm really curious about," Rose said, deciding it was time to change the subject. "Who is the other Keeper? All this time, I always imagined the Keepers to be incredible war heroes, like maybe Max the Warrior!"

Rylan laughed, and he looked grateful Rose had changed the subject. "I'm pretty glad, to be honest. It would be a lot of pressure to be bonded to Max the Warrior my whole life!"

At these words, Rose felt a roar of jealously ripple through her throat. Somehow, it hadn't occurred to her this meant Rylan was bonded to some random girl now. What kind of bond was it, anyway? Were they, like, soulmates now or something?

"Well, the other Keeper has to be someone your age, right?" Rose asked, trying to make her voice sound as casual as she possibly could. "It's not Lyla, is it?"

Rylan looked surprised, and he jolted his head to look at Rose with such force he nearly knocked himself out of the tree, which was the first time Rose had ever seen him look uncomfortable to be dangling in the sky.

"Lyla?! What, no! It couldn't be her. The other Keeper was a human, remember?" Rylan exclaimed defensively. Rose felt her cheeks blush, and she couldn't help but wonder if Rylan's ears were also turning red.

"Oh, right," Rose said, a small smile creeping onto her face. She felt a little relieved to know Rylan wasn't bonded to Lyla for life. Rose and Rylan both turned their eyes back to the world beneath them. Most of the festival was cleaned up at this point, and the world was growing quiet as more and more Wood Dwellers disappeared into their huts for the night.

After a moment of silence, Rylan tauntingly said, "So, would that bug you if I was bonded to Lyla for life?"

The blush that appeared on Rose's face had just started fading away, but this comment brought all the heat back full force. Rose stammered, somehow forgetting how to form real words with her mouth, and Rylan cackled with a laughter that floated comfortably over the village of Mavarak.

"I don't, I mean—no, I—Lyla is—I don't even—" Rose stammered, trying to decide how to properly respond to Rylan's question. Deciding evasion was the best tactic in this scenario, Rose instead blurted out, "Well, I suppose we should be turning in now! It's getting late!"

Rylan agreed and the two climbed out of the tree together, Rylan helping her along the way. Rose couldn't help but notice, though, Rylan glowed with a knowing smile the entire walk back to the hut.

***

For the first time since accidentally entering Mavarak, Rose had a hard time sleeping through the night. She kept waking up, feeling dread wash over her for fear the morning had come.

This was the morning Rose would be taking the potion that was supposed to return her home.

When the morning sun finally began filtering through the window of the Small's spare treehouse, Rose sadly lifted her head off the pillow and clambered down the tree and into the kitchen. Upon entering, she saw Rylan was already awake and eating a fruit salad breakfast. He was slumped over the kitchen table and picking at the various fruits with a grumpy look on his face. Rose wondered if he was as sad about her leaving as she was.

As the two ate breakfast, the gravity of drinking the potion hit her. She was going to leave this world and reappear back in her own. How would it happen? Would she suddenly wake up and be in bed at her grandparents' cabin? Would she be convinced it was all just a dream? Would she remember Rylan?

The time eventually came. Rose and Rylan stepped out of the hut and walked somberly toward the thick of the woods. On the way, they passed Max, who looked hard at work with two other warriors transporting supplies. When Rose and Max's eyes met, he gave a calm but warm smile and waved high above his tall head. Rose's heart thumped in her chest as she waved back and smiled half-heartedly. Max had no idea this would be the last time they'd be seeing each other. Rose knew she would miss him and his passion for protecting his home.

Rylan and Rose stopped walking when they entered the thick of the woods. Rose knew her time with Rylan was running out. She looked into Rylan's soft blue eyes and deflated. She needed to get back home. It was time to say goodbye. Rylan pulled the potion out of his back pocket, where he had kept it during their walk through the village. He handed the potion over to Rose, and she popped the lid off the jar.

"The river you fell into isn't far from here," Rylan informed Rose as she quizzically eyed the contents of the jar. He pointed into the woods. "It's only about 40 feet in that direction. I'm going to walk there as soon as you drink the potion. If something goes wrong and you don't find your grandparent's house, but you teleport away from me, meet me there, okay? I'll wait there today and pop back in tomorrow, just in case."

Rose nodded absentmindedly, only partially

listening to Rylan and mostly focusing on the unappealing brownish color of the potion.

"If you don't know where you are, find the river, okay? Once you find it, stay on the east side of land, and walk downriver. Eventually, you should come across Mavarak again. If you come across a lake then you've gone too far, turn around and walk back upriver. Don't trust anyone else but me, okay?"

"Okay," Rose said, taking a whiff of the vile-looking potion. It smelled fishy, like pond water. She stopped herself from gagging. A silence fell over the pair, and Rose realized Rylan was out of things to say. She looked up at Rylan, and his ears were down against his head. Her heart sank as she said, "Well…I guess this is goodbye…"

"Yeah," Rylan agreed, looking deep into her eyes. It looked like he had something he wanted to say but couldn't bring himself to say it. "Goodbye, then."

For a short time, Rose and Rylan stood in silence and stared at each other. Then, in a moment of bravery, Rose closed her eyes and tilted the contents of the jar into her open mouth. She swallowed fast before the salty, sweaty, bitter taste hit her.

Rose meant to hand the jar back to Rylan once she finished, but before she could, her hands involuntarily shook, causing her to drop the jar on the ground. She looked up at Rylan. He was moving his mouth, as if talking to her, but she couldn't hear anything but a distant whirring sound. Then the small distance between Rose and Rylan began stretching before her, and she watched as he grew farther and farther away.

Rose looked down and saw the ground beneath her was gently spinning. A glance toward the sky told her the trees were spinning too, though not as slowly as the ground. In fact, in the fraction of the second it took for her to realize they were spinning at all, the trees began spinning faster and faster until they were just a blur of green. Rose felt the potion rising in her stomach and could feel the heat of it burning her throat.

Rose was just beginning to wonder what would happen if she threw up the potion before she made it back to her grandparents' house when the spinning stopped in an instant. Rose felt as though she had slammed into a wall going forty-five miles per hour, and her body dropped in pain to the ground. There was a loud splash, and Rose realized she had just dropped into a shallow river.

Before Rose could register what was happening, she rolled over and vomited violently. With the burning contents of the potion out of her system, Rose felt much better. She pulled herself to her feet and peered around her.

She was sitting directly next to the boulder from her dreams, the boulder that started this all, the one that sent her plummeting face-first into the river and into the world of the Wood Dwellers.

Rose turned her attention away from the boulder and in the direction of her grandparents' house. In place of the familiar cabin, Rose saw a distant village. The village of Mavarak, exactly where it had been the first time she had appeared in this river.

In the moments that followed, she experienced a medley of emotions. First, she felt relief and excitement to know she would be seeing Rylan's face soon. In fact, according to what he had been saying before she drank the potion, he should be appearing any second now.

Soon after the relief and excitement, though, Rose experienced frustration, anger, and desperation. The potion had been their last hope. She was sure it would work. Had they mixed it wrong? Was it because Rylan had put the sweat into the potion without first mixing the pond water and scum? Had Rose mixed up the directions that she needed to stir the potion in? Had she thrown it up before the potion was complete?

Without being able to help herself, Rose felt a scream of rage bubble up through her stomach and rip through her throat. Without thinking, she began thrashing through the water in what could only be described as a temper tantrum. She kicked the rocks up from the riverbed, she splashed water into the air, she ripped shards of grass up from the ground. After a few moments of being completely overtaken with rage, Rose slammed herself down on the ground just beyond the river, opposite the boulder that started it all.

Gasping for air, Rose glared at the boulder. For the second time, a scream ripped through her throat, and she threw her head into her fists and screamed. She had heard once before that screaming can help relieve frustration, and right now it was the truest thing she had ever heard. Sending her shrill, angry screams into the open sky felt so satisfying to her that she let herself keep doing it until her throat hurt.

Finally, her screams quieted down, and Rose brought herself to look back up at the world of Mavarak. From the woods across the river, she could see Rylan's figure appearing through the trees. From the distance, Rose could just detect a look of notable relief on Rylan's face in seeing the potion had clearly not been successful. Here was Rose, sitting at the riverside, screaming her head off and staring angrily at the boulder.

Before Rose could overthink too much about the look of relief that crossed Rylan's face (was he hoping the potion wouldn't work because he didn't want her to leave yet?), the look of relief disappeared from Rylan's face. It was replaced with a look of pure terror.

First, he looks relieved, then he looks terrified? Rose thought irritably. *Make up your mind. Do you want me here or not?*

Rylan broke out into a full sprint, closing in the gap between himself and the river. "Rose!" he screamed, and his voice sounded urgent.

Rose opened her mouth to call out to Rylan and let him know she was okay, maybe inform him he could look a little happier to see her, when she felt a large hand slam hard over her face. A gruff arm wrapped roughly around Rose's gut, pinning her arms to her side, and whisking her off her feet. She tried to scream out to Rylan, tried to call for help, but the meaty hand covering half her face easily muffled her cries.

She watched as Rylan stopped dead in his tracks, just on the other side of the river. His face was pure shock and terror, white as a ghost.

And that's when Rose realized how dangerous it was to cross onto the Other-Side of the river.

Chapter 10

The House with the Many Windows

Despite her kicking and screaming for help, the Other-Sider who crept up behind her was able to easily whisk her away from the river and from the safe haven of Mavarak. Rose knew Rylan was entirely useless in this situation, as he had stopped running toward her at the edge of the river and was still safely hidden by the powerful magic of the Guardians. She was relieved he was protected, and all the other Mavarakites were safe as well, but it didn't do much in the way of comforting her.

Soon after Rose had been captured by the Other-Sider, he spun her around, clasped both her hands behind her back, and forced her to walk herself away from Mavarak and toward the Other-Side. He didn't even bother covering her mouth to muffle her screams. It seemed he was unconcerned about anyone in the vicinity coming to her rescue. Rose kept up her shrill scream regardless, in hopes one of the Other-Siders would see what was happening and stop Rose from being kidnapped.

That didn't happen.

It only took about a minute of walking through the woods before the trees and sky opened to what could only be described as a dense, overpopulated, industrialized city. In its entirety, the Other-Side was only slightly larger than Mavarak, but it was much taller and had a lot more buildings crammed into the space. The beautiful trees making up the woods had been hacked away, and the green, healthy grass had been covered with pavement. There were busy roads packed bumper to bumper in heavy traffic. Rose had to crane her neck to see the tops of the gray buildings. Several giant apartment buildings surrounded the city center, and at the heart of the city was the building Rylan had showed Rose on the first full day she had been in Mavarak: The House with the Many Windows.

Even though all the looming buildings seemed dark and gray, the House with the Many Windows was still the darkest and eeriest of them all. It was covered top to bottom in windows, and each window was tinted with such a dark black that it would be impossible to see anything going on inside the building. It was reflective, so Rose could see the other buildings of the Other-Side reflected in the House with the Many Windows.

As the Other-Sider who had captured Rose forced her to pass from the beautiful green grass of the woods and over the curb that marked where pavement began, Rose saw a large group of soldiers who appeared to be guarding the entrance to the city. None of them appeared hard at work, as they all stood around talking to each other and puffing on cigarettes.

"Help!" Rose shouted toward the soldiers. She expected the man who caught her to slap his hand back over her mouth as she called for help, but he did no such thing. The group of soldiers, six men all wearing black clothing emblazoned with a blue emblem, lazily looked up at Rose. She felt encouraged by their acknowledgment, however lackluster it was. "Help, I've been kidnapped! This man is taking me against my will!"

Two of the soldiers looked at each other and snickered, the others lazily returned to their conversation.

Rose's heart deflated. None of them cared she was being taken hostage. She thrust her body around in the Other-Siders arms, attempting to twist herself out of his grasp. She was unsuccessful in escaping, but she was able to get a good look at the man who forced her forward. She only caught a glimpse, but she noticed he had a short, well-groomed beard, a nonchalant expression on his face as though this were a regular occurrence for him, and a black uniform with a blue emblem that matched the soldiers Rose had called out to.

Rose turned forward once again and let out a blood-curdling scream, beginning to feel her efforts were futile. No one cared she was being marched into the city kicking and screaming. It was a soldier who led her there, so none of the other soldiers were going to stop it. If anything, they would likely help the soldier out if they thought Rose had any real chance of escaping his grip.

Which she didn't.

As Rose passed the tall apartment buildings and other business centers, it became apparent the soldier was leading Rose straight to the House with the Many Windows. For some reason, this made Rose more apprehensive than if she had discovered she was being led to any of the other dark, looming buildings she was now surrounded by. Just looking at The House with the Many Windows made her skin crawl, the same way her skin felt after she saw a spider and felt like there were more crawling on her. She felt a chill go down her spine as she was led past the last skyscraper surrounding the House with the Many Windows. She swallowed hard as the soldier grasped the handle of the sleek, black building and thrust it open, shoving her inside.

Rose took in a sharp deep breath and prepared to scream, but shock overwhelmed her enough to distract her from the scream she had mustered. Around her was what appeared to be an entirely normal business office. The plain interior in no way matched the dark, foreboding exterior of the building. With a quick glance at the wall of the building, Rose realized the windows that made up the entire building were actually those one-way mirrors, so Rose could see straight through the windows to the outside world even though they had appeared reflective from the outside looking in. The room she was now being pushed through looked like her dentist office, minus the pictures decorating the wall and perhaps lit more poorly. There was even a receptionist desk in the room, but there was no receptionist sitting on the other side answering phones. In fact, the room was entirely empty, which was the oddest part considering the streets were so full of traffic, leading Rose to believe there were many Other-Siders living in the city. Where were they all heading now, if not to the epicenter of business in the city?

Where all the evil happens, Rylan's words echoed through Rose's head. An uncontrollable shiver sent goosebumps across Rose's skin.

The soldier led Rose through the lobby and to an elevator. The elevator played no music, and once again it looked exactly like one in a typical dentist office but darker. It was like someone had taken a picture of a usual dentist office and then added a dark filter over it.

The elevator took Rose and the soldier up several floors. At this point, Rose had given up on screaming entirely. She no longer felt in danger, but rather extraordinarily curious. This was the place the Mavarakites lived in fear of? The soldier wasn't exactly being a sweetheart to Rose, pinning her hands behind her back and forcing her into the building, but he also hadn't hurt her, nor had he taken her to a jail cell or anything that scared her.

The elevator door opened to a long, plain hallway with several closed doors. He pushed her through the open elevator door and kept pushing her all the way down the entire hallway, until they reached the final door on the right. None of the doors were marked in any way, nor did any of them contain windows to see what was on the other side, so Rose had no idea what to expect when the soldier lightly rapped on the door and then gently pushed it open.

"Sir," the soldier spoke for the first time since capturing Rose, which made her jump unexpectedly. "I found this child screaming and throwing a fit in the river nearby Point C. She appeared unaccompanied."

Rose could not react to the soldier's words. In fact, she could hardly hear them. Her breath caught in her throat and her eyes bulged so wide she thought they might pop out of her head.

Sitting in the room, opposite a nearly empty desk with a pencil suspended in hand above a single paper—as though interrupted while writing an important document—was Black Eyes.

Rose recognized him the second she saw him, despite being sure she had never met him before. Obviously, she had seen an actor portrayal of him at the harvest festival, but it was nothing like the real life individual. Black Eyes had a powder white face, which was stark in contrast to the dark, black eyes he donned. His eyes were entirely black. There was nothing else to them, no white, no hues of dark brown or hazel, just entirely black holes making up both eyes. He had a salt and pepper beard that was as short and well-trimmed as the soldier who had brought Rose to this place. And when the man shifted his gaze up to Rose and a sly smile spread across his face, Rose was sure she felt her soul leave her body.

"Well let's not be rude to our visitor," Black Eyes said, and the words crawled out of his mouth icily. "Release the child. Come, sit down, make yourself at home."

Black Eyes beckoned toward a cushioned seat sitting on the opposite side of the desk he sat at. Rose felt her hands begin to shake involuntarily as the soldier released them and pushed her toward the seat. Even though he was a soldier for the Other-Side, Rose found herself disappointed when the man who had brought her up to Black Eyes slid out of the room and closed the door behind him, leaving Rose alone with the dark eyed man.

"Welcome to our city," Black Eyes growled, his words sounding welcoming but his voice coming out like black ice. "How did a young child like yourself find your way here?"

Rose didn't know what to say. She knew she couldn't reveal that she had seen Mavarak. This would put herself and all her friends at risk. On the other hand, she knew nothing about the woods beyond Mavarak and the Other-Side. How was she supposed to explain accidentally stumbling upon the Other-Side?

If he knows I'm an outsider, maybe he'll let me go! Rose thought to herself. *Just imagine this is one week ago, before I ever met or even heard of a Wood Dweller. Act clueless and confused!*

"I-I honestly don't know," Rose finally answered, her voice cracking and her hands shaking furiously as she lowered herself into the cushioned seat Black Eyes had offered to her. "It doesn't make any sense. I f-fell into the river by my grandparent's house, and when I came out it was like the world had changed…"

Rose paused, trying to get control over her stuttering, shaky voice. Then she continued, saying, "When I came up from the riverbank, I looked around and didn't see my grandparent's cabin anymore. I got scared and yelled for help, and that's when your soldier found me. So, I'm not normally from here…"

Instead of looking disappointed by Rose's lack of information, Black Eyes seemed to grow more and more giddy with every word she said, absolutely glowing with dark greed and excitement by the time she finished.

"Is that so?" Black Eyes asked, his face still spread in a wicked looking smile. "You fell into the river and came out in a different world, did you? Was there anything peculiar about the river when you fell in?"

Rose's heart was slamming against her chest. She got the distinct feeling she had said the wrong things. She tried again.

"No, nothing was weird about the river at all. In fact, I'm sure it's all totally fine. I think I must have been dragged downstream for quite some time when I fell in. If I could just get back to the river and walk upstream for a little while, I'm sure I'd find the cabin and be able to go back home," Rose replied.

Black Eyes leaned forward intently, placing his chin on his hands and eyeing Rose like she was a specimen for study.

"Did you meet anybody in the woods before finding this place?" Black Eyes asked interestedly.

Rose felt irritation boiling inside her head. Did Black Eyes really believe she was going to give away the Mavarakites?

"Nope," Rose answered stubbornly. She realized almost immediately she had probably answered too fast, possibly raising further suspicion.

"No?" Black Eyes pressed. "You were just walking along on your own through the woods when you came across a lovely city and started poking around?"

The irritation in Rose's chest was growing to outright anger. "I didn't go poking around anywhere, I was down by the river when your soldier dragged me into the Other-Side against my will!" Rose snapped.

The dark holes of Black Eyes' face twinkled with delight.

"The Other-Side?" Black Eyes drawled. "So, you've met some of our little Wood Dweller friends, have you?"

Rose was sure her heart stopped right then. She hadn't meant to give anything away. She didn't realize the Other-Siders were only called that by the Mavarakites. It never even crossed her mind that, had she been truly clueless, like she was a week ago, she wouldn't have known what to call the city.

Rose dropped the act and snarled angrily at the man sitting before her. "Don't call them your friends. You just want to find them and kill them all."

Black Eyes stood suddenly from his perch in his desk chair, and Rose filled in an instant with terror. She flinched, prepared to take whatever attack Black Eyes had planned. Instead, however, Black Eyes did something that surprised her. He turned away from her, leaving himself vulnerable and giving her the opportunity to attack or flee. He walked to the window of his office and stared down upon the ugly city he had built.

"Is that what they told you? That we want to kill them all?" Black Eyes asked, staring intently out the window. Rose remained silent, not sure how to respond to this. "Of course, we don't want to do that. They are our offspring. We caused their existence. Why would we hurt them?"

Rose silently glanced behind her, gaging how far the door was. If she jumped up and dove for it, she would probably make it there before Black Eyes could get around the desk and grab her. Of course, there's no telling where the nearest soldier was. For all Rose knew, the soldier that had led her here could be standing guard directly outside the door.

"You see, the Wood Dwellers fear us, but we don't want to hurt them. We only want to help," Black Eyes continued, his voice still dripping with ice.

"Help them?" Rose snapped, finally taking the bait Black Eyes was dangling before her. "How are you helping them?"

"You've obviously spoken with at least one, possibly several," Black Eyes stated, still staring out the window. Rose considered fight rather than flight and weighed her options. She didn't see any weapons she could use to attack him, other than the pencil that he had held when she first entered the room. It was now sitting on his desk. "But have you seen the way they live?"

Rose didn't answer. She wasn't about to confess she knew where Mavarak was. Likely, this was just Black Eyes' way of tricking her into admitting she could be used to locate them.

"They live in shambles, child," Black Eyes continued when Rose didn't answer. He turned back toward her, his black holes for eyes boring into Rose's skin. "They have nothing to their names. They live off the land, they have no electricity, no running water, no form of government or currency. We don't want to hurt them. We want to introduce them to a more efficient way of living."

Black Eyes gestured toward the city he had just been staring at, and Rose shifted her gaze out the window as well. She saw billows of smoke emitting into the air from several buildings, polluting the land and destroying the earth.

"They nurture their homes. You destroy it for your own selfish gain!" Rose argued, swelling with defensiveness over Rylan and the other Wood Dwellers.

"We take some calculated risks on the destruction of parts of the earth. But look; we remain on a small piece of land, so the trees and nature can flourish around us. You saw the river and the woods nearby. Was any of that polluted?"

Rose didn't answer.

"Let me ask you, child," Black Eyes said, but Rose, who was feeling defiant toward this man, interrupted in anger.

"Rose," she snapped. "Stop calling me child."

The same creepy smile spread across Black Eyes' face, and Rose's heart pounded. Had she made a mistake in giving him personal information?

"Excuse me. Rose," Black Eyes corrected. He walked toward Rose again and slunk back into his desk chair. "Back in your grandparents' home, do you have lights?"

Rose didn't answer. She glared at him angrily instead.

"What about a toilet and a sink. Do you use those?" Black Eyes continued, the same eerie look of delight in his dark eyes. Rose remained silent still.

"And heating or cooling, are you familiar with these advancements?" he pressed on, watching Rose's reactions. Rose couldn't bring herself to admit that yes, she had all those things. Her mind flashed to her cell phone currently perched on the nightstand next to her bed in Grandma's guest room.

"And let me ask you, Rose," Black Eyes continued, "do any of these make you a bad person?"

For a fleeting second, Rose wondered if it were in any way possible the Other-Siders truly didn't want to hurt the Wood Dwellers. Maybe they had no intention of killing them, but truly did want to introduce their technological advancements to them.

But isn't that still wrong, to force their species to live like the Other-Siders live, to abandon their way of life and join the Other-Siders in damaging the earth?

Well, yes, it might be a little wrong, but still isn't on the same level as mass genocide. Why would the Wood Dwellers tell Rose the Other-Siders want to kill them if they didn't?

It's possible they just wanted Rose to hate them as much as the Mavarakites hated them. Maybe they embellished the story a little bit to paint the Other-Siders out as evil. After all, it is fair the Wood Dwellers fight against the industrialization of their homes and community. But like Black Eyes said, Rose isn't evil, nor is her family, and all of them lived in industrialized cities…

Plus, Rose was *dying* to take a warm shower. She had splashed around in the river multiple times, but her hair was long past the greasy stage and could definitely use a little shampoo. Is it the end of the world for the Mavarakites if they're introduced to a little shampoo themselves?

"I think we may have gotten off on the wrong

foot," Black Eyes interrupted Rose's thoughts, leaning back in his chair comfortably. "Let's start over. Tell me a bit about yourself, about your childhood."

Rose eyed Black Eyes suspiciously, which prompted him to smile his creepy smile and add, "You don't have to tell me anything that might reveal where our little Wood Dweller friends might be."

Rose racked her brain for information that would be entirely safe to give to Black Eyes. She needed to give him enough information so he wouldn't become angry or prod harder, but that would still protect the Mavarakites.

Finally, Rose determined it would be safe to tell Black Eyes, "I live with my mom and my dad and I'm an only child."

"Interesting, I thought you were in search of your grandparents' home. Do you not live with them?" Black Eyes asked innocently.

"No," Rose answered. She considered whether it would be dangerous to give more information, then carefully added, "I'm only staying with my grandparents for the summer."

"Ah, well that must be fun," Black Eyes said warmly, or at least as warmly as a voice of ice could become.

"Not really," Rose snapped without thinking.

"No? Why not?" Black Eyes asked, and Rose couldn't tell if his voice was filled with genuine concern or not. She decided to give a half-truth.

"There's nothing to do. I'd rather be hanging out with my friends."

"Well, can't you go back to your parents' house then, if you aren't having any fun?" Black Eyes questioned. Rose became serious, and her mind turned to her parents. He didn't need to know about them. He didn't need to know about the pain Rose felt every time she thought of her mom and dad.

Black Eyes must have sensed Rose's tense mood or noticed the sadness in her eyes. He hissed, "I sense there is more to it you're not telling. Perhaps it would make you feel more comfortable opening up if you knew a little of my home life?"

"Sure," Rose shrugged, quite certain she would not want to reveal more after hearing about Black Eyes' life.

"I was the second youngest of eight boys," Black Eyes said, turning away from Rose and staring intently at the wall, as if watching his childhood played out on a screen there. "Quite a large family, I envy you as an only child. Anyway, my parents came by little work in their lives, and the work they did come by wasn't well paying. With such a large family, they rarely had enough food to go around. My siblings and I would switch off who got to eat for the day, sometimes going two to three days between meals. A bit of a sob story, some might say.

"Anyway, food being stretched thin led to difficulty in the family. There was some arguing about how to deal with eight hungry, growing boys. Mom thought we needed to move to a smaller house, Dad thought any smaller of a home wouldn't be able to house the number of kids living there. Mom always said Dad needed to get a higher paying job, Dad always said Mom needed to do better at rationing money and food. It was always finger pointing and arguing, never working together to overcome the issue."

Rose had been staring intently at her fingernails and picking dirt out of them during most the story, but once he got to the end, Rose looked up at Black Eyes' face with interest. She was surprised to discover a look of sadness had overcome him. She wondered if the look he had was the same one that always came over her face when she thought of her parents fighting, and she felt her heart pang with sympathy.

"It was always the worst part when I could hear them arguing," Black Eyes murmured, and he turned his dark holes of eyes to look at Rose. "And the sinking feeling that it was partly my fault."

Rose felt goosebumps rise on her arms as she listened to someone else voice her own exact concerns out loud.

"My parents fight a lot too," Rose admitted. Black Eyes gave her a look of concern, and she was quite certain this one was genuine. "My mom thinks my dad is irresponsible. He used to make her laugh all the time, but he doesn't anymore…"

Rose felt tears welling up in her eyes. She said the words out loud that had been clawing at the back of her throat for years. "They're getting a divorce and it's my fault."

Black Eyes watched Rose sadly as she wiped away the tears falling down her cheeks. While it felt nice to have someone who understood what Rose was going through, Rose felt an overwhelming desire to have Rylan hugging her tight while she cried once again.

"I'm truly sorry you feel this way," Black Eyes responded, voice filled with concern.

"How did you get over it when your parents split up?" Rose asked, wiping the tears from her face, sniffing hard, trying to stifle any more tears from falling down her cheeks. She failed almost instantly.

"Oh, they didn't split up. They are still together, happy as can be!" Black Eyes exclaimed, his smile once again crawling across his face.

"Really?" Rose asked, looking up at Black Eyes in shock. "How? I mean, how did they get past all the fighting so they could make things work?"

Black Eyes' smile flashed dangerously, and his dark eyes twinkled in delight. "That was my doing. You see, I have certain…abilities. I made a trade long ago with a powerful being. It was quite simple. This is important, Rose. Almost everything in life requires sacrifice. I only had to make a small sacrifice, and I was given powers beyond your understanding."

Rose blinked, thinking about the play she had seen at the harvest festival. All it took was a blood sacrifice to unleash the bond that hid Mavarak from the Other-Siders.

"What did you have to sacrifice?" Rose asked. Black Eyes leaned forward, and Rose felt herself become entranced by those dark holes taking up his face. The dark, endless holes that shadowed his face in constant foreboding. Black Eyes didn't have to tell her what he sacrificed. She knew. No one is born with those eyes.

Black Eyes seemed to understand that Rose had found the answer to her own question without his help, because when he talked again, it wasn't to answer her. Instead, he continued with his story of sacrifice, saying, "I now obtain certain powers beyond the normal human capabilities. For example, I was able to repair the love bond between my parents that was broken by money. I could complete a similar reparation if you would like. I could repair the love bond between your parents broken by irresponsibility."

"You could?" Rose asked hopefully, sitting up straight in her chair eagerly.

"I could. But, of course, you know what that would take?" Black Eyes prodded. Rose thought for a second, then answered.

"A sacrifice?" Rose asked. Black Eyes nodded. "What kind of sacrifice?"

"It could be quite small," Black Eyes answered, leaning toward Rose intently. She felt herself pulled in by him, and she realized she too was leaning forward on the edge of her seat. She could practically feel the power Black Eyes held pulsating inside him. "In fact, it could be as small as a simple secret."

"A secret?" Rose asked, and her head began buzzing with secrets from her life. Lacie just told Rose she had a crush on Jack Lemmings from Social Studies. Or Rose could admit she once stole a tube of Chapstick from Walmart. Or—she felt herself begin to blush at the thought of admitting it out loud—if she really had to dig up a dirty secret, perhaps she could admit she had recently developed a crush on someone...

"A secret, of course, about the Wood Dwellers," Black Eyes added casually. Rose felt herself begin to tense up. Of course. This was all just a trick to find out where the Mavarakites are hiding.

"I'm not telling you where they are," Rose snapped defiantly, falling back into her chair. She felt all the hope that had built up inside her chest release in an instant, and her body flattened like a balloon releasing all its air.

"You wouldn't have to," Black Eyes explained, flashing an encouraging smile. "Any secret will do. It doesn't have to be something that will reveal where they are hidden. In fact, it can be a teensy tiny little secret. I don't mind what secret you tell. I wouldn't even need a secret...I'd be willing to repair the bond for free. But the magic requires it."

Rose considered this, her mind once again filling with secrets, this time about Mavarakite. What could she tell Black Eyes that would have absolutely no consequence for the Wood Dwellers, but would result in her completing the requirement of a sacrifice?

"It doesn't have to reveal their location at all?" Rose inquired, eyeing Black Eyes quizzically. He still had a giant smile plastered to his face.

"Not at all!" he replied, opening his hands toward her in a vulnerable position, as if to prove he had nothing to hide.

"And if I tell you one tiny secret—a secret that in no way reveals where the Wood Dwellers are hiding—you can make my parents get along again?" Rose asked, raising an eyebrow in doubt. Black Eyes' smile never faltered.

"Absolutely. Tell me Rose, would you like to see your parents laugh together again? Would you like to forget they ever fought?" Black Eyes pressed. Rose felt her heart pound in her chest. The truthful answer was yes, she would very much like to see her parents laugh together again. She remembered the days when her dad used to flash his million-dollar smile at Mom, crack one of his infamous Dad jokes, and Mom's laugh would fill the room. Her heart ached to see that again.

Still, she hesitated. What was the catch? Why a secret about the Wood Dwellers if it didn't give away their location? What good did that do for Black Eyes?

"After all," Black Eyes continued when Rose didn't answer, "it is sort of your fault they fight so much anyway…isn't it?"

Rose felt her heart break. Black Eyes was right. It was her fault.

Rose searched every corner of her brain for knowledge about the Wood Dwellers both secret and entirely harmless to reveal. Finally, she settled her mind on one detail she had just recently come across. She looked up at Black Eyes, who was watching her intently and eagerly.

"Have you heard of the Guardians?" Rose asked, her heart pounding so hard she could hear it in her right ear.

Black Eyes smiled back wickedly. "Of course, I know of the Guardians. If I didn't, I would know where our friends hide, wouldn't I?"

Rose gulped, then made her decision. After all, even Black Eyes just admitted, he wouldn't be able to find any of them as long as the Guardians kept the path hidden. There was no way he could bring any harm to them, right?

"Well, one of the Keepers is a Wood Dweller who lives in Mavarak," Rose said, staring into the black holes for eyes that stared intently back at her. The smile plastered on Black Eyes' face was unmoving but eagerly awaiting the secret. Rose mulled it over one more time. *He's safely hidden by the Guardians.* Rose assured herself. *There's no way Black Eyes can hurt him.* "His name is Rylan the Small."

As soon as the words fell out of her mouth, Rose felt a sharp, searing pain flash white-hot on the fleshy part of her right palm. Rose cried out in shock and looked down at her hand. The scar that spread across her palm was sliced clean open, as though a knife had just pierced through the skin, and it was gushing blood. The skin around the scar was red with irritation, and the pain coursed through her body and brought fresh tears to Rose's eyes.

"Ow!" Rose screeched, jumping up in shock and confusion and grasping the wrist of her damaged hand with her good one. Behind her, the door to Black Eyes' office opened, and the soldier who had captured Rose entered. "My scar! I've had it since I was a kid, but somehow it just opened!"

Black Eyes didn't even blink. He was entirely unconcerned for Rose and her ripped open hand. He didn't even seem to care about the blood streaming down Rose's arm and dripping onto the clean white carpet.

"Thank you, Rose, for that enlightening information," Black Eyes said, smiling triumphantly and standing to attention, turning so he was once again facing outside the window and peering on the city that surrounded him. "Take her away."

The hands of the soldier clapped around Rose's shoulders, and he dragged her out of the office, blood streaming from the scar on her hand, and away from the haunting smile of Black Eyes.

Chapter 11

The Betrayal

Rose was dragged down the long hallway for the second time that day. This time, her screams had been renewed, shrill and bloodcurdling all over again. It didn't matter. Black Eyes had looked entirely unconcerned as Rose was forced out of his office, and she hadn't even seen another human in the building.

Attempting to escape the soldiers grip, Rose clung to every doorway they passed in the hallway. All that had done was smear the blood dripping from her hand all over the white walls and doors, and possibly further irritated her open scar. Soon, Rose was once again forced into the elevator they had come up. It took them down to the second floor. When the elevator shaft opened again, Rose noticed the hallway looked identical to the top floor corridor they had just come from. Aside from the smears of blood Rose had just left behind, there was no way to distinguish this floor from the other.

The soldier slammed into Rose's back, shoving her out of the elevator and down the hallway, which gave Rose more gusto in screaming her head off. Someone, somewhere in this terrible, earth-killing city had to hear her, right? It couldn't be possible every single Other-Sider would approve of their leader's kidnapping actions! Someone must hear Rose's cry for help and want to stop what was happening!

Just as she did on the top floor, Rose left her mark on the white, undecorated walls and closed doors by clinging to them with her bloody hand. It served to help her just as well as it had the first time, which was not at all. On the fifth closed door, the soldier stopped in front of the doorway and pinned Rose down using only one hand. With his other, he opened the door. Before Rose could react, he shoved her body into the room.

Rose only had time to register the room she stood in looked like an empty, abandoned classroom, with a whiteboard covering most of the far wall and a blinking fluorescent light. Those were all the details Rose was able to take in before she hurriedly slammed her arm and shoulder into the crack of the door the soldier was shoving closed behind her. The door slammed hard onto Rose's shoulder and she cried out in pain. The soldier pressed hard against Rose, attempting to push her through the door and pull it closed behind her. Her foot, which was also pressed through the crack of the door, caught on the edge and tripped her into the room. The door slammed hard, and Rose could hear the soldier fumbling with keys to lock her in.

Rose scrambled to her knees, ignoring the screaming pain now emitting from both her shoulder and her bleeding hand. She clutched the handle to the door, but before she could make her move to fight against the soldier and reopen the door, she heard a noise from out in the hall that made her stop in her tracks.

First, there was the sound of someone spitting. Then, there was a loud thud, which sounded distinctly like a body hitting the floor. Rose paused, still bent on her knees, and gripping the handle with both hands. Her heart pounded in her chest as she felt the handle twisting open, a movement being caused from the other side of the door.

The door pushed open, knocking Rose back to the ground. She peered up, and her face split into a giant smile. Standing in the doorway was Rylan, looking heroic and standing tall above the snoring figure of the Other-Sider. Next to Rylan was an unamused Kearn, shaking out her mane gruffly.

"You have no idea what I have been through," Rylan said, his voice scolding but his eyes and smile bright. "Kearn and I searched nearly every floor of this building looking for you, only to realize the rescue party had gotten here before you even *needed* rescuing! We've been wandering these halls for the last twenty minutes for no reason!"

"Rylan!" Rose cried, jumping to her feet and throwing her arms around Rylan's neck in glee. She screeched into his ear, "How did you find me?!"

"Hey, watch it!" Rylan laughed, rubbing the ear Rose had just yelled into. Rose released Rylan and looked into his eyes, which were stunningly beautiful as they shimmered with excitement. "It was pretty easy, actually. Has anyone ever told you that you have the shrillest scream in the world?"

Rose and Rylan paused for a second, beaming at each other. Then, it seemed to hit Rylan how close they were standing to each other, for he clumsily stepped backward and awkwardly cleared his throat, filling the space in the room with noise.

"So, uh—" Rylan stammered, seeming to forget what they were doing. Then his face became serious as the situation dawned on him. "Right, we need to get back to Mavarak as fast as possible. Did they hurt you at all?"

"Not too bad," Rose assured. She held up her hand, showing the slowing bleeding. "It doesn't hurt much, but it is bleeding a lot. Oh, and I probably have a small bruise on my shoulder from trying to wedge through the door before it was closed all the way."

"We need to stop the bleeding," Rylan said, carefully taking Rose's injured hand in his and investigating it closer. "What did they use to cut it?"

"Er—" was all that came out of Rose's mouth in response. How was she supposed to explain that Black Eyes had used absolutely nothing to cut open her hand? That she was just sitting there, talking, when it ripped open all on its own?

Before Rose could answer, the elevator made the familiar *ding!* that sounded whenever it stopped at a floor. Both Rylan and Rose snapped to attention, and Rylan used the injured hand he was already holding to yank Rose in the direction of Kearn.

"We have to get out of here," Rylan directed, bounding onto the Trusk's back. Rose didn't have time to think about the last time she had sloppily mounted the creature. She jumped swiftly onto Kearn's back just as the elevator shaft slid open.

"Hey!" Rose heard the commanding voice of an Other-Sider cry out from behind them, but she didn't have the chance to turn back and look at him before Rylan dug his heels into Kearn's side and directed her forward. The trio bounded down the hall, and Rose heard the scrambling of feet running after them. Kearn gracefully made it to the end of the hall in a matter of seconds and burst through a swinging metallic door. Just as the trio entered a stairwell, Rose made a quick and terrified glance backward in time to see the scrambling figure of a black-and-blue clad soldier sprinting desperately down the hall. The door slammed shut behind Kearn, and she bounded with one large jump down the staircase. She spun around in one easy movement and hopped over the second half of the stairwell, then burst through the doors that led to the empty lobby Rose had been dragged through earlier.

Kearn set off toward the tinted glass doors at full speed. Rose expected to see a wall of soldiers awaiting her outside the building, but that was not the case. In fact, the scene Rose could see through the one-sided mirrors of the House of the Many Windows didn't seem quite right to her. All the traffic that had been clouding the streets earlier was abandoned. Rose couldn't make out the figure of any soldiers guarding the city on the streets. As Kearn tore through the doors of the building and took to the sky, Rose scanned the streets of the Other-Side. They were empty. Deserted.

"Rylan, something's wrong!" Rose called over the sound of the gushing wind around Kearn's wings. "Look around; where are all the Other-Siders?"

"Doesn't matter," Rylan called back over his shoulder. "It helps us out a lot. Look at how easily we're escaping. We're almost to the river."

Rose looked up ahead and saw the river from her dreams rapidly approaching. She tried to convince herself Rylan was right, that it was a good thing there were no soldiers or Other-Siders wandering around the city. But something wasn't sitting right with her. What about the group of soldiers standing along the outskirts of the city when Rose was first captured? Where had they gone?

That's when Rose saw it. Up ahead, approximately the distance of the Mavarak clearing, was a billowing cloud of black smoke. Rose sniffed at the air, recognizing the crisp smell of fire. Then, as Kearn flew them closer to the village center, Rose heard the chaotic sound of shouting.

"What's going on?" Rose asked. Rylan didn't answer. Instead, he leaned forward, directing Kearn to gain speed. His ears were flat against his head, and Rose knew Rylan also realized something was wrong.

Long before they entered the clearing, they were able to see the scrambling figures of the Wood Dwellers. Rose watched as the children and women were being rounded up and led out of the clearing by Mavarakite warriors. In the meantime, others were carrying loads of spears out of the Weaponry Hut and passing the weapons one by one to a crowd of warriors. Standing on the same raised platform used for Bryce the Leader at the harvest festival was Max the Warrior. He was red in the face and was shouting commands at the top of his lungs, pointing warriors in various directions. As soon as Kearn dropped down to the ground in the clearing, Rose watched Max turn his attention to her and Rylan. He looked insane with ferocity and anger.

"Rylan!" he shouted above the clamor of the city. He stepped down from the platform and sprinted toward Rose and Rylan, and the warriors parted, making a pathway for Max. Without pause, Rylan practically pounced from Kearn's back and ran toward Max to meet him halfway. Rose scrambled off Kearn to follow, just catching Max's words above the sounds of the terrified village.

"Where have you been?" Max snapped at Rylan. At first Rose thought Max was simply furious with him. Then he demanded Rylan follow him, and Rose realized Max was also terrified and worried.

Rose struggled to keep up with Rylan and Max's long strides, but through sheer determination she was able to elbow her way through the mass of people to follow them. But when they reached their destination, Rose's heart shattered in such a way she almost wished she had just stayed with Kearn back by the arsenal.

The billowing smoke was coming from Rylan's hut.

The hut had clearly been ravaged. The insides of the hut appeared, at least from a distance, as though it had been gutted. The door was unhinged, leaving a gaping hole into the hut. The hut and parts of the tree had clearly been set on fire, with several parts scorched and blackened. The leaves that made out the words, 'It's the Small things in life!' were mostly either charred or gone, so all that could be read now were 'Small things.'

"Where are my mom and brother?" Rylan asked, his voice wavering. With one quick glance, Rose saw Rylan's shining blue eyes were brimming with tears.

"They're in the Medical Hut," Max explained sadly, shifting his dark, brooding eyes across the clearing to what Rose assumed to be the Medical Hut. Rose had never seen any Wood Dweller enter or exit the hut before. Today, she could see warriors and civilians streaming in and out of the hut like mad.

Without another word, Rylan turned and began marching toward the Medical Hut. Before he got far, Max reached out his muscular arm in front of Rylan and stopped him dead in his tracks.

"Rylan, there is something you need to understand," Max said, his voice grave. "This was the doing of the Other-Siders."

Rose's heart sank. She had known the streets of the Other-Side were too desolate for comfort. She had felt instantly something wasn't right.

"It happened in a matter of minutes. They surrounded us, ravaged your home, and are currently attacking us from all sides. We have warriors holding them off for now, but it won't last. We can only hope it is long enough to get the woman and children into hiding. But we have to know right now if there is any reason the Other-Siders would have attacked your home first?" Max demanded. Rylan paused, mulling the question over, then firmly shook his head. Max looked disappointed, but he quietly thanked Rylan for his deep consideration and then made for the arsenal to return to shouting directions.

Meanwhile, Rose stared intently at the leaves on Rylan's hut. It's the Small things in life. Small things.

One of the Keepers...His name is Rylan the Small. The words rang through Rose's head. The secret she had told to Black Eyes was that Rylan was one of the Keepers.

"The only way for a pathway to be revealed,"

Rylan growled, his face dark as he stared hard at his destroyed home, "is for a Keeper to betray Mavarak…"

He turned to Rose. His normally bright, wide eyes were narrowed. His normally smiling, smirking, mischievous face was pinched into a hard stare. In that moment, Rylan looked at Rose with a face of complete disdain, a look she had never seen cross his face before.

"You. You were the other Keeper."

Rylan's words were a slap to the face and Rose took a sharp step back, eyes tearing up. How is this possible? How could she be the second Keeper? She had never even heard of Wood Dwellers or Other-Siders before all this, she was just minding her business when she accidentally stumbled upon this world. She couldn't be!

Like a montage, memories flitted through her brain. The strange, recurring dream. The little Elf-Boy in the dream, the one that looked just like Rylan but much younger. The boulder he always perched on, the one that was identical to the boulder by the river next to her grandparents' cabin. The way Robin had greeted her with her full name and a giant hug, like an old friend. Rose had recognized Black Eyes in the play at the harvest festival, as if she had met him before. Then there was the little human girl in the play. And when she reenacted the blood sacrifice, they had sliced open the palm of her hand. Rose looked down at her bleeding scar, the one she had mysteriously had since childhood that her parents could never explain. The one that appeared after Rose nearly drowned in the river all those years ago. The one that had ripped open and gushed blood the moment she had betrayed the Mavarakites, the moment she had betrayed Rylan...

Rose closed her eyes, and the recurring dream she had so many times growing up flashed through her mind. The details weren't at all foggy as they always had been before when Rose tried to remember. This time, they were crystal clear. Rose was in the water, looking up. She could see the sun reaching toward her through the surface of the water. Then, partially blocking the sun, was the silhouette of a little boy with sharp ears. His hand reached out, stretching toward her through the water. Her hand stretched out before her, her fingertips reaching out for his—

It wasn't a dream. It was a memory.

Rose was the other Keeper. And she had betrayed the Mavarakites and revealed the pathway for the Other-Siders.

Rose had been in Mavarak before. The first time she had fallen in the river, she had seen the little door just like this most recent time. She had grabbed onto it and was transported into Mavarak. She had looked up through the water and caught a glimpse of Rylan's silhouette peering back down at her. Rose had met Whitney, Cecily, Robin, and Rylan before. Rose was the other Keeper.

"What did you tell them?!" Rylan's voice demanded, snapping Rose out of her reverie and back into the real world. Rose's eyes shot open and she looked up at Rylan, who stood angrily against the backdrop of his burning home.

"I—I thought it would be okay..." Rose stammered, not sure how to explain to Rylan she had led the Other-Siders to his hut. "I never—I didn't—I wouldn't have thought I was the—"

"WHAT DID YOU TELL THEM?" Rylan screamed, his voice slicing through Rose with such force that she physically stepped back, as though she had been smacked in the face.

Nearly inaudibly, Rose told Rylan. "I told them you were one of the Keepers..."

A face of furious disbelief fell over Rylan. He stood stunned, staring ferociously at Rose. Then, before Rose had a chance to explain her thought-process —that she believed Rylan to be safely protected by the Guardians—Rylan turned on his heels and sprinted away. Calling after him, Rose chased Rylan, but he soon disappeared into the crowd of anxious and bustling Wood Dwellers. Rose kept calling for him, but her voice was drowned out by the roar of warriors shouting commands to each other, children crying, and family members calling to their loved ones who were preparing to head into battle.

Rose continued to chase Rylan in the direction he had disappeared long after she lost sight of him. She threw elbows against Wood Dwellers walking in the opposite direction as her, she pushed past Wood Dwellers who demanded she follow the other women and children, she ducked below spears and other weapons being passed out. Then, just as she pushed between two warriors and made to break out into a run toward the Medical Hut, she nearly ran face first into Whitney the Wise.

Rather than calling out toward loved ones, or scrambling to gather supplies, or preparing to head off to battle, Whitney was just standing stock-still in the center of the chaos. His calm demeanor against the hysterics caused Rose to stop dead in her tracks. The part that really confused Rose was, while he stood in the center of the village where the densest crowd was, his eyes were focused entirely and unblinkingly on Rose alone.

Chapter 12

The Beginnings of War

Whitney's unconcerned demeanor beckoned to Rose. Curiosity got the best of her, and she approached him carefully. Although the world around her was still hectic with Mavarakites searching for their loved ones and trying to find a safe haven amidst the ensuing war, it seemed as though time slowed down. The world had been muted. Rose's focus was on Whitney, and why he was so calm.

Once she reached Whitney in the crowd, he knowingly stated, "The bond has been broken."

Rose felt a pang of guilt, but Whitney's voice wasn't angry or emotionally charged in the slightest. It was just a matter of fact for him. The bond had been broken. One of the Keepers had committed a Betrayal. The Guardians had fallen.

Without another word, Whitney turned on his heel and began walking calmly through the mass of Wood Dwellers in the direction of his treehouse. He hadn't signaled for Rose to follow, but she couldn't help but feel she was meant to.

It was much easier to follow Whitney to his treehouse than it had been to follow Rylan, as he moved at a much slower pace. He entirely ignored the panic around him. Once they left the center of the village and worked their way through the outskirts, it became much quieter and less crowded. Rose could still hear the panicked sounds of the village floating through the woods, but it was a distant memory as they moved farther and farther away. Occasionally, Whitney and Rose would pass one of the hidden huts that filled the outer parts of Mavarak and found a family packing small bags of their belongings. One pair of elderly Wood Dwellers were in a silent embrace, and Rose could tell by their shaking shoulders they were sobbing together. Rose swallowed hard on her guilt and looked away.

Once they approached Whitney's treehouse, he reached for the ladder and clambered up. He hadn't looked back or spoken to Rose on the entire journey, but nevertheless Rose got the distinct feeling he knew she was following and wanted her to continue to do so. She obediently took hold of the ladder and began the ascent. She was able to move slightly faster, as she had begun getting used to climbing and tall heights.

When Rose pulled herself through the opening in the floor of the treehouse, she saw the familiar clutter of Whitney's home and heard the familiar sound of buzzing bees. Just as he had been the first time Rose entered the treehouse, Whitney was sitting carefully on the worn couch facing the entrance. One leg was crossed over the other and he sipped carefully on a steaming cup of tea.

"Would you like some tea?" he offered. Rose couldn't decide if she wanted to laugh or cry at the sight of Whitney sipping tea while the rest of the Mavarakites were packing their bags in preparation to flee their attacked village. She ended up not being able to bring herself to either reaction.

"No, thank you," Rose said politely, quite sure she wouldn't be able to stomach anything just then.

Whitney beckoned for Rose to take a seat on the couch beside him, and she did so somewhat awkwardly. Whitney didn't seem to notice her uncomfortable demeanor in sitting on his dingy couch in his crowded treehouse with him, basically a total stranger, while the rest of the village was falling to pieces.

"Aren't you scared?" Rose asked after a moment of awkward silence on her part. The only sound filling the treehouse was the slurp of Whitney drinking his tea.

"Of what precisely?" Whitney asked. Rose blinked. Was he joking?

"Well, the Other-Siders attacked Mavarak…" Rose informed.

"Ah, that's where you're wrong," Whitney replied, setting his cup carefully on the armrest of the couch and turning to smile at Rose. "They are presently still attacking Mavarak."

Whitney took Rose's hand gently and tugged her to her feet, leading her to the nearest window. He pointed a finger in the distance, but Rose didn't need any help finding what he was pointing to. From this high vantage point, Whitney and Rose had a view that reached over the surrounding trees to an open field behind the village center, just beyond the surrounding cluster of trees. From there, she could see many black and blue clad Other-Sider soldiers battling against a far smaller number of gray and brown dressed Mavarakite warriors.

"Mavarakite blood has already been shed. And much more is to come." Whitney informed Rose calmly, still staring out the window toward the epic battle.

Rose watched as a Wood Dweller was overcome by soldiers on all sides. She turned away, covering her face with her hands and allowing herself to do what she had wanted to do since she realized she had caused this; she burst into tears.

"It's my fault," Rose sobbed. "All of this is because of me. I betrayed Mavarak. It's all my fault."

Rose wiped at her tears and looked up at Whitney, prepared to argue with him when he tried to tell her it was no one's fault, and she shouldn't be so hard on herself. Instead of saying anything of that nature, Whitney simply nodded, moved back toward his tea and dingy couch, and stated, "Indeed, this is your fault. It was always to be this way, for it is told in the stars."

This caught Rose off guard for a fleeting second. Then she burst into a second wave of tears, feeling even worse than she had before. He acted calm and unconcerned, but clearly even Whitney was angry with her. And why wouldn't he be? She had led the Other-Siders to his home, caused many of his people injury or even death, and forced the Wood Dwellers to have to move from their village and find a new place to live. The last Crusades went on for years, and this one could go on for an even longer time.

"What do I do?" Rose asked, sniffing hard as giant tears rolled down her cheeks. "How can I fix this? How can I make this up to—" Rose nearly said Rylan, but caught herself just in time, "—Mavarak?"

"To right a wrong—" Whitney began, then paused to take a long slurp of tea. Rose waited anxiously for the wise words Whitney had to offer. "—sometimes there is sacrifice involved."

Rose remembered Black Eyes' words. *Almost everything in life requires sacrifice.*

"What kind of sacrifice?" Rose asked, thinking about the last sacrifice she had willingly offered. A Mavarakite secret.

"The magic of the Guardians is ancient, but quite simple," Whitney explained, beckoning for Rose to join him on the couch once again. She didn't this time, as she was paralyzed by fear at what he was about to say. "The Betrayal can be reversed, and the bond can be mended, if one of the Keepers performs the Ultimate Sacrifice."

"What is the Ultimate Sacrifice?" Rose blurted. Her heart was beginning to race. It didn't matter what the Ultimate Sacrifice was. She needed to fix her mistake. She needed to make things right.

"Ah, yes. That is the question, isn't it?" Whitney asked, a knowing smile crossing his face. He sipped his tea, leaving Rose staring anxiously at him. He had the demeanor of someone who had just finished a conversation, but Rose felt nowhere near finished.

She blurted out the question that had been weighing on her mind since she heard the words Ultimate Sacrifice. "Is it death? Is the Ultimate Sacrifice death?"

Whitney looked her in the eye, and she could see a world of wisdom swimming behind those mysterious eyes. "Is it?" Whitney asked.

Rose took that as a yes. It had to be, right? What is more ultimate of a sacrifice than giving up your entire life?

Feeling as though she had received all the information she needed, Rose hurriedly turned and scrambled to the opening in the treehouse. She knew what she needed to do.

Just as he had the first time Rose had met Whitney, he stopped her before she left his treehouse for one last tidbit of information.

"Rose," Whitney said, and she stopped with

one foot out the treehouse and on the first rung of the ladder. "I want to reiterate one tiny detail about the ancient Guardian magic. Notice I said the bond can be repaired if a Keeper performs the Ultimate Sacrifice? That is to say, if *either* Keeper performs the Ultimate Sacrifice, not necessarily the Keeper who committed the act of Betrayal." Whitney looked at Rose importantly, and his next words gave Rose all the push she needed to rush back to the clearing. "Rylan too is aware of the Ultimate Sacrifice."

As soon as Whitney said this, Rose could hear Rylan's voice in her head as though he were standing right next to her. *I would do anything to prove my loyalty to Mavarak.*

Rylan was going to sacrifice his life to repair the bond. Rose had to hurry.

She practically flung herself down the rung ladder, not particularly caring if she toppled off and hurt herself in the process. She needed to find Max the Warrior.

Although she had never been through the woods without someone to lead her, she didn't hesitate to take off at a full sprint through the trees in the direction she confidently knew led to the village center. She hurriedly jumped over rocks, ducked below low-hanging tree branches, and bounded around bushes and boulders. It was like she was a new person from the scared little girl that had first walked through the Mavarak terrain. Now she had an internal compass helping her on her journey. Plus, it didn't hurt that the village center was alive with panic and she could hear the terrified Mavarakites from a great distance.

    Once she made it to the clearing, she noticed the panicked crowds of Wood Dwellers had thinned out. Between the warriors heading into war and the women and children going into hiding, the village center now mostly consisted of Wood Dwellers making and transporting the weapons. Rose caught sight of two warriors who were just at the far end of the clearing, arms full of bundles of arrows. Rose broke into a sprint chasing them before they disappeared into the trees behind the far end of the clearing, opposite the direction of the river and little door that had brought Rose to Mavarak.

    Rose caught up to the two warriors not too far into the thick of trees beyond the clearing and followed them to a green and brown tent that had been erected in the thickest part of the trees. Rose was glad she had caught up to them because the tent was almost entirely camouflaged by the greenery of the woods and she surely would have missed the tent if she hadn't been led there. Rose dashed into the coverings of the tent and realized immediately she had just entered an arsenal to store extra bows and arrows for the Mavarakite warriors. Aside from weapons, the tent was almost entirely empty. There was a small, wooden table off to one side of the tent that contained one large bow and a sheaf of arrows. Max hunched over the table, brows furrowed, deep in thought. He didn't even glance up when the two warriors entered the tent followed closely by Rose.

"Arrows in," the female warrior called as her and the man both dropped bundles of arrows. They turned on their heels and nearly plowed Rose over. The male looked Rose up and down, narrowing his eyes at her rounded, fleshy ears, and the female reached instinctively for a sharpened wooden knife tucked into her pants.

"Leave her," Max directed. The two warriors exchanged glances, then left the tent without another word.

Rose turned her attention to Max. Every time she had ever seen him, he had looked stern and serious. Now, however, it looked as though he had aged ten years overnight. His face looked wrinkled from all the furrowing his brows had been doing, and his eyes looked full of anger and frustration. Rose waited for Max to say something, but he didn't. The tent instead fell into dead silence. Max's eyes were trained on the table he stared at, deep in thought. From a distance, Rose could hear the sound of battle.

Finally, just as Rose was about to break the silence, Max spoke. "We should have been preparing for this for a long time," he said, his voice dark and dispirited. "We all knew it was a possibility the Guardians would fall one day. We were even told it would happen. We all knew the Other-Siders outnumbered us. But we became lazy. We celebrated our victory from the Crusades and ignored the dangers that awaited us. We were foolish."

Rose swallowed hard. She didn't know what to say, so she waited silently for Max to say more.

Almost inaudibly, as if speaking to himself rather than Rose, Max added, "Twelve warriors have already died."

At the words, Rose's mouth fell open and tears filled her eyes. Twelve Mavarakites had died already? She thought of the one she had watched from the window of Whitney's treehouse. She wondered if he was one of the twelve.

"We have sent messengers to find the Farcriers, our sisters in battle," Max said, his voice a bit louder than before. "Unfortunately, at this rate, most of our warriors will be dead before the Farcriers get here."

Rose watched in stunned silence as a single tear rolled down Max's cheek. A moment of silence passed as Rose's heart broke for Max and his beloved village. Then, without another word, Max straightened up, wiped the tear away from his face, and took up his bow and arrows. Then he turned determinedly toward the far end of the tent, the direction of the battle, and made to leave.

"I want to fight," Rose called after Max before he stepped out of the tent. He stopped dead in his tracks and turned an incredulous face toward Rose.

"Wood Dwellers are dying out there," he said, looking Rose up and down.

"I know," Rose replied, her heart aching to make things right. "That's why I want to fight."

Max seemed to consider Rose's request. Then he asked, "Do you know how to use a bow and arrow?"

Rose glanced at the bow and arrows lining the walls of the tent. Her thoughts turned back to the harvest festival, where Rylan had playfully showed her how to shoot. He had laughed at her as she shakily pulled the arrow back and launched it toward the target. It hadn't even come close.

"Yes," Rose answered firmly. She knew in her heart she barely knew how to use it, and there would be soldiers fighting against her who had trained their whole lives to use these weapons to kill. She would be dead within minutes.

That's the point. Rose told herself, thinking back to Whitney's news of the Ultimate Sacrifice. The sooner she performed it, the sooner the Wood Dwellers would return to safety. The sooner she died, the less Wood Dwellers have to die with her.

Max pressed his lips together. He clearly didn't believe Rose knew how to use a bow and arrow, and for good reason. He seemed to understand Rose wouldn't last in battle against the Other-Siders. Nevertheless, he collected a spare bow and arrow for Rose. He handed it to her silently, nodded once to give his thanks, then turned and exited the tent, leaving Rose alone with her new, mostly unfamiliar weapon and her final thoughts of life and her family.

I'm sorry Mom and Dad. Rose thought, her mind turning to her parents one last time. She wondered if Black Eyes repaired their broken relationship like he said he would. Perhaps her parents would at least have each other to lean on as they mourned the mysterious disappearance of their only child. Maybe the Wood Dwellers would find a way to return her body to them so they would at least have closure on her disappearance. It made Rose's stomach turn to imagine her parents spending the next several years hopefully searching the woodlands around her grandparents' home.

Just as Rose took a deep breath and prepared to head into battle, she heard the distinct sound of Trusk wings beating against the wind in flight. Just outside the tent, she heard a Trusk landing hard against the dirt.

"Kearn, stay," Rose heard a voice say from outside the tent. Her heart jumped into her throat and she had about half a second to prepare to see him before Rylan came sprinting through the opening of the tent.

He skidded to a stop, and the two Keepers of the Guardians looked each other deep in the eyes, both knowing what the other planned to do.

Chapter 13

The Battle

Rylan took one look at Rose, eyes flittering to the bow and arrows held awkwardly in her hands, then gave her a reproaching look.

"You have no right to be here," he bellowed, his voice hard, angry.

"Max gave me permission to fight alongside the Mavarakites," Rose answered, watching Rylan carefully. She stood in between him and the weapons lining the wall of the tent, the stacks of spears and arrows in bundles.

THE LITTLE DOOR

"He doesn't know what you did," Rylan answered back, his voice spitting at Rose like venom.

"Doesn't he, though?" Rose asked. It wasn't a question. She had seen the way Max looked at her. She was quite sure he at least had his suspicions.

Instead of responding to Rose, Rylan gruffly pushed past her, nearly knocking the bow and sheaf of arrows out of Rose's hands. He scanned the options before him, his eyes lingering momentarily on the bow and arrows, but instead reached out for a sharpened spear. Rose's heart knocked in her chest. He purposefully selected a weapon meant to be used in close quarters. He planned to walk right up to the Other-Siders and fight head on. Rose realized Rylan was far braver than her. She had found solace in the knowledge that, at least fighting from a long distance with a bow and arrow, she wouldn't see her assailant coming, wouldn't know of her impending doom.

"I've spent my entire life proving my loyalty to Mavarak," Rylan said, turning confidently toward Rose with the spear firmly clutched in his hand. "After today, the loyalty of my family will never be questioned again."

Rose shook her head and neared Rylan carefully. "You don't have anything to prove, Rylan. You kept your loyalty. You never betrayed your people. It isn't your fault your grandpa did. It isn't your fault that I did. You're the most loyal Mavarakite there's ever been—"

Although her words were meant to be comforting, they seemed to have the opposite effect on Rylan, triggering something deep inside him. "Shut up!" he yelled, pulling back from Rose just as she was reaching a comforting hand toward him, toward the spear. He clutched the weapon firmly, and Rose saw tears appear in his eyes.

"Shut up, shut up, shut up!" Rylan yelled again, even though Rose hadn't attempted to speak again. She stood stock-still, confused and hurt by his sudden harshness. "You don't understand! You have no idea what you're talking about!"

His voice cracked with the urgency and anger in his words. Though his features were fierce and hard, he had the appearance of a small child, and it struck Rose how young Rylan was to be bearing the weight of his village's safety on his shoulders.

"Rylan—" Rose tried again, but he cut her off instantly.

"No, you don't understand. You can never understand how much my loyalties waver," Rylan said, his ears turning red and his eyes filling with moisture. "You can never understand I think about leaving every single day."

Rose was surprised, but she didn't interrupt. She felt Rylan needed to get this off his shoulders. He needed someone to trust, and though Rose had proven herself untrustworthy, she was determined to not ruin this moment.

A tear rolled down Rylan's cheek, but he continued. "I've thought so many times about leaving late at night when everyone is asleep. Just taking Kearn and flying away. I think about how mysterious and endless the world beyond Mavarak is. There are so many places to go, sights to see. I think about it when I take care of the Trusks. I think about it when I walk through the village center. I think about it when I help my mom gather berries. I think about it in everything I do here—every mundane, boring chore I'm given. Every day, exactly the same as the one before. Before you got here, I hadn't had a real adventure in…longer than I can remember."

Rose watched Rylan carefully. His ears laid down against his head, the way they did whenever he became upset. His eyes and face fell, looking at the spear he held in his hands. "Why do you think I wanted to help you so much? Because when you got here, it was the first time in my whole life something was new or different. It was the first time in my whole life I wanted to stay right where I was…"

Rose's heart fluttered in her chest. She wanted to tell him she understood exactly what he meant, that he made her want to stay in Mavarak, that she had been relieved when the potion hadn't taken her home. She was just considering laying it all out there for him as he had just done when the mood shifted, and Rylan hardened.

"But then you betrayed us. You betrayed me," Rylan snapped, his glare hard. "Mom and Drew are in the Medical Hut, my home is gone, and my people are dying. Because of you."

Then, Rylan dashed out of the tent, sprinting away from Rose. She gasped, realizing she had been so entranced by Rylan's speech that she had forgotten what she was supposed to be doing. In one swift movement, she flung the sheath of arrows around her shoulder and chased after him. When she stepped out of the camouflaged tent, she heard Rylan give a long, low whistle, then the beating of Kearn's wings. Rose located Rylan's disappearing body through the thick of the trees, but just as she made to run after him, Kearn's giant body dropped between them.

Rose was sure Rylan had purposely sic'd Kearn on her to stop Rose from entering the battlefield. Kearn noisily gathered spit in her mouth, preparing to lull Rose asleep, but Rose slapped her arm over her eyes as a shield. Peeking at the ground from behind her arm, Rose attempted to dive around Kearn. The Trusk's large body was able to easily blockade the way, sending Rose in several different directions unsuccessfully.

"Rylan!" Rose yelled after him, her voice shrill and desperate. She knew the battlefield wasn't far away, and the Mavarakites were so outnumbered that the Other-Siders were likely closing in by now. It could be a matter of minutes that Rose had to catch up to Rylan before he would be killed in battle. She called after him a few more times, knowing well it was futile. He couldn't hear her, and even if he could, he wouldn't stop and come back for her. She needed to find a way to get to the battlefield before he did. She needed to complete the Ultimate Sacrifice and reinstate the fallen Guardian before Rylan could. She owed it to him and his people. She needed to make it right.

THE LITTLE DOOR

Rose tried again to sidestep Kearn while simultaneously shielding her eyes, but the creature's large body held her back with ease.

Rose racked her brain. She needed to come up with a way to get to the battlefield before Rylan. At this point, with Rylan having such a solid lead, it was nearly impossible. Rose would have to sprout wings and fly to the battlefield to get there before him.

It was as if a lightbulb appeared over Rose's head. She knew exactly what she had to do.

Rose carefully unshielded her eyes for about half a second, just long enough for Kearn to see her naked eye and spit at them. Then she slapped her arm back over her face, letting the sticky wetness splatter over her. Once Rose heard the low gurgle of Kearn gathering more spit, she made her move. As Kearn readied herself for another shot at Rose's eyes, Rose dropped her arm and dove toward Kearn's side, directly under her left wing. Rose gripped the animal and thrust her body onto Kearn's back. Then she dug her foot into Kearn's side the way she had seen Rylan do before, and Kearn flapped an angry wing.

"Kearn, listen to me!" Rose shouted desperately, clinging to the animal's back as she attempted to fling Rose off. "Rylan is in danger, and I'm the only person who can stop it from happening, but only if you help me! So, *please help me!*"

As Rose pleaded with the animal, she dug her foot into Kearn's side once again. She needed this to work, and she needed it to work fast.

From behind, Rose could see Kearn twitch an

ear, tousle her head, and then, as if by some miracle, she began taking the familiar bounds that meant she was about to take flight. Rose held onto Kearn for dear life, wishing she had Rylan to help her. But it was her turn to help Rylan. The animal took to the sky, and the moment Rose had a bird's eye view she began scanning the world below. It didn't take long to find the battle ensuing nearby. Rose guided Kearn toward the battleground, keeping the animal low enough to hide in the trees if a soldier from the Other-Side saw them.

The sight Rose saw was sickening, and it made her want to bury her head into Kearn's neck and sob. Across the small stretch of open land, there were a few dozen warriors bearing Mavarakite colors. These warriors were fighting with everything they had, clutching spears and yelling battle cries as their weapons clashed against the armor-clad soldiers. Closing in around the warriors, Rose saw, were at least triple the number of Other-Siders. They were relentless, slamming into the Mavarakites' wooden spears with their sharp metal swords. Rose could see at least twenty fallen warriors littering the battlefield, either wounded or dead, which the Other-Siders easily stepped over.

The one saving grace for the far outnumbered Wood Dwellers was that there were obviously several hidden warriors among the trees with bow and arrows, which became apparent to Rose as she watched arrows shoot from the depths of the woods and into one of the Other-Siders arms, who cried out in pain as a warrior overtook him.

Just beyond this exchange, Rose saw, with a sinking heart, Rylan had beat her to the battlefield. She pulled on Kearn's reigns, directing her toward Rylan and closing in the gap between the two. Kearn closed in on the battlefield, spitting in the direction of one of the Other-Siders, who fell to the ground in a slumber.

As Kearn brought Rose closer to Rylan's fighting figure, she was able to catch a glimpse of the soldier he was in battle with. Her heart leapt into her throat as she realized it was none other than Black Eyes himself who fought against Rylan.

Rose watched, feeling helplessly out of reach, as Black Eyes sliced Rylan's leg with his shining sword. Rylan screamed in pain as Black Eyes raised his sword high and then brought it down against Rylan's chest in what could clearly be a fatal blow. Luckily, Rylan stopped the sword from piercing all the way through his chest by using the spear to hold it back. The spear snapped against the weight and Rylan fell to the ground, blood already beginning to pour out of his shallowly pierced chest. Black Eyes raised his sword above his head, the dark holes boring into Rylan, prepared to pierce him through the heart.

Kearn reached Black Eyes just in time, tackling her front hooves into him and sending him flying backward, the sword clanging to the ground. The moment he hit the ground, Kearn landed hard and bucked Rose off, lifting herself to her hind legs in attack. Landing hard against the ground knocked the wind out of Rose and sent pain through every joint of her body, and for the first several moments of Rose being on the battlefield, all she could do was watch Kearn protect the warriors with all her might.

Black Eyes called for help as Kearn prepared to bring her large body down against him. Several soldiers began overtaking Kearn, stabbing into her with swords and standing around Black Eyes with weapons ready so Kearn couldn't attack him as she had prepared to do. She whined in pain and anguish as more soldiers surrounded her, spitting at the nearest ones as fast as she could gather her defensive spit.

"Kearn!" Rose yelled desperately, pulling her aching muscles into action and clambering off the ground. She couldn't move fast enough. "Kearn, get out of here! Fly away!"

The beautiful, majestic creature ignored Rose, spitting at a soldier and kicking another one to the ground. Another sword sliced into Kearn, and Rose could see the Trusk was bleeding in multiple places now.

"Kearn, fly away!" Rose screamed, holding her bow up shakily and preparing an arrow. She watched as the subject of her aim, a particularly large Other-Sider, brought his sword high above his head and prepared to stab deep into Kearn's side. Rose's heart pounded hard in her chest. She needed to protect this creature she brought here. She sent a shaky arrow flying toward the soldier, but it missed him entirely and collapsed pathetically against the ground.

Without missing a beat, Rose swiftly pulled another arrow out of her sheaf and shakily prepared that one as well. She aimed the arrow at the soldier, but she could see she was too late. He was already bringing his sword down, closing in on the Trusk as Kearn distractedly kicked a soldier on her other side.

Just as Rose lost hope entirely, the soldier's sword stopped mid-swing, as if someone had hit a pause button on the soldier. He completely froze. Then, he fell slowly to his side, revealing Max wielding a now empty bow. He quickly and precisely unsheathed a second arrow and sent that one flying toward another attacking soldier, rescuing Kearn from what could have been the last attack she could bear. Meanwhile, Kearn kicked down another soldier, leaving only one attacker.

Max looked downright ferocious. He didn't pause even for a second as he shouldered his bow—now in too close of proximity for a bow and arrow attack—and pulled a sword out of the hands of a fallen Other-Sider. Now bearing one of the swords from the Other-Side, he engaged in a duel with one of the soldiers who had been closing in on Kearn.

As Kearn used her strong legs to battle and Max sword fought one of the soldiers, Rose took this opportunity to check on Rylan. She scrambled to him and dropped to his side, tossing her weapon to the ground, and peered down at him. His beautiful blue eyes glittered in the sun, almost glazed over as he fought for his life. He was clutching the open wound on his chest, which was bleeding profusely onto the grass around him. Rose gripped him, lifting his head tenderly off the grass and onto her lap.

"Rylan, can you hear me?" Rose asked urgently.

Rylan sputtered unintelligible words, his body shaking from the pain gripping him.

As Rose racked her brain in panic, she heard the loud and distinct sound of a large creature falling. She looked up and saw Black Eyes once again on his feet, holding a bloody sword over the now collapsed Trusk. Rose watched as Black Eyes walked purposely toward Max from behind, just as Max triumphantly defeated the other attacking soldier.

"Max!" Rose screeched, warning him of Black Eyes' sly approach. Before she could say anything beyond his name, Black Eyes swiftly attacked. He thrust his sword clean through Max's chest. Time seemed to stop as the bloody sword erupted through the front of Max's body. Max's eyes shot wide in shock, then his face froze. The sword he had used to duel the soldier released from his hands. Blood seemed to rain down from Max's body. Then, Black Eyes pulled his sword back, and Max crumpled to the ground in a lifeless heap.

"NO!" Rose screamed, tears stinging her eyes. She began to shake as, all around her, friends were falling to the ground like flies. In her lap, Rylan barely clung to life. Kearn had collapsed and it was unclear whether there was any life left in her. And now, Rose watched as Black Eyes slaughtered the greatest living Mavarakite warrior. The reality of Rose's impending death became all too real and Rose realized the number of allies was dwindling rapidly.

I can still save Rylan. Rose thought, standing on her shaking legs. *I can still fulfill the Ultimate Sacrifice.*

I can still protect the Wood Dwellers. And maybe, just maybe, I can take down the leader of the Other-Side with me.

Black Eyes turned to face Rose; a wild look overcoming his features. He seemed to realize, like Rose, her chances were dwindling. What he didn't realize, however, was that Rose had no intentions of surviving the battle. In fact, she *needed* to die so Rylan could be taken to the Medical Hut and revived. What Black Eyes didn't know was that Rose's goal wasn't to survive, but to take him down with her.

With this knowledge in mind, Rose dove toward Black Eyes. She used her height to her advantage and kept low to the ground, diving below Black Eyes' arms as he struck the air above her. As he was now facing the wrong direction, Rose took the split second she had before he turned around to army roll toward Max's lifeless body and retrieve the sword he had battled with. She held it somewhat awkwardly in her hands, having no idea how to fight with a sword but knowing only that she needed to send the blade through Black Eyes' body before he did the same to her.

Just as Rose had realized her size was her greatest advantage, Black Eyes clearly believed his brute strength was his. He brought his sword high above his head and swung the weapon down heavily. Without thinking, Rose countered the move with essentially the exact opposite motion, swinging her blade upward so the two swords clashed above her head, and Rose successfully blocked what would have been a fatal blow.

Gaining newfound courage in response to her successful defense, Rose decided to attempt an offensive move next, lunging at Black Eyes' chest. Her sword clashed against Black Eyes' armor, leaving not even a dent. Black Eyes next move came too fast for Rose to defend against, and his sword gave her a piercing slice through her arm. As Rose cried out painfully, Black Eyes lunged at her hands, giving Rose another painful slice through her skin. The excruciating pain jolted through Rose's entire arm, making her drop her sword and fall to the ground.

This is it. Rose thought to herself, blinking up at Black Eyes as he drew near. *I wasn't even able to scratch him for the Wood Dwellers.*

Rose glanced over her side at Rylan, who was still lying on the ground unmoving, clutching at his chest. For a brief second, Rose felt a shimmer of hope surge through her as she thought there might be a chance Rylan could still survive. That he could return to Drew and Robin and be revived in the Medical Hut. That the warriors could drive the Other-Siders out of their home. That the Guardians would return to their former glory, the path to Mavarak would be hidden once again.

Those glorious thoughts of hope were dashed from Rose's mind, however, as Black eyes stepped menacingly overhead, nearing Rose. He had a wicked smile covering his face, and his sword was at the ready. Rose was defenseless, weak, and small. She would die a coward, just as she had lived.

Just as Black Eyes raised his sword, ready to kill her, Rose heard a low but shrill whistle envelope the battlefield. Though it was just one lone sound, the entire atmosphere of the battlefield immediately shifted. The fighting that had surrounded Rose stopped, and Rose watched as a look of pure terror fell over Black Eyes. He gradually brought his eyes up to the Mavarakite side of the field, and Rose watched the color drain from his face, the smile that had wickedly danced upon his lips seconds ago was now a distant memory. Rose whipped around on the ground to see hundreds of what could only be Farcrier warriors standing at the edge of the battlefield. Their ears were pointed just as the Mavarakites, but they all wore robes of maroon and brown colored silky fur and large fur boots.

Black Eyes seemed to forget Rose existed. He no longer looked at her as he began taking steps back, looking terrified at the new number of warriors he faced.

"Fall back!" Black Eyes' voice echoed across the field. Before a single soldier could move, however, an identical shrill whistle sounded. Suddenly, the Farcriers stampeded into battle, with battle cries lifting over the field.

Rose watched as Black Eyes turned around and ran away from the fight, yelling "Fall back!" above the cries of war, and many other soldiers who had yet to be met by Farcry warriors too began dashing away from the stampede.

"Fall back!" Black Eyes continually screamed,

leading his terrified soldiers away from the battlefield. He soon disappeared into the distant trees, as many of his soldiers followed suit, all the while crying his mantra of 'fall back' for as long as he could be heard. Meanwhile, the soldiers who were not able to flee were left behind to fight the Farcriers and surviving Mavarakites, and the sound of clashing metal and shouts of pain filled the air around Rose.

From the corner of her eyes, Rose noticed Rylan stirring, as though he were trying to sit up. As if this were a call to action, Rose hurriedly jumped up and ran to his side. She leaned down and gently put her arms around him, attempting to help him sit up. He cried out in pain and collapsed back to the ground, his arms and chest sponging up the blood pouring from his wound. She could tell that he was in a lot of pain, and his injuries needed immediate medical attention, or he would end up being the Keeper to complete the Ultimate Sacrifice after all.

"Rylan," Rose said to him, her voice firm and commanding. "You're not going to die today. Not as long as I can help it."

And she meant it.

Chapter 14

The Ultimate Sacrifice

Rose was pretty sure she had seen on TV before that someone on the verge of death needed to stay awake or they risked never waking back up again. Her goal was to get Rylan back to the Medical Hut for intensive care without letting him fall asleep. This was difficult, as every time Rose looked away from him even for a fleeting second, his eyes would begin fluttering closed once more.

"Rylan, stay with me," Rose cried urgently, yelling at him from about an inch away from his face. He stirred once more, his eyelids drifting open.

From a distance, Rose could see several Mavarakites who had not been fighting in the battle were collecting the fallen warriors now that the Farcriers had caused the Other-Siders to flee. She needed to wave down some of these stronger Mavarakites, as she knew she was too small and weak to carry Rylan herself. Although he wasn't exactly a large Wood Dweller, he was still bigger than her and couldn't help carry any of his own weight.

Rose looked back down at Rylan's once more closed eyes. "Rylan!"

With his eyes again flittering open, Rose turned back to spot the nearest medics. She waved her hands above her head and called for help. For the first time since she had seen Black Eyes slash Rylan in the chest, he made an intelligible noise. He was shushing Rose, telling her to be quiet.

Rose looked down at him desperately and saw his beautiful blue eyes wide with fear. "I need to get someone to help you or you're going to die!" she said urgently.

"That's the point," Rylan answered, his voice sounding choked and forced. It looked like it hurt him to talk, but Rose regained hope at seeing him form words and keep his eyes alert long enough to hold a conversation. "You need to let me die."

Rose's eyes filled with tears and she shook her head forcefully. "No, I'm not going to do that. Help! Over here, somebody help me!"

Several Wood Dwellers heard her this time, and

she watched as four Wood Dwellers came running toward her from across the field.

"Rose!" Rylan snapped, and then winced in pain. He was using too much energy to talk. Rose tried to hush him, but he pressed on anyways. "I need to die for the Ultimate Sacrifice to be complete! This is the way it's supposed to be!"

"It wasn't supposed to be this way! It was supposed to be me who died!" Rose sobbed, tears streaming her cheeks. "Not you, or Kearn, or Max. It was supposed to be me."

She checked on the progress of the approaching Wood Dwellers. They had almost reached Rose and Rylan, and they could definitely hear their conversation by now. When they reached the body of Max the Warrior, one of them let out a choked sob and dropped to his knees before the fallen warrior.

Rose looked back down at Rylan, but his eyes had remained open this time. He looked determined to tell her something before the medics picked him up and began fussing over his body. "Rose, you have to listen to me. You're going to make it back to the river. When you do, the little door is going to reveal itself to you. You'll go back home, and all of this will become a dream again."

Rose was shaking her head insistently, refusing to accept any of this. But Rylan was set on it. He had accepted his fate already.

"You'll be with your family again," Rylan said, his voice weak. Around her, the medics arrived, pulling out a stretcher made of vines, leaves, and rope.

"I'm not leaving," Rose assured Rylan, knowing she was out of time. Knowing he wasn't going to fight for his life. Knowing when this conversation was over, he would close his eyes and let himself slip away. Knowing this was her last chance to say what she needed to say to him. "I'm staying here, Rylan. I'm not running away back home to my parents from a war I started. I'll stay here and help nurse Robin and Drew back to health. I'll help you make a full recovery."

Rylan's eyes had gently closed somewhere in the middle of her speech. The Wood Dwellers grabbed onto his body from every side and lifted him onto the stretcher. Rose stepped back, allowing them space to work.

Rose's thoughts flickered to her parents sobbing and searching for her body in the woods and in the river, but the thoughts remained there for only a second. Then they flipped to Robin and Drew, devastated by the news of their son and brother. Rose's mind was firm and made up. Before the medics whisked Rylan's body away, she assured him one last time. "I'll stay here, Rylan. I'll stay here and fight for Mavarak until the day I die."

Then, Rose felt a warm, tingling sensation spread across the palm of her hand. She looked down at the place where her scar had been ripped open when the bond was broken. It had long stopped bleeding and the flaps of skin hung loose, brown with dirt, and the skin beneath was angry and red. But at this time, all of it was glowing yellow like something out of a fairytale. Inside the cut, Rose's skin felt like it was crawling, like the fibers of her skin were moving on their own. She scrutinized it and realized her skin was stitching itself back together.

The bond was being repaired.

Rose choked back more tears. It was done. The Ultimate Sacrifice had been completed. She looked up and watched the Wood Dwellers carry Rylan's lifeless body away. Off to the side, another stretcher had been placed next to Max's body. Beyond that, Farcriers and Mavarakites were working together to honor the fallen warriors and bring them back home.

"Rylan, no..." Rose whispered, new tears stinging her eyes once more. She jolted into action, running to Rylan's side as the Wood Dwellers carried his body across the battlefield. Rose grabbed Rylan's hand, wishing he would open his eyes and talk to her again. Her heart slammed hard against her chest.

As if her wishes had been granted, Rylan's fingers squeezed Rose's, and his eyes fluttered open once more. Rose was shocked and confused. Through Rylan's pain, although his body was battered and lifeless and he was nearing death, Rylan looked up at Rose, his eyes glittering, and somehow, he smiled.

"The bond has been repaired," he explained, his voice raspy and quiet.

"Wh—how?" Rose asked, hurrying alongside Rylan's body. The Wood Dwellers entered the thick of the woods, leading Rose to what she assumed would be the Medical Hut.

Rylan smiled an award-winning smile. "It wasn't my sacrifice."

Then, the Wood Dwellers reached a hut that had been set up in the thick of the woods near the battlefield, presumably for the warriors who were injured during battle.

Rose stared at Rylan in confusion. As Rylan was brought into the hut, a nurse stepped between Rose and the stretcher, preventing her from following. Rose watched Rylan disappear into the hut, feeling unsatisfied and needing more answers.

"You need to go this way, we're treating minor injuries over here," the nurse directed Rose away from the direction Rylan had just disappeared. Rose stared after him, wanting desperately to run to his side and demand he explain. What did he mean it wasn't his sacrifice? Rose was certainly far from death. She had sustained much less injury than him. She hadn't given her life or even a limb as a sacrifice. But she was the only other Keeper, so if it wasn't Rylan's sacrifice, it had to have been hers. But what had she sacrificed?

Rose pondered this as a nurse began prodding at her injuries from her battle with Black Eyes. She continued to ponder Rylan's words over the next several days as she awaited the answers to her questions.

**

The next few days were frustrating for Rose. She was kept in the Medical Hut as her injuries healed because apparently they had been far worse than Rose had originally thought. The slice on her hand from Black Eyes' sword hadn't bothered her much, but the gash on her arm screamed with pain and was, according to Patricia the Healer, at major risk of infection.

After two long days of being treated and forced to rest, Rose had grown entirely restless. Patricia did eventually allow her to leave, and she instantly demanded to be taken to Rylan. She was relieved to hear he was stabilized, and she would be allowed to see him, but she was disappointed to find he was resting and was in no state to have conversations, particularly ones that were emotionally jarring. Rose was directed, specifically, not to attempt discussion on the battle, the wounds Kearn had faced, or Max's fate. Rose had considered breaking all the rules and discussing each of these topics with Rylan, but it didn't matter much anyway. Rylan was asleep when she reached his bedside.

Rose stayed with Rylan overnight and the next day, which Rylan slept through most of. He did wake up at one point, but he was confused and, as the nurses had informed Rose already, not in a state of mind for discussion.

That night, Rose did receive a wonderful surprise. Robin and Drew's burns had healed enough that they could leave the main Medical Hut permanently set up in the center of town. As soon as they entered the room, Robin burst into tears and flung herself over Rylan's lifeless body. Drew stayed back a bit, but he too was choking back tears. Rose only needed to be embarrassed for a moment that they had walked in on her grasping Rylan's hand, because no one mentioned it or seemed to even notice. Rose was relieved Robin hadn't seen Rylan the day he sustained his injuries; if this is how she reacted to his stabilized and resting body, Rose couldn't imagine how devastated she would have been to see Rylan on the verge of death. She also couldn't imagine how Robin would have been if Rylan had completed the Ultimate Sacrifice the way he wanted to.

Another day went by with Rylan mostly sleeping or in a state of confusion when awake, and Rose was grateful for Robin and Drew's company. Robin and Drew informed Rose there would be a Mavarak funeral service in honor of Max the Warrior and the other warriors who gave their life protecting Mavarak the day of the battle. Then, Drew began prodding Rose, trying to get the juicy details Rose didn't have to give.

"So, the Other-Siders haven't tried to attack Mavarak again since the first attack," Drew said nonchalantly. Rose could sense he was gaging her reaction to this information.

"That's good," Rose replied, feeling truly relieved. Though she had seen her scar glow and magically heal, and Rylan had claimed the bond had been repaired, Rose frequently had her doubts since she had no clue how this could have happened.

"It seems like the Guardians are hiding the pathway once again," Drew added, still attempting to be nonchalant. He picked at some dirt under his fingernail as he talked.

"That's such a relief to hear," Rose answered genuinely, smiling at Drew.

Drew finally erupted. "How did you do it?! What did you have to sacrifice?! Everyone knows the Ultimate Sacrifice requires giving up your life, and both you and Rylan are alive!" he cried desperately, spilling all the thoughts that had been whirring around his brain. Admittedly, Rose felt as exasperated as Drew did in wondering.

"I honestly have no clue," Rose said, furrowing her brow and looking hard at Rylan's sleeping form, as though he held all the answers. "I've been wondering myself. Maybe Rylan died temporarily and came back to life?"

"How would he have come back to life?" Drew asked, and Rose admitted she hadn't a clue.

"Maybe the Guardians messed up," Drew suggested.

"Maybe..." Rose agreed, but even as she said it, she knew it wasn't right. Something happened that day, something the Guardians accepted as an Ultimate Sacrifice. But what? Perhaps the sacrifice can be done by any true Mavarak and not just a Keeper, so the Guardians accepted Max's honorable death as a sacrifice? Or maybe the Ultimate Sacrifice was an exaggeration, and it was just another bloodshed sacrifice? If that were the case, there had been a lot of sacrifices given by both Rylan and Rose.

Rose would have run these theories past Drew to see if he thought anything of them, but Robin looked like she was itching for a subject change. Apparently, she didn't like the thought of her son in battle, especially when he nearly died. Rose decided instead to ask Drew whether the berry salad at the main Medical Hut was any better than the infirmary. Drew informed Rose that after eating his mom's cooking, nothing in Mavarak would ever taste as good. Robin smiled, seeming grateful for the change of subject, and Drew continued to tell Rose about some of the great dishes his mom cooked during the cold season.

Finally, on the third day of being with Rylan and the fifth day after the attack from the Other-Siders, Rylan woke up enough to talk. When he first woke up, Rose decided to leave the hut and give the family some privacy. After a while, though, she made her way back to Rylan, who was animatedly telling Drew about his fight with Black Eyes (so much for not discussing the battle), and she quietly sat on the tree stump seat farthest from Rylan.

Drew listened to Rylan with eyes wide, hungry for every detail, but Robin seemed like she might become physically ill.

"—and then after that, I was kind of in and out of consciousness. I remember watching Rose battle Black Eyes, then I blacked out for a little while. Next thing I know, I'm talking to Rose, I can only remember bits and pieces of the conversation, then I was being carried away on a stretcher." Rylan finished his story. Rose had already detailed her battle with Black Eyes to Drew, so he was uninterested in hearing that part of the story. However, this last bit Rylan said was the part Rose was most interested in. She perked up and decided it was time to intervene.

"Do you remember the last thing you said to me?" Rose asked. Robin and Drew exchanged glances.

"I think we'll leave you two to catch up," Robin

said, smiling knowingly at Rose. Drew snickered and the two left, leaving Rose staring quizzically at Rylan.

He racked his brain, trying to remember. Then, as if a lightbulb went off over his head, it dawned on him. "I do. I told you the sacrifice wasn't mine."

"Right," Rose exclaimed. She was so close to the answers she had been waiting days for. She moved from the seat she had taken far away from Rylan to the one Robin had been occupying, the closest to him. She leaned against the bed he rested on. "What did you mean by that?"

Rylan smiled. "I meant you made the sacrifice. Obviously."

Rose rolled her eyes. Even after nearly dying and five days of unconsciousness, Rylan still pushed all of Rose's buttons.

"*Obviously*," Rose mimicked in a high-pitched, nasally voice. Rylan laughed, but Rose ignored this and pressed. "But I thought the Ultimate Sacrifice was death?"

"I thought so too at first," Rylan said, shifting in his seat. Rose knew he must have been sick of sitting in the same bed in the Medical Hut that had been thrown together the day of the attack. "I mean, I tried my best to get myself killed…probably could have done a lot more damage to Black Eyes if I had been trying to live, of course…"

Rose smiled. "Of course,"

Rylan cleared his throat. "Anyway. I was confused at first too. But then I realized. The Ultimate Sacrifice isn't necessarily dying. It's giving up your life."

Rose blinked. Did he not just say the same thing twice in two different ways?

"Rose, let me ask you something. Don't think at all, just say the first thing that comes to your mind, okay?" Rylan said. Rose nodded her agreement, and Rylan asked, "What is the one thing you want more than anything else in the world?"

"To be with my mom and dad again. Together. As one happy family."

"Right," Rylan exclaimed, as though Rose had just solved his riddle. She still didn't understand though, so Rylan continued. "And what was the promise you made to me before I was taken away by the Medics?"

Rose thought for a second, then whispered, "I told you I would stay here."

Rose's Ultimate Sacrifice was giving up her hope of being with her mom and dad again as one happy family.

Rylan nodded. "I first took 'sacrifice' to mean death as well. But that's not what a sacrifice really is, is it? Sometimes it can mean giving up what you want most for those you love. You taught me that." Rylan smiled, and it was the most beautiful and genuine smile Rose had ever seen. It made her feel warm, and she couldn't help but smile back at him.

"And you know what that means?" Rylan continued, his smile still warm and genuine and touching Rose's heart.

"What?" Rose asked, eager to hear more words of wisdom.

Rylan's smile turned mischievous in a split second. "It means you like me more than you admit."

Rose's smile disappeared and she rolled her eyes, swatting Rylan on his arm.

"Ow! You can't hit me, I'm injured!" Rylan laughed, grabbing his arm as though Rose's hit had left him in pain.

"I'm injured too so that makes it okay!" Rose said, lifting her hand as though prepared to hit him again.

"You're not injured as bad," Rylan argued.

"Yeah, only because I can fight better than you," Rose teased, smiling smugly at Rylan.

"I'm sure you're more experienced because of your cold, cold heart," Rylan laughed. Rose swatted his arm again, and Rylan began yelling, "Help, I'm being attacked in here!"

Rylan's nurse—who was actually a Farcrier, and Rylan explained the Farcriers are more medically advanced than the Mavarakites—came into the room soon after Rylan's cries for help. Rose hurriedly explained Rylan was kidding—and further explained he was still kidding when he attempted to claim she was actually hurting him—but the nurse insisted Rose let him rest for a bit longer before he could return to normal activities. He told Rylan that he needed to stay in the infirmary for one more night, just to ensure he was really okay to leave, but assured that the next morning Rylan would be free to go.

As promised, the next morning, Rylan was permitted to leave the Medical Hut. He was reminded upon his departure he needed to rest a lot, avoid excessive physical activity, and drink a lot of fluids. But, with a wink in Rose's direction, was assured a few deserving swats to the arm wouldn't do any lasting damage.

The moment Rose and Rylan exited the infirmary, followed by Robin and Drew, they were elated to discover Kearn had made nearly a full recovery and was being tended to just outside the hut. She had many wounds on her body, but she was in full spirits and was whinnying and shaking out her mane as she had done before. Rylan had been informed of Kearn's injuries, and he practically burst into tears of joy when he saw her standing and full of life. He ran to her and threw his arms around her giant neck.

Rose felt joy swell in her chest as well. She felt terrible because she was the one who brought Kearn to the battlefield to be attacked. As Rylan hugged the animal around her broad neck, Rose approached carefully and patted Kearn's back.

"Thank you for protecting us, Kearn," Rose said. Kearn tousled her mane in response, and Rose smiled. She couldn't believe the first day she had met this beautiful creature, she had been terrified even to look at her.

From the depths of her throat, Kearn began gathering spit. Rose gasped and slapped her hands over her eyes. Alright, so there was still a small amount of fear left.

Rylan laughed easily and lovingly patted Kearn's neck. "Easy, girl. We're all rested up."

Since Kearn was too small to carry all four of them back to the village center, the group had to make their way on foot. Despite having no idea where the Medical Hut had been placed, Rose seemed to instinctively know her way back home. Along the way, they passed several tents made of animal hide, which Rylan explained was housing the Farcriers. Due to their long journey, and to ensure the Guardians really were back to their full power, the Mavarakites would house the Farcriers for a few days before they made the journey back to their village, which was also hidden by a certain magical power.

Once the group made it back to the village, Rose saw the clearing was particularly bustling with extra people. She could easily tell the Farcriers apart from the Mavarakites, as the Mavarakites were clothed in green and leaves and flowers while the Farcriers were adorned with reddish-brown, black, and white pelts and giant fur boots. The Wood Dwellers all mingled, though, and Rose could see the relationship between the two villages was good.

While Rose was distractedly looking at the contrast between the Mavarakite's grassy greens and the Farcrier's reddish browns, the entire Small family had been entirely captivated by another change that had occurred in the village. Rose didn't notice until she glanced at Rylan and saw a giant smile spread across his face, lighting his features and filling him with a childlike joy. Rose followed his line of sight and saw, to her delight, the Smalls' hut had been rebuilt during their stay in the Medical Hut.

The hut hadn't just been restored to its former glory. It was bigger and more beautiful than before. It was nestled between two trees, as it always was, but the wood was more smoothly carved, and the color was a brighter and more glorious color of brown. There were lavishly large, green leaves draped over the windows from the inside, acting as curtains, and the treehouses that were Rylan and Drew's rooms both had balconies overlooking the village center. Etched into the wood above the door, where it had previously read, 'It's the Small things in life,' there was a new saying. Above the door, the Smalls' house now read, 'No one ever became poor by Giving.' Surrounding the front door on either side of the tree was a medley of brilliant flowers.

"Do you like it?" a deep voice asked from behind Rose and the Smalls. All four of them swung around to face Bryce the Leader, who had a look of humble pride. "Many of the greatest builders from both Mavarak and Farcry came together to rebuild your hut from its ashes."

"It's beautiful," Robin answered earnestly. "The saying…"

"No one ever became poor by Giving," Bryce said, turning a smile toward Rylan. "You have given more to Mavarak in sixteen years than many Wood Dwellers give their entire lives. I don't believe you deserve the cruel name your grandfather earned before the first Crusades began. If you would like, your given name is yours. Rylan the Giving."

As he said his name, Bryce bowed deeply to him

as a show of honor. Rylan was beaming more than Rose had ever seen him beam before. Then he turned to Drew, bowed deeply in front of him, and added, "Sometimes the hardest gift to give is patience. Your gift will come in due time, and you will be a great and powerful Wood Dweller. Drew the Giving."

Drew smiled proudly as well, and then Bryce turned to Robin, who looked near tears. "You have given much to our community. You give your delicious berries. You gave your husband once so long ago. And you gave your son as a Keeper to protect our people. To be frank, this is long overdue, and I sincerely apologize it has taken so long. Robin the Giving." And Bryce bowed deeply to Robin, who swelled with pride and joy.

Rose was shocked when Bryce turned to her next. "And to our Keeper who fulfilled the Ultimate Sacrifice to right a wrong. Many are capable of greatness, but few achieve it. You are one of those, Rosalie the Great." Bryce bowed deeply. Rose felt awkward, until she made eye contact with Rylan, who was silently snickering. He pretended to bow to her behind Bryce's back, causing Rose to break out in a giant grin that matched the size of the Giving family's smiles.

Bringing himself to a full standing position once more, Bryce looked deeply into Rose's eyes. "Our village is home to you for as long as you would like to stay here. We hope you will stay for the funeral service being held in honor of the fallen warriors. I believe certain specific warriors would appreciate that greatly."

Rose's smile vanished, along with the smiles on Rylan, Robin, and Drew's face. She knew all thoughts had turned in an instant to the stoic face of Max the Warrior. Rose clenched her fist, her heart aching over the unfairness of Max's death. He had been the most loyal and brave Wood Dweller she had ever met. She knew he would be proud of his death, as it had been to protect the place he loved most. But Rose couldn't help but grit her teeth in anger as her mind replayed his death. Black Eyes' cruelness took Mavarak's greatest warrior from the world too soon.

"I will be there," Rose promised Bryce the Leader. "For Max."

Chapter 15

A Mavarak Funeral Service

The next morning, the morning of the funeral service, Rose woke to a knock on the tree bark outside the Smalls'—now Givings'—guest treehouse.

Rylan's face appeared through the window, clinging to the rope ladder that brought him to the treehouse.

"Merry to see you," Rose murmured, rubbing her eyes and sitting up in bed.

"Merry to see you," Rylan returned the greeting with a smile. "I want to show you something outside of the village center today before the service. Can you get ready quick?"

"Sure," Rose said, curiosity stirring inside her. Rylan disappeared as he began his descent down the rope ladder, and Rose wondered what it was he wanted to show her as she carefully changed into her light green leaf shirt and skinny brown pants. Perhaps he had taught Kearn a new trick. Or, more likely, he had discovered somewhere new and incredible while riding Truskback and wanted to show Rose.

With Rose now fully dressed and her hair tamed by the thistle brush Robin loaned her, Rose ventured down the rope ladder and into the main hut. The hut was quiet, and it seemed Rylan had woken Rose before either Drew or Robin had ventured out of their rooms.

Rylan was carrying a woven basket filled with bread and Sweet Berry jam (still left over from the harvest festival).

"So we can eat on the road," Rylan explained. And with that, he led Rose out of the hut and into the clearing.

It was still early enough for the leaves to be coated in dew and for the morning air to chill Rose just a bit. The earth had a fresh, oaky smell to it, one that only happened early in the morning in the woodsy air. The village was quiet, but there were a few Mavarakites who were already hard at work. Rose saw a few Wood Dwellers picking berries off the trees around the west side of the clearing, and one Wood Dweller was cutting down blocks of wood into smaller pieces.

Rylan led Rose out of the clearing and toward the river she had come to know so well. Once the pair got to the river, he turned and led Rose upstream. Her heart knocked against her chest. Did this have something to do with the little door in the river? Rose knew she couldn't go home; her sacrifice, the one that had reinstated the fallen Guardians, was that she would remain in Mavarak until the day she died.

After following the river for a few minutes and chatting a bit about Kearn's recovery progress, Rylan directed Rose to stop. She obeyed and found herself looking at a tree perched directly on the border of the river and land, its roots dipping into the gently streaming water. At the heart of the tree was a small tree hollow. Rylan took Rose's hand and gently pulled her closer to the hollow. Inside the hollow was an owl. At first, Rose jumped back. Then she realized the owl was unblinking, unmoving, and entirely gray, and it dawned on her that the owl was made of stone.

"The Owl Guardian," Rose said. She peered below the hollow and noticed an engraving. It read:

Rylan the Giving
Keeper of the Owl Guardian

The engraving was weathered and clearly the original words. Rose confusedly asked, "How did they know your name would be Rylan the Giving?"

"That was the Mavarak name I was given at birth," Rylan explained. "My grandfather was Samuel the Giving. Even though he betrayed Mavarak before I was born, it was still the name that I was born with.

Small was, in a way, just a nickname we were forced to go by."

Rose nodded, then studied the small stone owl. "So where is the other Guardian?"

"This one protects the northern entrance to Mavarak. The Snail Guardian protects the southern entrance," Rylan explained. With that, the two made their way downstream. As they walked, Rylan asked Rose to explain human schools. This conversation held them over until they reached the south border of Mavarak. Once again, Rylan directed Rose to stop walking. Unlike the first time, Rose didn't see any tree for the Guardian to be perched in. Instead, there was a large patch of tall grass. Rylan bent down, Rose following suit, and pushed some of the tall grass aside.

The stone snail was approximately the same size as the owl and was attached to a flat stone surface. The stone surface that housed the Guardian was where this engraving was held, reading:

Rosalie the Great
Keeper of the Snail Guardian

Just as she had been confused by Rylan's name, she was taken aback by her name. She had only been given the name the day before, yet here she was looking at an engraving that had clearly been here for ten years.

"Your Mavarak name was given to you on your first visit here ten years ago," Rylan explained, sensing her confusion without her voicing it. "You only proved you still deserved it with your second visit."

Rose looked at Rylan in amazement and wonder. "So, you knew the entire time I was the other Keeper?"

Rylan shook his head. "Wood Dwellers don't shorten our given names. I had no idea your full name was Rosalie. I just thought you had a similar name to the other Keeper. I should have known when Mom called you Rosalie and hugged you, the first day you met...I was too busy being embarrassed to think about it, though," Rylan said, laughing as he seemed to think back on the first day Rose appeared in Mavarak. Rose smiled too. Could it only have been two weeks ago that she was back at her grandparents' cabin? It felt like a lifetime had passed.

The two sat next to the Snail Guardian and the flowing river while they ate bread and Sweet Berry jam. Even when the bread wasn't fresh and warm, it was still heavenly when mixed with the tart sweetness of the jam. Rose and Rylan stayed by the riverside talking and laughing until the sun rose over the waking village of Mavarak. Soon, Rose knew, they would be mourning over the death of several brave warriors rather than basking in the sun.

***

As the saying goes, all good things must come to an end. Eventually, Rose and Rylan finished their bread and jam—leaving nothing in the basket but about a handful of sweet berries and two lone arrows Rylan mysteriously packed, which he insisted they would need later—and headed in the direction of the funeral. Rose discovered that the Snail Guardian was just about on the opposite corner of Mavarak from the funeral service. Even more surprising to Rose was the fact that the funeral was being held on the battlefield, where the gravesites were.

After the long trek through the trees, through the village center, and past the Medical Hut that had been Rose's home for nearly the past week, the trees opened to the large field. When Rose stepped onto the field, bad memories flashed through her mind. The most lasting memory was the image of Black Eyes' blade piercing directly through Max's chest, blood raining down in front of him.

Because of the long trek, Rose and Rylan were among the last of the Mavarakites to enter the battlefield. There were as many Wood Dwellers to see the service as there had been at the harvest festival, and Rose silently wondered if every Mavarakite attended every funeral service. Most of the Farcriers had already journeyed back to their homes, feeling confident the Other-Siders would not attack again, although there were a few who lingered along the back row of Wood Dwellers.

Every Wood Dweller stood at attention, and they all faced east. Rylan led Rose through the crowd to where Drew and Robin stood, which was about the center of the crowd. Once they joined Drew and Robin, Rose took the time to study the scene before her. Past the front row of Wood Dwellers standing at attention was a small gap, then fifteen graves lined up in a straight line across the battlefield. Rather than gravestones, the Wood Dwellers had stuck a wooden spear into the ground at the head of each grave to mark the spot the bodies lay. The ground looked freshly dug, and Rose knew the bodies of each warrior had already been placed into the ground prior to the funeral service.

All of Mavarak was silent for a long time. Many Wood Dwellers cried silent tears to mourn the death of the fallen warriors. Rose herself had to bite back tears as the image of Max's final moments flashed through her mind. Finally, Bryce the Leader stepped forward from the standing crowd of Mavarakites and turned around to face his Wood Dwellers.

"Family of the fallen first," was all he said. The Wood Dwellers clearly understood what this meant, however, as the words sprang the crowd into action. Several Wood Dwellers—mostly those in the front of the group—began forming a moving line. The procession of Wood Dwellers was led by the farthest on the left side and curved around until the line of Wood Dwellers walked along the foot of each grave. As they did so, Wood Dwellers occasionally dropped small items into the holes of certain graves.

Rylan leaned toward Rose as she watched the strange activity and whispered the word, "Offerings."

Rose nodded her understanding. As she did so, Rylan lifted the basket from their breakfast and retrieved one of the arrows. He handed it to Rose. Then he scooped up about half the sweet berries and handed those to her as well. Then he took the rest of the items in the basket into his own hand and placed the basket at his feet.

When the first group of mourning Wood

Dwellers finished passing each grave, they somberly wrapped around to the other side, so they assembled at the heads of the graves, clustering in small groups around certain spears. Rose assumed the families stood at the head of the warrior whom they lost. Her heart ached particularly for the spear seventh in the row. At the head of this particular grave stood only two people: a woman Mavarakite, probably in her late twenties, and a tiny child holding her hand.

    Once each family member reached the spear that stood at the head of their fallen warrior's grave, they all placed one hand gently on the surface of the spear. Once this was done, Bryce the Leader stepped forward and faced the crowd once more.

    "And the rest may follow," he instructed. Once he said this, the rest of the Mavarakites began following in the same pattern as the family members. As she waited her turn, Rose imagined Robin and Drew standing at one of the spears, mourning the death of Rylan. At the thought, she wanted to wrap her arms around Rylan's waist and hug him tight.

    Eventually, it was the Giving family's turn to step into the procession. As Rose followed Rylan to the graves, she realized each spear had engravings that read the names of the fallen. Rose read each name she passed. She knew the berries and arrow that Rylan had handed her were meant for Max.

    Max's grave was the last of all fifteen graves in the line. When Rose reached his grave, she peered down into the gaping hole that was there. Inside the hole was a large, sleek black box. It appeared to be wooden, but it was entirely unadorned, which was a stark contrast to the elaborate caskets Rose had seen at the few human funerals she had attended. On top of the box was only the offerings that had been dropped into the hole. Rose caught glimpses of several types of fruits as well as arrowheads, jewelry, and one small book. Rose didn't have time to register any other items before she had to drop the arrow and berries into the hole and move on.

Unlike the family members, the rest of the audience gathered back at the foot of the graves rather than rounding to the far side and gathering at the spears. Once the last mourning Wood Dweller dropped their offering into the grave right before Max's and returned to the standing, Bryce the Leader stepped forward and looked to the crowd once more.

He was silent for a few moments. He opened his mouth, as though to say something, but snapped it closed once more. Finally, he covered his eyes and his shoulders shook, and Rose realized he, too, was crying over the death of so many good Wood Dwellers. Rose realized the last time the Mavarakites had been this devastated was likely during the Crusades.

Eventually, Bryce managed to pull himself together and speak. "It is not often I am brought to tears in my life. I once thought this was a sign of strength. I realize now it was only a sign of general well-being in my life and in the life of those around me.

"Historically, this battle has been the most devastating battle to those of Wood Dweller kind. We lost fifteen great warriors during this attack. These Wood

Dwellers gave their lives so we might be safe once more. It brings me great joy to know this has not been in vain. Our Guardians are standing strong and protecting our pathways. We have learned much from this battle as a community, and we will rise from the ashes stronger than ever before.

"Normally, I would take a moment to speak on the fallen Wood Dweller and open up the opportunity for friends and family members to share memories and kind words. Unfortunately, with the great number we mourn today, we are unable to speak individually on the good of each warrior—" Bryce paused here, and Rose could tell he was once again fighting back tears. Rose glanced discreetly at the Wood Dwellers surrounding her. Most that she could see had shiny eyes. None smiled.

Rose's heart pounded hard against her chest. Several people down and in the same row as the Giving family, Rose could see Lyla the Beautiful. Her soft, beautiful face was coated in tears, and her ears—which normally poked through her wavy blonde hair—were lying back on her head and were entirely concealed instead. Rose saw the pain on Lyla's face and knew Lyla had cared deeply for Max and the other warriors. Rose could see the pain Lyla had felt was the same pain Rose had felt when she believed Rylan had passed. It was the kind of pain that could only be felt by someone who was losing a person who could never be replaced for them. Despite every bitter and jealous feeling Rose had ever felt toward Lyla, all she wanted right then was to reach out a comforting arm toward her. Instead, Rose turned back toward Bryce the Leader and again listened to his speech.

"What can be said for each of these individuals," Bryce continued, "is that they had a loyalty to their people that few can understand. They died in honor, and they will be remembered. At this time, I will name each of the warriors who gave their life so that we can live."

As Bryce named each warrior, the family members of the named Wood Dweller took up their shovels and tossed dirt over the offerings, filling the graves.

Rose registered each individual name as they were stated by Bryce. She wanted to ensure she truly honored each warrior by etching the name into her brain. Andrew the Aggressive. Stan the Friendly. Sage the Friendly. Kiana the Courageous. Kory the Bold. Reese the Energetic. Gray the Big Hearted. Willow the Wide Eyed. Bane the Determined. Nyla the Animal Whisperer. Jordan the Quiet. Alexa the Tall. Lexus the Loving. Liv the Maker. Max the Warrior.

As Max's name was called by Bryce the Leader, the weight of his death hit Rose all over again. She felt tears begin leaking down her face, and she quietly closed her eyes and allowed herself to mourn her friend's death. She was not alone. The Mavarakites around her all allowed themselves a moment of silence and pain.

Rose opened her eyes again when she heard Bryce's voice carry over the battlefield. "Together we live!" Bryce said, and the Mavarakites echoed his words. Rose regognized the words from the harvest festival, though it had sounded much happier that day. When the crowd finished their mantra, Bryce placed a fist over his heart. Rose watched as the family members all placed a fist over their heart in an identical fashion. Around Rose, each Wood Dweller followed the action, including Rylan, Robin, and Drew. Though Rose had never been explained the process, she understood instinctively. She placed her hand over her heart as well. Then a low, shrill whistle—one identical to the whistle that had announced the Farcriers appearance in battle—fell over the hushed audience. It began far in the back, probably from the Farcriers Rose had seen earlier. Then the low, shrill sound spread throughout the Mavarakites. It lasted for a few seconds, and then the sound dispersed. The Mavarakites waited patiently with their hands over their hearts as the family members, joined by several other Wood Dwellers, filled the graves. Once the graves were entirely filled, the Mavarakites lowered their hands from their heart.

After that, the Mavarakites began to disperse little by little. Without any words of passing, the Wood Dwellers simply turned and disappeared into the woods, homeward bound. Rose waited, her eyes glued to the spears marking the graves, her mind whirring. She thought of Max and every time she had ever spoken to him. She thought of the single tear she had seen roll down his face the day of the battle. She remembered the pain in his voice when he spoke of the fallen warriors up to that point. Her mind spun in various directions as the crowd around her thinned.

Eventually, the Giving family, Bryce the Leader,

and the family members of the fallen warriors were the only ones left. Then Robin and Drew eventually peeled off. Some of the family members filtered away from the battlefield. Then Bryce the Leader. And finally, the last of the family members, until Rose and Rylan were the only two left standing there.

Finally, Rylan leaned over to Rose. "You ready?" he whispered.

Something just didn't feel quite right to Rose yet. She felt unsatisfied. She felt there was something else she needed to do before she could leave the field.

"Rylan, are there any rose bushes in Mavarak?" Rose asked. Rylan looked confused, but he nodded and led Rose to the nearest bush without another word passing between them. She plucked one single rose and then trekked back to the graves, Rylan trailing behind her confoundedly.

With the funeral now over and all other Mavarakites back in the village center, Rose was able to walk directly up to the now filled grave of Max the Warrior. She dropped down to her knees at the foot of the grave, Rylan standing behind her and watching her in confusion.

Goodbye Max. Rose thought.

"What are you doing?" Rylan asked from behind Rose. She gently looked over her shoulder at him.

"This is how humans say goodbye," Rose explained. Rylan nodded, and a single tear fell down his cheek. Rose turned back to the grave and tenderly placed the rose on Max's grave. Then she stood, feeling accomplished, and turned to Rylan.

"Okay. Now I'm ready."

Chapter 16

The Decision

    The walk back to the village center was long and quiet. Rose and Rylan passed the last handful of Farcriers packing up their pelt tents and preparing to return to their homes. Rose felt her heart growing heavy as she thought of the Farcriers returning to their families. There would probably be a lot of hugs and tears, just as there would have been had Rose returned home.

    As the thought ran through her brain, she snuck a peek at Rylan. He was lost in his own head, his blue eyes swimming with thought and his ears tucked against his hair. He paid little attention to where his feet were taking him, yet he glided over the rocks and sticks gracefully without stumbling or even making much noise. Rose was shocked and proud when she realized that she, too, hardly glanced at her feet as she walked.

"Are you thinking about Max?" Rose asked carefully. Rylan's brain was working so hard she could practically see the gears turning, and she wondered if he had Max's final moments in his head as well. Rose wasn't even entirely sure Rylan was fully conscious for that.

"Um, no, actually I wasn't..." Rylan said, his ears perking up. Rose noticed the tips of them were turning a light shade of pink, and she wondered if he had been thinking about her. "I was thinking about the new hut..."

"Oh," Rose responded, attempting to hide her disappointment.

"It's a lot bigger than the old one was," Rylan said, ducking below a low-hanging branch distractedly.

"Yeah," Rose agreed absentmindedly, not fully interested in a discussion on huts.

"There's space for another person to live there comfortably..." Rylan added, his voice trailing off. Rose was caught off guard and she nearly tripped over nothing.

"Oh," Rose exclaimed, fighting back a blush from spreading over her cheeks.

Rylan stopped dead in his tracks. They were nearing the village, and Rose could hear the sound of young Wood Dwellers laughing and playing. Rose stopped as well, facing Rylan.

"You could stay," Rylan said. "Mom wouldn't mind it at all. She would probably love to have another girl in the house. And we could find you a job in the village you love doing. You could even help me with the Trusks if you want!"

"Rylan," Rose said slowly, confusedly. "I have to stay, remember? My sacrifice to the Guardians was that I would stay in Mavarak and fight until the day I die."

Rylan looked down at his dirty bare feet. "That's not exactly how the sacrifice works. You already paid the price. You obviously meant it when you promised you'd stay, or the sacrifice wouldn't have worked. You gave up your life. Now that the sacrifice has been completed and the Guardians have been restored, you can leave. If you want to."

Rose pondered the offer. Since the moment she had been told her promise is what restored the Guardians, she was under the impression she must keep the promise, or the Guardians would fall again. Now that she knew otherwise, she had a decision to make.

On the one hand, she missed her parents a lot. On the other, she had come to love Mavarak and the way the Wood Dwellers lived. The way they survived off the land in harmony with nature was beautiful. Taking to the skies on Truskback was wild and adventurous. Climbing trees and splashing in the river and walking through the woods had become second nature to her. And now that she thought about it, she had never had so much fun in her entire life. It was as if she belonged here, like she was born into the wrong world, that she had been meant for the life of a Wood Dweller.

Plus, Rylan was here...

Rose looked into Rylan's eyes and felt her heart hammering in her chest. His eyes were wide with hope and his ears were perked so he had the appearance of a begging puppy.

"The Other-Siders haven't been defeated," Rose said, thinking out loud. "They could strike again at any time. Mavarak needs warriors..."

Rylan smiled gently. "That's true."

Rose continued thinking, her brain turning now to her mom and dad at home. "But if I stay, I'll never see my parents again..."

Rylan continued to smile gently. "That's also true."

"But we're bonded," Rose continued, looking deep into Rylan's eyes. She wished he would just make the decision for her. She didn't want to.

"Yes, this is true as well," Rylan said, entirely unhelpfully.

"So, what does that even mean? To be bonded?" Rose asked, hoping he would give her a clue about what she should do.

"It means...well, it means we'll never leave each other," Rylan answered.

Rose puffed her chest, an air of finality in her

voice. "Then I have to stay, right?"

Rylan shook his head, but his face was still gentle. "No, Rose. It means we'll never *really* leave each other."

Then, just as the Wood Dwellers had all done at the funeral, he placed a firm fist over his heart. Rose felt a single tear spring into her eye as she decided what she needed to do.

As the tear gently fell down her cheek, Rylan reached out his hand and cupped her chin, using his thumb to wipe the tear away. Then he wrapped his arms around her waist, and Rose dropped her head onto his chest. She never said the words out loud, but she knew her unspoken words had been heard.

It was time for her to go home.

After a moment of silent embrace, Rylan broke the hug. Without another word, they turned and walked together through the woods. They passed the village center and began the now familiar walk to the river.

The sparkling water beckoned Rose as it had done the day she first discovered the little door. It felt like a lifetime had passed since she had fallen into the water and into the world of the Wood Dwellers. By now, she was likely presumed dead by the search party that had come after her. Her parents would cry tears of joy when she arrived. She had no clue what she would say when they asked her where she'd been the entire time. She decided she would cross that bridge when she got there.

Rylan stopped a few feet short of the river, but

Rose continued. She stepped carefully up to the boulder that she had fallen from, crawled on top of it, and peered down.

There it was. As if it had been there the entire time, Rose could see a little door nestled in the soft dirt of the riverbed. Waiting for Rose to finish what she had started ten years ago.

A thought struck her, and Rose couldn't help but let out a soft laugh. *He was right.* Rose thought, her mind flickering to Whitney the Wise, in all his zany glory. Rose lifted her eyes from the little door nestled in the riverbed to the direction of the Other-Side. *All I had to do was look in a different direction.*

Rose turned back to Mavarak, the only side she ever wished to face, and her eyes landed on Rylan. He had leaned back against the nearest tree, his leg bent so one foot rested against the rough bark of the tree, and his arms crossed over his chest. He looked as mischievous and playful as the day she met him. She considered a quick told-you-so regarding the existence of the little door, but for some reason it didn't quite feel right. Instead, she asked one final question.

"Will I remember you?" Rose asked, thinking back to her strange dreams of the elf-boy that had brought her to the river in the first place.

"Only if you want to," Rylan answered. Rose nodded, knowing she would remember him, and turned to face the little door once more.

She laid herself on her stomach and dipped her fingers gingerly into the cool water. She sunk her arms deeper and deeper still, until her fingers just brushed the riverbed. Then she reached through the cool, green-tinted water toward the handle of the little door.

The last thing she could remember, her fingers just brushed the little door, and she felt the rest of her body fall into the river after her.

Then, black.

∗∗

Rose woke with a start. As soon as she opened her eyes, she knew where she was. There was the familiar occasional beep of the heart monitor, and the room around her was white. She was perched on a clean hospital bed, and a drafty hospital gown draped loosely over her.

"She's awake!" Rose heard a familiar female voice cry. Before she was able to look up into her mother's eyes, she was entwined in a hug. Mom's hair was a mess, and it tickled Rose's nose as she peered past her mother's figure.

Her dad was standing hurriedly from a hospital chair he had clearly been perched in across the room. He crossed to Rose and threw his arms around her and her mother. Also standing from hospital chairs were Grandma and Grandpa Greenwood, looking flustered and concerned but relieved to see Rose awake.

"Mom? Dad?" Rose said, trying to make sense of the situation. She could tell she was in a hospital bed, but how had she gotten here? And why? "What's going on?"

"Rose, we've been worried sick," Mom exclaimed as her and Dad released Rose from their clutches and gave her a bit of breathing room. Mom sat in a chair next to the hospital bed, most of her weight leaning against the bed itself. Dad stood nearby behind her.

"You fell into the river, Freckles," Dad informed. "Your grandma found your body caught in some rocks on the edge of the water. It looked like you hit your head going down. We're lucky your body got caught before your head went underwater, or you might have drowned."

Rose blinked in confusion. She was feeling too groggy for all the information being thrown at her.

"You had a huge gash on your arm, a giant bruise on your shoulder, and some cuts on your hands and legs as well," Grandma Shirly explained. Rose blinked again, then peered at her arm. Just as Grandma had said, there was a huge bandage wrapped around her arm where she had clearly been injured.

Just where Black Eyes hit me. Rose thought, and all the memories of Mavarak flitted through her mind. She had been gone for weeks. When did Grandma find her body?

"How long have I been here?" Rose asked, struggling to sit up straight amidst all the wires connected to various points of her body.

"Stay down, honey, you need rest," Mom said, pushing her body back down. "You've only been here a couple hours. Maybe 7."

"I'm sorry," Rose rushed to say, the beeping heart monitor informing her that her heart rate was picking up. "You all must have been worried sick looking for me for the past couple weeks. I think I—"

Before Rose could make up an excuse for her long disappearance, her dad cut her off to ask, "Weeks? What do you mean?"

Rose looked individually at all the adults in the room. Grandma and Grandpa Greenwood were looking at her like a poor, lost animal they had found in the rain. Dad looked confused, and Mom looked like she wasn't even listening because she was just so relieved to have her baby back.

"Wasn't I missing for two weeks?" Rose asked, still looking between all her relatives.

"I told you she'd have a concussion," Grandpa Roger barked as Grandma Shirly swatted him and told him to quiet down.

"Freckles," Dad said as Mom brushed a mess of hair back from Rose's eyes, "we only dropped you off at your grandparents' cabin yesterday."

It felt like the world had come to a halt. She had been dropped off only yesterday? How is that possible? She hadn't exactly been keeping track of the days, plus there were many days spent in the Medical Hut that sort of just slipped by, but she had definitely spent many nights in the comfy spare treehouse in Robin's hut. The timeline didn't make sense.

"But...I thought..." Rose stammered, trying to make sense of the situation.

"Shh, let's not upset her please," Mom said, pushing Rose gently back down so she was resting against the hospital pillow. "Rose, sweetie, you need to rest. We're here for you if you need us. You just worry about dreaming sweet dreams."

Dreaming sweet dreams. The words toyed with Rose's brain. There was no way she could have dreamt it all up. The Wood Dwellers, the Other-Siders, the Farcriers, the Guardians and the blood sacrifice it took to bring the Guardians to power. Whitney the Wise, Max the Warrior, Lyla the Beautiful.

Rylan...

Rose closed her eyes and attempted to lull herself back to sleep. She knew it had all really happened. She knew it was real. She just wasn't sure how.

***

The summer was about as exciting as Rose had thought it would be. Although it did cause another fight between Mom and Dad, eventually Rose was allowed to return to the cabin—after she promised she wouldn't revisit the river unsupervised.

The fighting hadn't ceased one bit. Rose wasn't sure if Black Eyes had lied outright, or if he had mended the bond originally but then broke it again when the pathway was once again hidden by the Guardians. It didn't really matter anyway. Rose knew her mom and dad loved her, and they were still a family even if things looked different now.

Luckily, Rose was able to take her mind off it most days by spending her time in the woods. She kept her promise to her parents not to get too close to the river unsupervised, mostly due to her grandma's watchful eye every time she left the house. Just as she had done with Rylan in Mavarak, Rose had tried poking the riverbed with a stick many times. She had also scouted up and downstream in search of the places where Rylan had showed Rose the Guardians.

Grandma and Grandpa allowed Rose to go alone into the woods as long as she took a ball of yarn and wrapped it around the trees she walked past to track her steps, ensuring she wouldn't get lost. It actually came in handy, as the woods were entirely unfamiliar and not at all the woods she had come to know in Mavarak. There was no clearing, no large battlefield, no treehouses or huts or anything of that nature. There were a few times Rose discovered interesting looking berries, but always in a bush instead of a tree as they had grown in Mavarak. She hadn't dared eat them since she couldn't be sure they weren't poisonous.

Eventually, the summer came to an end. When Rose returned home, she moved into her mom's new apartment a few cities away from her dad's house, which now sported a for sale sign. The apartment mom lived in was a bit too far from her new school, so Rose now had to take the bus.

The first day was the scariest. Rose waited by herself at the bus stop, preparing mentally for the first day of high school. To make herself relax, she texted her best friend from her old school, Lacie, as they both prepared for their first day of high school. Lacie wasn't exactly a ton of help, as she just kept reminding Rose that the worst time to move to a new school in a brand-new town was the first year of high school.

Thanks, Lacie. Tons of help.

Rose thought it would be like in the movies

when she stepped onto the bus, where everyone stared at her because they knew she was the new girl. Instead, everyone just ignored her. This was just as bad.

Rose found an empty spot on the bus and plopped down, immediately looking out the window. Her mind turned to a certain, specific, messy haired Wood Dweller she could never stop thinking about. She was trying to train her mind to think of other things aside from him, though, so she instead thought about the day Dad sat her down and told her she would be going to a new school.

"You gonna be okay, kiddo?" Dad asked, driving Rose toward Mom's new apartment. Rose's bags were stuffed into the back seat, bringing with her about three quarters of her clothing. She would only stay at her dad's house every other weekend, so she figured it would be best to take her cutest clothes with her to Mom's.

"Yeah, I'm okay," Rose nodded. She had been asked this question by her dad about a million times already, and each time she assured her dad the same thing. He seemed to struggle believing her.

This time was the first time the conversation had gone beyond that. Dad didn't seem to know how to comfort Rose. His usual response in this scenario would be to change the subject to something that would make Rose laugh.

"You know I'm going to miss you bunches, right?" Dad asked, keeping his eyes trained on the road ahead of him. He always got a bit awkward whenever he had to be serious for longer than twelve seconds.

"I know," Rose said confidently, looking over at her dad and smiling. She placed a fist firmly over her heart. "It's okay though. We'll never *really* leave each other."

Dad smiled back at her. With one hand on the steering wheel, he reached his other arm out and tousled Rose's hair. "Did I send you away for the summer or for an entire year?"

Rose laughed. "I'm growing up, Dad."

Dad placed the free hand over his heart and gripped, as though he were in pain. "Stop it, you're killing me!"

The thought of her dad's playful smile distracted Rose during the entire bus ride to her new school. With her face pressed up against the glass of the bus window, she was given a great view of the school building as they pulled into the bus parking. Before her was a three-story building built of a brown-red brick. The school yard crawled with teenagers who all seemed to recognize each other, throwing their arms around their friends they hadn't seen all summer long and screaming in delight.

Rose didn't notice any of this. Directly outside the window, she had caught sight of a glorious thing. An amazing, glorious sight.

It was Rylan.

The back of his messy blond head was bobbing away from the bus Rose was stuck on. She couldn't see his pointy ears from the distance, but she could see his tall, skinny build looming over the smaller kids around him. The moment her bus stopped, Rose pounced up from the bench and bustled to the sliding doors and toward the figure.

"Rylan!" she screamed through the opening bus door. She bounded through them quickly, the first person on her bus to push to the exit. He was crossing the school yard, heading toward the looming building.

Rose broke into a run after him. The other students surrounding her were too loud for him to hear her call his name over the ruckus.

"Rylan!" Rose yelled again, this time close enough that she knew he'd be able to hear her. She caught up to him, grabbing him by the elbow and pulling him around. "Ry—oh!"

Her heart dropped in her chest as she saw the boy standing before her had beady green eyes rather than the wide, puppy-dog eyes Rylan sported. His ears were round and fleshy—clearly human—and his face twisted in confusion upon seeing her.

"Um, it's Nick," the boy, Nick, responded, shaking Rose's hand off his arm.

"I'm so sorry," Rose said, feeling a blush spreading across her face. "I thought you were—er—someone else..."

That wasn't the only time she had seen Rylan around town. She saw him everywhere over the next few months. She even once could have sworn she saw the pointy ears poking around the messy blond hair. But it was always the same, with the boy looking at her confusedly and Rose stammering an embarrassed apology.

As the weather became cold and Rose grew

accustomed to her new school, new friends, and new home, she sometimes fell into despair and began to wonder if it really had all been a dream. There was nothing to prove it had ever happened. No momentums, no evidence, no souvenirs, no way to communicate. Rose had a few scrapes, but those could easily be explained from her tumble into the river.

Due to this, Rose jumped on the opportunity to return to her grandparents' cabin the first chance she had. Rose begged her mother to let her travel up to the cabin once more when winter break came around. At first, her mother refused. Every time Rose had been there, she had fallen into the water and nearly died. Rose promised she would stay away from the river, insisting it would be frozen over anyway. Mom made her promise she wouldn't try to mess around with it even if the ice looked thick, then eventually agreed to let Rose visit her grandparents.

Rose hadn't been there longer than a day before she trekked into the woods, bundled with a thick, marshmallow coat and a scarf. She kept her promise to her mom—she had no intentions of playing on the ice. Instead, she carefully climbed on top of the infamous boulder, facing the direction Mavarak should have been but was replaced instead with her grandparents' cabin, closed her eyes, and let her thoughts drift away to a happier place.

What would Mavarak be like during the winter? How did the huts stay warm? The Farcriers were all bundled with warm pelts and fur boots, so they were well equipped for the colder seasons. Did the

Mavarakites have similar clothing and equipment for the cold? Does Mavarak even get cold, or is it summer weather all the time there?

Rose looked down at the river, wishing there could be a little door she could travel through. She wished she could come and go as she pleased, having both her family and her Wood Dweller friends at her convenience.

But some things in life require sacrifice.

Rose closed her eyes and the image of Rylan's smiling face filtered into her mind. *We'll never really leave each other.*

With a sudden thought, Rose's eyes popped back open. She stood carefully on the boulder, staring intensely into the woods where the Mavarakites should have been. She placed a fist firmly over her heart in true Mavarak fashion. Then, she let out a low, shrill whistle; the same whistle the Wood Dwellers had done at the funeral service and during the battle.

Rose listened carefully to the world around her. Then, sending goosebumps of excitement over Rose's arms, she heard a whistle sound deep inside the woods.

Rose's face split into a grin and she prepared to run into the forest, whistling along the way. "Rylan?!" Rose screamed.

"*Rylan?!*" Rose's voice repeated back to her over and over again, until it faded away. Rose's face fell.

It was just an echo.

She turned away and stepped carefully off the boulder, defeated and cold, ready to return to the cabin.

Then, she stopped, turning one ear back over her shoulder, listening intensely. Rose could have sworn, for a fleeting moment, she heard a whistle. She spun slowly to face the woods once more. Carefully, she whistled again, listening intently.

Don't be stupid, Rose, Rose thought, shaking her head, turning away. *It was just an echo.*

Then, she heard it again. The echo.

It was just an echo.

Or was it?

Printed in Great Britain
by Amazon